The Outpost

A Novel

The Outpost

A Novel

Ben Date

COSMIC EGG
BOOKS

Winchester, UK
Washington, USA

JOHN HUNT PUBLISHING

First published by Cosmic Egg Books, 2024
Cosmic Egg Books is an imprint of John Hunt Publishing Ltd., 3 East St., Alresford,
Hampshire SO24 9EE, UK
office@jhpbooks.net
www.johnhuntpublishing.com
www.cosmicegg-books.com

For distributor details and how to order please visit the 'Ordering' section on our website.

Text copyright: Ben Date 2023

ISBN: 978 1 80341 472 0
978 1 80341 473 7 (ebook)
Library of Congress Control Number: 2022922855

A CIP catalogue record for this book is available from the British Library.

Design: Lapiz Digital Services

UK: Printed and bound by CPI Group (UK) Ltd, Croydon, CR0 4YY
US: Printed and bound by Thomson-Shore, 7300 West Joy Road, Dexter, MI 48130

We operate a distinctive and ethical publishing philosophy in
all areas of our business, from our global network of authors to
production and worldwide distribution.

Chapter 1

On the Road

Joseph had taken cover behind the counter of a dilapidated gas station that was set off to the side of a desolate highway, situated in the middle of nowhere. The gas station had been abandoned for years, and all but one window had been broken by a combination of vandals and violent nuclear storms. There was a visible layer of dust that covered every exposed surface like a light blanket of grey snow. The only source of light came from outside as the sun attempted to pierce through the perpetual cloud coverage, resulting in colourless rays of murky illumination that filled the dreary building.

Joseph sat on the floor with his back against the counter and his legs pulled up to his chest. A lone cockroach wandered by his battered boots in search of a morsel of food that had been overlooked by looters or other hungry creatures of various sizes. Joseph paid no attention to the insect passing by; he was only focused on reloading his now empty revolver. A bullet whistled over the counter and slammed into the back wall, making Joseph flinch. His hands trembled as he tried to load his final bullet into the revolver, a now seemingly impossible task. It felt as if he were trying to thread a sewing needle while wearing a pair of winter gloves.

After what felt like several minutes, but in reality was only a handful of seconds, Joseph got the bullet into the gun and clicked the chamber shut. One more bullet whizzed by, striking an empty Coca-Cola can that had been lying on its side on the back shelf across from him. The can spun off the shelf and rattled to the floor as another bullet struck the counter that he was hiding behind. This bullet was accompanied by "You're dead! You hear me? Dead!"

Joseph had been trailed by a duo of bandits for several miles before he decided to cut his losses and make a stand at this depressing little gas station. He tried to initially talk things out, but there was no bartering with these men. They wanted everything he had, including the boots off his feet. If he did not oblige they would try to kill him, but if he did give in to their demands he would be a dead man walking anyways without his supplies. Joseph decided to take a chance and participate in a shoot-out, so here he was, trying not to catch a bullet as he sat behind the counter.

He had managed to shoot one of the bandits when the firefight initially started. He wildly took a shot when they drew their guns, before ducking down behind the protective barrier, and tagged the bandit on the right in the lower abdomen. At first he had screamed in agony, but his screams quickly settled down to a low moan as his life force leaked from the hole in his stomach.

Joseph was now sitting behind the counter, terrified. He only had one last shot after all, a bullet that he had been planning to save for himself if the right moment, or wrong moment for that matter, ever came. Joseph heard something clatter to the floor behind him, and the remaining bandit let out a string of profanity. He was reloading and Joseph knew it. Joseph sprung to his feet and aimed the gun at the lone bandit. The man's eyes widened and he dropped his gun, raising his hands.

"Please..." the bandit mouthed, too frightened to utter an actual word as he stared down the barrel of Joseph's revolver.

"I'm...I'm sorry," Joseph whispered as he squeezed the trigger and sent a bullet sailing between the eyes of the bandit. He knew that if he let him live the bandit would likely trail him again until he got another opportunity to strike, probably whenever Joseph was forced to sleep.

His body crumpled to the ground just outside the entrance to the gas station, next to the still-breathing body of his partner.

Joseph cautiously approached the two and locked eyes with the bandit he had first shot, who was clinging to his final moments of life. He could see the fear in the dying young man's big brown eyes. He was young, much younger than Joseph: 15, maybe 16 at most. A tear ran down Joseph's cheek, but he knew he did what he had to do in order to survive. He had been forced to kill before and he knew that he would have to kill again if he was to continue surviving in this new world of nightmares. The bandit who was lying on the ground clutching his stomach let out a final ragged breath and was gone from this world forever.

Perhaps he was the lucky one, Joseph thought. There wasn't much left to live for anyways. He slowly made his way into the bathroom. A small window near the ceiling let in enough light to see, but it was very dim and smelled putrid. Joseph entered one of the stalls and removed the cover to the back of the toilet tank, careful to not let any dust particles fall into the water basin. He scooped water with his hands, wiping the sweat and dirt from his face. He then proceeded to replenish his canteen and drink heavily. Once he was hydrated and his water reserve was full, he replaced the cover on the toilet tank to preserve what little water remained for the next wandering soul.

As he exited the graffiti-covered bathroom stall, he came to a halt as he saw a strange man watching him. This unfamiliar man was himself. He stared into the large bathroom mirror, which had a jagged crack running from left to right, and squinted at the face peering back at him. His once clean-shaven face was concealed in a short beard. It's funny—as a teenager Joseph had never imagined being able to grow a beard. As it turned out, all it took was several months of not shaving or grooming and he could achieve a real mountaineer's style.

His once bright-blue eyes that were full of life now seemed like windows to an empty shell of a man. His hair was long and unkempt, and he looked untrustworthy by traditional societal standards. Joseph was only 28, but he could probably pass for his mid-forties at this point. It was truly remarkable how much he had changed over the past 24 months.

***

Two years ago, Joseph had recently passed the bar on his law exam and had a promising career lined up at a local law firm to become the next hotshot criminal defence attorney. He had found success defending a handful of clients for petty crimes and was working his way up to tackling more high-profile type cases such as murders. It was a Friday night and he had declined an invitation from a group of his lawyer friends to hit the bar, although Joseph was much more keen to refer to them as acquaintances. Joseph preferred to keep to himself whenever possible and was going through the difficult break-up of a three-year relationship at the time. His reclusive tendencies had kept him isolated for most of his life, but on that particular Friday night his introverted persona saved his life.

At the time the year was 2048. The global economy was at an all-time low and resources were depleting at a rate far too fast to replenish, even with the growing technologies surrounding preservation. Of course it wasn't North America that suffered; it was the 'global south' countries and continents enveloped in poverty. North Americans just kept them out of sight and out of mind in order to continue enjoying their luxuries and commodities guilt free. Tensions between the West and the East were at an all-time high, making the once petrifying Cold War seem like a silly schoolyard scuffle. In the end, all it took was one unhinged dictator to launch a barrage of nuclear warheads aimed at North America. The West retaliated with a similar response and both continents were virtually obliterated.

A few nations survived the initial bombings and remained standing among the ashes of the supposed free world. Instead of rallying together to help survivors and rebuild civilization, these remaining few nations battled it out for global supremacy. In the end they too were reduced to dust, leaving the world ripe for the taking, not that there was much left to take or anyone left to take it.

The Friday night that Joseph had spent secluded in his basement apartment playing video games, like he did so many other Friday nights, was the beginning of the end of the world as he knew it. Nuclear Armageddon had arrived. Cellphones were blowing up across the nation with SMS alerts, and people began scrambling for shelter. Estranged relatives made amends and old lovers rekindled lost flames. In a disturbingly twisted way, the world seemed to fill up with love and become a better place for an hour in the countries that were facing certain doom. This resurrection of love and a desire to make peace occurred primarily behind closed doors, however, and the subsequent silence in the streets was deafening.

Joseph was slumped in a beanbag chair, a purchase that he regretted tremendously as it offered no lumbar support whatsoever, playing your typical shooter game. He had heard the warning go off on his phone and didn't bother to check to see what it was about; very rarely were they anything relevant to him. He had started to hear people panicking over the in-game voice chat and he initially believed it to be a prank. As more and more people started disconnecting, Joseph had finally made his way across the room to check his charging phone. He read the message in utter disbelief over and over again until his phone rang, which he answered on the first ring. It was his mother calling and she was frantically crying. They lived hundreds of miles apart and she was calling to hear her son's voice one last time in her final moments. They talked but mostly cried, while Joseph urgently tried to gather up as many supplies as he could in his small basement apartment to take into the old cement wine cellar. Eventually his mother's line cut out and that was the last time he heard her voice.

Joseph stuffed blankets, clothes, a couple of bottles of water, canned goods, an old painting mask from when he helped his brother renovate his new condo in Atlanta, and other miscellaneous items into the cellar and pulled the thick wooden door shut behind him. He waited in the dark, just listening for something to happen. He heard the upstairs door burst open, the stomping across the floor above, and the pounding knocks on the door that separated him from his upstairs neighbours. They were screaming for him to let them in before it was too late. Joseph was too scared to even move and knew that he wouldn't have enough supplies to keep his two neighbours and himself alive for very long. He continued to sit alone in the dark and damp wine cellar, ignoring the pleas for help coming from above him.

A few minutes later he felt the ground gently shake and heard a distant explosion that sounded not much louder than a burst of thunder on a stormy night. That wasn't so bad, he had thought. Shortly after his foolishly optimistic thought, the entire upstairs of the house was ripped away along with the upstairs tenants, rocking the house's foundation to its core. The earth itself began to violently shake in protest, and the handful of bottles that Joseph had actually stored in the cellar for special occasions fell to the ground and shattered, drenching him in cheap grocery store wine. The freezing cold basement suddenly felt like a sauna and caused Joseph to begin sweating profusely. Unfortunately, the cellar lacked that familiar smell of cedarwood that was present in most steamy saunas, instead reeking of hidden mould and Cabernet Sauvignon.

Joseph kept his head covered with his arms for what felt like almost an hour and waited until the world stopped shaking. Joseph was no fool; he was aware that surviving the initial blast of a nuclear bomb was the easiest part. The real danger would be in the coming days as nuclear fallout rained down from the sunless skies. Nuclear bombs at the time had been designed to be more explosive than traditional nuclear bombs manufactured during the Cold War, but less radioactive to reduce collateral damage to unintended targets. Nonetheless, high levels of radiation were still present in these advanced warheads, and some of the less affluent nations continued to utilize the more primitive versions loaded with copious amounts of traditional radiation. Joseph hoped that the more sophisticated and less radioactive nuclear warheads had struck the West, which indeed was the case. Unfortunately for Joseph and the rest of the world, the radiation compounds present within these modern warheads were still relatively unstudied at the time of launch. As a result, people could survive massive doses of this new type of radiation but would suffer from adverse side effects that transformed them into things other than human.

Joseph had remained in that sturdy little wine cellar for an entire week. He had ventured into the main room for bathroom purposes, taking whatever precautions he could to protect himself from radiation, such as heavily layering up before leaving the cellar and always wearing that archaic painting mask. He tried to consistently do his business in the same corner of what used to be the living room, but it was always dark and the floor above had caved in, making the once quaint room unrecognizable. He spent most of his days daydreaming, reminiscing, having conversations with himself, and crying. He hardly slept, too scared and paranoid about the small spiders that would periodically crawl across his exposed hands or face. Water, or the lack thereof, was what eventually drove him out of his shelter. He had run almost completely out of that precious life-sustaining liquid and he knew that he would have to find more soon in order to survive.

The first several months were the hardest for Joseph. He was a strong and muscular young man, but he lost almost 30 pounds over the first couple of months and could feel his strength quickly fading away. He had pneumonia from staying in the damp wine cellar, filled with mildew and mould, but he naturally believed it to be radiation poisoning and had to battle that nasty illness without the aid of medicine. His city had been completely levelled, forcing him to travel long distances to towns and cities that hadn't been hit as hard in search of supplies.

He spent most of his time drifting in and out of cities, scavenging and stealing whatever he could in order to stay alive. It wasn't until the one-year mark that he started encountering other survivors somewhat frequently, and small settlements began popping up sporadically. Within the most recent 12 months, more and more survivors had been coming out of hiding, and a plethora of settlements had emerged. These communities, however, rarely survived more than a month or two before being decimated by raiders and people so damaged by radiation that they were now more similar to animals than humans. As promising signs of post-apocalyptic civilization began to emerge, so did new and unimaginable threats. Unfortunately for Joseph, his hardest days were yet to come.

***

Joseph averted his gaze from his face to his apparel. He wore a tattered brown leather jacket that he had taken from a corpse a few months back. A dirty black T-shirt was visible underneath and he wore a pair of very well-loved jeans. His black boots were coated in mud, and the seams at the back of his right boot along the heel looked at risk of bursting. A black backpack rested on both of his shoulders, bulging with supplies. He let out a long sigh thinking about how much he had taken a simple haircut for granted before the nuclear Armageddon.

He exited the bathroom and froze in his tracks, his blood turning to ice in his veins and his heart sinking down to his stomach. He *heard* what was there before his eyes could register what he was witnessing. He could hear the unmistakable crunching of bones being broken and an uncomfortable wet slurping sound. A grotesque and deformed humanoid figure knelt over the two corpses in the doorway of the gas station exit. Not everyone had been as lucky as Joseph during the explosions. Some had been much luckier, and others much less. The figure by the bodies was one of the much less lucky ones, a victim of the perils of the untested radiation present within the advanced nuclear warheads.

A chunk of the survivors got hit hard by the radiation, really hard. Joseph had referred to this population as 'The Sick', since they had become sick in all aspects of their mind, body, and soul. There were a lot of different names given to this group, but the most darkly humorous name Joseph had heard for them was 'Orvilles'. The name stemmed from a pre-war microwave popcorn brand called Orville Redenbacher's. The name was applicable since their brains had been fried from radiation as if they'd stuck their heads into a microwave and the blisters on their ravaged flesh would pop like popcorn. Whatever they were called, these people were nightmarish and they were dangerous.

They often lost most of their nails, but for some peculiar reason they rarely lost their teeth. They were hairless from head to toe and their skin was often a sickly yellowish hue like a smoker who had smoked one too many cigarettes or someone dying of scurvy. It varied from individual to individual, but most of the Orvilles possessed physical deformities and were maimed in a multitude of ways. The most problematic aspect of The Sick was their lacklustre mental capacity—their brains might as well have been nuked in a microwave. Complex decision-making was almost non-existent and they had become more animal than human. The Sick often engaged in cannibalism as their main source of food, sometimes even consuming one another.

Human flesh was exactly the delicacy that this particular Orville was partaking in. It must have begun its feast shortly after Joseph had gone into the bathroom because the young man that he had shot in the stomach was now unrecognizable. Joseph gagged and the Orville quickly looked up and glared at him. Joseph took out his revolver and checked the wheel, only to see that it was empty. A part of him had hoped that a new round would have magically appeared since he ran out of ammo, but no such luck was in store for him.

The Orville snarled; most of its upper lip had been bitten off, presumably by another Orville.

"If you're going...to shoot me...shoot me already."

Verbal communication was a tremendous struggle for The Sick. For some more far gone, it was impossible.

"I'm not going to shoot you. I just need to get by you so that I can leave," Joseph replied, trying to hide the tremble in his voice.

The Orville stood to its full height, its face and hands dripping with blood, and it was barely clothed. Now identifiable as a male, the Orville was about 6 feet tall and terribly gaunt. Joseph stood a mere 5 feet and 8 inches. It was uncommon for Orvilles to travel alone as they often hunted in packs like wild dogs. This particular Orville was undeniably malnourished and he likely had had to flee from his brethren in order to avoid being cannibalized himself.

"What's stopping you? Come on out..." The Orville's voice was light and raspy, like he was speaking through a fan.

Joseph slowly walked towards the Orville and stopped about 5 feet away, his empty revolver in hand and aimed at the Orville's head. Joseph doubted that this frail creature would try to pick a fight with two fresh corpses ready to be consumed. Then again Orvilles were unpredictable and did not share the same logic a normal person had. He could smell necrotic flesh on the Orville, and the air reeked of iron from all the blood.

"Could you please step aside?" Joseph asked, as confidently as he could.

"C-could you p-please step aside?" the Orville mocked with a sinister grin that revealed bits of flesh stuck between his rotten teeth.

They peered into each other's eyes for a second, the Orville's eyes bloodshot and shifty. After a few moments the starving Orville stepped aside and made a grand gesture for Joseph to move past him. Joseph did so quickly and turned to observe the Sick man once more. Joseph almost felt bad for him. Almost.

"What're you waiting for? Move along, flesh bag, or you'll be my next meal!" The Orville snapped his teeth and Joseph backed away quickly.

Joseph promptly began walking down the deserted highway once more. He came across the occasional abandoned car that had run out of gas long ago and he would check for anything of value, often coming up empty-handed. It was a small two-lane highway surrounded by a vast forest void of leaves and other signs of life. He quickened his pace, hoping to reach a new source of shelter before nightfall and more than happy to put as much distance between himself and the human buffet spread out on the floor of that damned gas station.

Chapter 2

Homestead Living

Joseph had been walking for a couple of hours before his aching feet persuaded him to take a break. He was currently sitting on the trunk of an old and beyond-rusted Toyota Corolla, eating a can of cold baked beans with a plastic spoon that he had found on the floor of a filthy diner a few weeks back. He had always enjoyed baked beans, often opting to have them with his breakfast. Of course he preferred them to be served hot and by now he was getting tired of beans. Nonetheless, he was relatively content to be resting his feet and filling the seemingly eternal void of hunger in his stomach.

He hadn't seen a sign for the next city for the entirety of his walk from the gas station, but it was possible that they had been knocked down when the bombs dropped. At least that's what Joseph kept telling himself. The highway had expanded into four lanes, which indicated that he was getting closer to a major city, a promising sign to say the least. There hadn't been any signs of life besides the occasional bursts of gunfire that echoed across the empty land. Joseph had hoped to make it within city limits before nightfall, but as the sun began to set it became increasingly apparent to him that he'd have to spend another night on the road.

The Sick often hunted in packs during the night. It was unusual to see them in the day, although if they were desperate enough they would come out to scavenge for food on occasion. The ultraviolet rays from the sun, even from behind the never-ending coverage of blackish grey clouds, wreaked havoc on their already damaged skin. For this reason Joseph was none too pleased to be spending another night on the road. Last night he had slept in a resilient bush that still had some foliage off the side of the highway and had gotten caught in a downpour of rain. There was very little protection from the elements or from being seen in the forest as the majority of vegetation had been wiped out by the contaminated rainwater, with the exception of a few pockets of greenery that defied all odds.

On Joseph's left was an endless forest of dead trees. If he looked carefully enough he could find a few scarce patches of sacred green, but not enough patches to count on two hands. To his right, the forest had given way to farmlands. The crops were almost completely dead and Joseph wouldn't risk eating whatever did still grow anyway. A few rundown-looking farmhouses could be seen in the distance, although it was impossible to know whether they had always looked so rundown from neglect or if they had more recently suffered from the vicious nuclear blast waves. Either way, they were an eyesore to say the least.

Joseph was finishing up his can of beans, trying to figure out where he should spend the night. He was strongly considering one of the unattractive farmhouses, but he was hesitant since they were a prime location for The Sick to raid in the middle of the night so that they could feast on unsuspecting sleeping victims. On the other hand, the highway was well travelled and someone would likely stumble across him sleeping if he were to set up camp in the back of an old sedan. The forest was out of the question after the miserable sleepless night he had endured the night prior.

He investigated the bottom of his now empty can hoping to find one last bean. There wasn't one. He tossed the can and watched it roll noisily across the lane and come to a final stop against the tyre of an old pickup truck. Joseph had originally tried to take a car, but it was almost impossible to find one that still ran. Even if he could get one going, assuming someone was generous enough to leave the keys conveniently behind in the car, the highway could become quite congested at certain points. Not to mention that everyone nearby would literally kill for a ride. It just wasn't practical, and so walking was Joseph's primary transportation of choice.

He sat on the hood of the car for a moment more, swinging his legs and listening to the silence. A couple more gunshots could be heard coming from the direction of the upcoming city, but this was no surprise. At this point Joseph had made up his mind that he would take his chances spending the night at one of the farmhouses. He was just about to get moving again when something caught his attention out of the corner of his eye. One of the smaller farmhouses, one that used to be bright red but was now a depressing dirty brown, had smoke wafting out of the brick chimney and up into the evening sky. It was risky having a fire out in the open, especially at night. Smoke wasn't as bad, but still a gamble no doubt.

Joseph slid off the trunk of the car and let out a laboured grunt. His feet were sore and swollen; bloody blisters that had eventually become numb covered his heels and the tips of his toes. He was hesitant to head towards the smoke, especially now that he was unarmed minus the 6-inch pocket knife that he kept in his right jacket pocket. He was so lonely though; he hadn't encountered a friendly face for days. Joseph had also learned that talking to whoever was willing to talk was a great way to learn about what was going on across the ravaged country. It was extremely difficult to find a working radio, let alone batteries. Word of mouth was really the only way of gathering any kind of information. Joseph could really use a friendly conversation right about now anyway.

He began making his way towards the once quaint and cosy-looking farmhouse that now looked ready to fall down at any moment. The field was muddy and wet. Joseph's boots would sink into the mud and make a loud squelching sound when he tugged his foot free with each step. It was as if something deep within the earth was trying to pull him down and trap him beneath the surface as a punishment for his sins.

The half-a-kilometre walk was exhausting. Joseph had to stop multiple times to catch his breath, and his legs were on fire. The lack of proper sustenance and the toll from the radiation did not make the walk any easier. Eventually Joseph made it to the front porch of the farmhouse. There were two old white rocking chairs on the porch, one lying on its side. The white paint had begun to chip away, exposing rotting wood beneath. It made Joseph sad, but he wasn't quite sure why.

He stood on the porch trying to listen for sounds coming from inside. He could hear voices just beyond the aged wooden door. He could clearly make out a female and a male, but he couldn't quite hear what they were saying. They sounded friendly enough, and Joseph decided to take a chance. He took a deep breath and knocked on the front door, something he hadn't done for what seemed like forever. No one really had property any more, let alone the courtesy to knock on a door.

The voices were abruptly silenced by the knock. Joseph could hear rapid whispers, now realizing that there was likely a third party inside as well. The door opened a crack and a funny-looking older man, probably in his late fifties, peaked out at Joseph from behind round gold-framed spectacles. No one spoke for a few seconds. It was Joseph who broke the silence first.

"I saw the smoke from the highway...I'm just looking for a place to spend the night. Maybe trade supplies and information, you know?" Joseph said, not feeling quite as scared seeing the little man who answered the door.

"See? I told you that fire was a bad idea!" a deep bellowing voice said from behind the door, out of sight.

"I don't want any trouble. I can move along to the next farm if you want," Joseph said sheepishly.

"No, no, no, come in! Come in! We've got plenty of space and we haven't met a fresh face in a while," the older man replied in a very grandfatherly tone.

The old man opened the door fully to reveal himself and a man sitting on a tattered dark-green sofa near the fireplace, next to a young girl. The man looked a little bit older than Joseph, but he was very burly. Clean-shaven, surprisingly, with deep-set eyes that seemed like they could read a person like a book. The large man was bald and wore beige cargo pants to go along with a tight-fitting, navy-blue T-shirt that revealed a sleeve of tattoos on his right arm.

The girl next to him looked to be around the same age as the bandit Joseph had shot in the stomach. She wore a black sweater two sizes too large and matching black jeans with sneakers that once upon a time used to be white but were now a shade closer to black. Her long blond hair was a mess of knots and went down beyond her shoulders. She looked terrified to see the stranger in the doorway.

The old man who was holding the door open was even shorter than Joseph. He wore a get-up that was likely extremely fashionable when it was clean and not tattered. A torn blue blazer rested upon his torso, a stained pink vest beneath. He wore a pair of faded corduroy pants, although it was hard to tell what color they were supposed to be. It was strange to see brown hiking boots on his feet; Joseph expected to see the complete look with loafers and maybe a pipe. He supposed hiking boots were more practical.

The living room was just as dusty as the gas station, but the fire gave off the kind of warming orange glow that made Joseph want to curl up and fall asleep. He stepped into the living room and the old man closed the door behind him. Joseph could feel the three sets of eyes focus on him. He was completely aware of the fact that he looked like an absolute mess and probably even a little shady. He walked over to the fireplace and shrugged off his heavy backpack, allowing it to drop to the floor with an audible thud. He then proceeded to grab a small footstool to sit on near the fire, basking in the warm embrace of the flames. The interior of the farmhouse faintly reminded Joseph of the small family camp he used to frequent in the summer months with his mother when he was a young boy.

The old man joined the scene by sitting in an enviously comfortable-looking La-Z-Boy recliner. Joseph could see foam bulging through the torn seams, but that only made the chair look even more comfortable. This time the old man broke the awkward silence.

"What's your name, son?" he asked gently.

"Joseph."

"Well, Joseph, I'm William and that is Greg and Hillary," he said, nodding at the two on the couch as he introduced them. Joseph nodded at the two in acknowledgement but did not get a response back.

"Where are you headed?" William asked.

Joseph shrugged. "Nowhere in particular. Wherever I can find food and shelter, really."

The man on the couch, Greg, straightened up a bit.

He looked at Joseph and asked, "Which way are you headed? North or south?" His voice was loud and commanding, a stark contrast to the gentle voice of William.

Joseph paused for a moment. He had never paid much attention to which direction he was travelling. It never seemed to matter.

"North. I came from the south," he replied after a few seconds of consideration.

"Are you going to the PAR outpost on the far side of the city?" Hillary asked excitedly. This was the first time she had spoken since Joseph had entered the farmhouse.

"The...PAR outpost?" Joseph's face registered visible confusion.

"Yes, Outpost Zulu! You *have* heard of PAR, haven't you?" Hillary asked with a hint of irritation in her voice. Joseph shook his head.

"Seriously? They had some pretty awesome social media accounts before the war. Did you live under a rock or something?" Hillary was only half joking.

"Yeah, something like that," Joseph replied with an awkward laugh.

Joseph previously had a minimal presence on social media. He found that the supposed 'social' networks only made him feel more alone and reminded him of his lack of a real social life. He never had an abundance of followers and if he were to post anything at all he was lucky to get perhaps three likes, one of them consistently being his mom. As a result, Joseph was often out of the loop when it came to the newest trends and gossip. He tried to keep up with the news, but in the sombre months leading up to full-blown nuclear warfare he had begun to tune even that out. All the local news channels would fixate on the increasing nuclear tensions between the West and the East, and Joseph could live without the daily reminder of the imminent end of the world.

"PAR is short for the Post-Apocalyptic Republic," William interjected. "They were founded by some ex-Russian general named Reznoff and were privately funded. PAR was supposed to be a contingency plan for if the country actually fell apart, which it did. I'm not sure how big they became though. They were still in their infancy when the bombs dropped."

"Don't worry, Joseph," Greg spoke up with a sly smirk. "I hadn't heard about PAR either until I met these two. I always had my head buried in the engine of a truck."

Joseph was glad that he wasn't the only one out of the loop.

"Anyways," Hillary continued, "they were created to help survivors in the event of, well, you know, this." Hillary made a grand gesture with both her arms, referring to the world that they all now lived in.

"So, how'd you hear about this outpost on the far side of the city?" Joseph asked. He had visited the upcoming city, Hathbury, on numerous occasions to visit his partner, which in the end turned out to be a tremendous waste of time and money. If there was some kind of nuclear outpost being built prior to the war, he surely would have caught wind of it from his wretched ex-partner who loved to lie and spread rumours.

"With that, William said as he triumphantly pointed to an old CB radio perched on a thin, single-plank wooden shelf above the fireplace. Joseph swivelled on his stool and craned his neck upwards to see the ancient relic. The radio was a fairly big black box with four dials and a mouthpiece that resembled a walkie-talkie connected by a curly grey cord. It was the kind of radio that Joseph would imagine every trucker to have, the kind of radio a lawyer such as himself would have never seen.

"Whoever used to live here generously, or foolishly, left it behind," William explained.

"You can see for yourself. It's almost seven o'clock." Hillary was watching an old grandfather clock that was tucked away in the back corner of the room. It was a beautiful cherry-wood clock that stood over 6 feet tall. The bronze pendulum swung gracefully from side to side and Joseph became aware of the rhythmic ticking sound that filled up the small room.

Joseph stood and carefully retrieved the radio. He stood there examining the radio for a while, unsure of how to even turn it on.

"Give it here," Hillary demanded and extended her arms.

Joseph obliged and carefully transferred the radio to her as if they were exchanging another nuclear warhead. Hillary balanced the radio on her lap and began fidgeting with the dials until the rhythmic ticking of the grandfather clock was drowned out by the harsh white noise of static. She gently placed the radio on the ground in front of her and folded her hands politely. The static droned on for a while and then the grandfather clock struck back, noisily declaring that it was seven o'clock with a melodious chime. The chime faded away and the static remained for a few more moments, accompanied by the occasional pop from the crackling fireplace, which had lost its once mighty flame and had become a pile of dark-orange embers. Finally, there was a break in the static.

"Attention, all survivors." A strong authoritative female voice that demanded respect emitted from the CB radio. "I am Commander Ventress, leader of the Post-Apocalyptic Republic. There is a safe haven on the north side of Hathbury called Outpost Zulu. Follow the arrows located downtown. We have food, shelter, and security. We are here to help. This message will repeat every hour. Do not lose hope."

The alluring female voice left the room and was replaced by that abrasive static once more, which Hillary quickly put a silence to by switching the radio off. The room had cooled off significantly and the sun was starting to set on the horizon just above the tree line that was visible from the kitchen window in the next room. Joseph had butterflies in his stomach; could such a safe haven really exist?

"We're heading there tomorrow morning at first light. Care to make this a party of four?" William offered.

"Yeah, for sure!" Joseph blurted without hesitation. He hadn't been this excited since he found an unspoiled can of peaches three months ago in the backpack of a dead nomad.

"Great," William said as he clapped his liver-spotted hands together, "it's a plan then!"

"Joseph, would you mind coming out back with me? There's an old well with a hand pump and I'd like to gather a few buckets of water before it gets dark," Greg said as he tore himself away from the soft couch.

"Sure, no problem," Joseph replied as he rose to his feet, eager to get off the uncomfortably low footstool that made his knees almost touch his chest.

"Be careful, you two. And try to be quiet out there, okay?" William pleaded nervously.

"Don't worry so much, old man, you'll give yourself a heart attack." Greg laughed and pulled a Glock from the back of his waistband. "See? We'll be fine."

Greg started towards the back door and motioned for Joseph to follow. The two stepped out into the backyard and began making their way over to the stone well that had been dug a hundred yards away. There was no mud here, just overgrown grass that came up to their knees. Joseph had enjoyed nature growing up, but there wasn't much natural beauty left any more. Even the tall grass was turning yellow—most of the rainwater was filled with radioactive contaminants. Joseph predicted that he'd only live for another ten years if he was lucky. He couldn't imagine what kind of radiation poisoning he'd picked up over the past couple of years, even *if* the West had been hit with the more sophisticated nukes.

The two arrived at the well and went to work. They took turns pumping the large wooden lever, and progress was slow.

"Joseph," Greg said in between laboured breaths—it was his turn to work the pump. "We have no idea if this place still even exists."

"What do you mean? That broadcast seemed pretty promising." Joseph kept an eye on their surroundings, making sure that there were no prying eyes from the outlying forest.

"For all we know, that broadcast went out over a year ago and has been on replay ever since. Who's to say Outpost Zulu hasn't been ransacked by raiders or freaks by now like every other settlement?" Greg explained as Joseph took a turn cranking the pump. They had filled the first large wooden pail and were working on the second one now.

"I mean, yeah, that's true. But wouldn't an organization created for end times be ready for something like that?" Joseph asked as they both picked up a bucket and began slowly walking back to the farmhouse. Joseph knew as well as anyone that the longevity of settlements was not very promising.

Three months ago Joseph had set up camp inside a small settlement that had been built up in the remains of an old highway-side community. There were 15 permanent residents, including Joseph, and the occasional drifter who would show up for a place to rest or for a disappointingly warm beer that had become the specialty of a makeshift tavern located in the basement of a cheap bungalow. It was a good set-up and Joseph had been prepared to live out whatever time he had remaining there. He worked with a small scavenging party that would gather supplies for the settlement in exchange for free goods and services. The settlement had a vague resemblance to pre-war civilization for a while. Unfortunately, The Sick eventually caught wind of the settlement and began nightly raids. At first the citizens of the community were able to keep the Orvilles at bay, but as time went on the raids grew more violent and frequent, prompting people to flee the settlement. Eventually the population had dwindled down to six people. Joseph ultimately had to pack up and hit the road again, which is where he had been ever since.

"Maybe you're right," Greg admitted. "I'm sure something called the 'Post-Apocalyptic Republic' would be prepared for raider attacks. I'm just worried that anyone with a radio will be headed there."

"Maybe that's a good thing. Maybe this is a chance to actually set some roots and rebuild," Joseph replied optimistically. He needed this; he needed something to believe in. Outpost Zulu was the first bit of good news he had received since prior to the war.

"Yeah, I'll keep my big mouth shut. I'm sure it'll be safe. Besides, it can't be worse than what's out here," Greg said with an ironic laugh.

The two new acquaintances hauled the heavy wooden pails up the porch steps to the back door. Joseph struggled significantly more than Greg, but he made sure not to show it. Joseph felt good about things. He had finally found a group of seemingly trustworthy companions and he finally had a surefire destination. It felt good to not have to wander, to have a landing place in mind. Joseph cracked a smile and followed Greg inside.

Chapter 3

Night Is Short for Nightmare

When Greg and Joseph returned to the farmhouse the embers in the fireplace had completely died out, leaving no trace that there ever was a fire except for the slight smoky aroma that lingered within the room. Daylight was receding quickly and the nights had become impossibly dark. The permanent thick coverage of clouds blocked out the moon and the stars, canvassing the world in darkness. It was far too dangerous to have any source of light at night as it would act as a beacon, alerting any nearby Orville or bandit of the group's whereabouts.

William was telling Hillary about his old German Shepherd that he had before the bombs dropped. The dog, Ollie, had been in the backyard at the time of the explosions and had run off. He had been thoroughly spooked when the first bomb erupted about 45 kilometres away from William's countryside home. That was tragically the last time that William ever saw Ollie. Nonetheless, he was making it a pleasant story about his old companion, talking about their times hunting together before the world fell apart.

"Lots of fresh water to go around," Greg said. "Help yourselves."

Everyone drank whatever water they had left and refilled their bottles and canteens. Joseph had filled a small pot from the kitchen to use the water to wash his face off. His beard had accumulated an abundance of dirt and other unruly things. By the time the group had consumed their fair share of the refreshing cold well-water, the inescapable shroud of darkness that accompanied the night had enveloped the land.

William had a stash of ammo in an old green duffel bag, partially ripped along the zipper, that he had stealthily stolen from a raider camp. He had a handful of .45 magnum rounds for Joseph's revolver, which he traded for a few cigarettes. Joseph had tried smoking a few times in university, but he never understood the appeal. The taste was terrible and the smoke made his lungs burn. It was probably for the best anyway as cigarettes turned out to be a highly valuable commodity during the end of the world. Nobody was concerned about cancer any more; there were far more pressing dangers, and cancer seemed inevitable for both smokers and non-smokers alike.

The little farmhouse had three bedrooms upstairs. Each bedroom was relatively the same, consisting of a bed, a wardrobe, and a dresser. William supposedly got the master bedroom, which really only had a slightly bigger bed and an en-suite bathroom that did not have functional plumbing any more. The previous owners of the house had evidently been minimalists. Greg had volunteered to take the couch downstairs by the front door, a place that Joseph certainly would not have wanted to sleep. Everyone said their good nights and went to their respective rooms, except for Greg who remained in the living room. His long legs extended beyond the length of the sofa and forced him to curl up into a ball like a scared child in the foetal position cowering from a thunderstorm.

Joseph was lying in his bed trying to get comfortable on the lumpy mattress and gazing out the window. There wasn't anything much to see other than the eternal void of darkness. Joseph thought that he might be able to see where the moon was trying to break through the perpetual cloud coverage when he focused on seeing with his peripheral vision, a trick that he had learned at camp as a young boy. It had helped him spot evening frogs and other critters while he patrolled the sandy beach.

Joseph had taken the smallest of the three rooms available, but he actually preferred smaller rooms. He felt safer in them, like there weren't as many places for something to be lurking in the dark. The room likely was that of a child a long time ago. The now peeling wallpaper had been a bright blue at one point in time and the duvet that now covered Joseph's weary body was patterned with astronauts and stars. Joseph believed that the only time he would ever be able to see stars again with his own eyes would be by looking at this musty blanket that once might have inspired dreams of planetary exploration in a curious child. It was like a sick joke from the universe.

Joseph had lain on his left side looking out the window for quite some time trying to find the moon before finally falling asleep. He had to actively reassure himself that he was safe; he suffered from constant paranoia at night. He always felt like something was watching him and waiting for an opportunity to strike.

***

Greg had no problems falling right to sleep. He had put a sweater on before he went to bed and he was now lying perfectly straight with his arms folded across his chest and his feet dangling over the end of the couch. He was sleeping peacefully and gently snoring when something awoke him with a startle. He could've sworn that he heard a loud thump outside the front door. Greg remained perfectly still, listening for whatever he heard to happen again. This time he heard footsteps on the creaky front porch. Greg slowly leaned over and grabbed his Glock from the floor beside the couch, while still lying down and being careful not to make a sound. He slowly sat up and stared out the window beside the front door, but it was far too dark to see anything. Greg could hear his heart thumping in his chest; he was terrified that whatever was just beyond the thin wooden wall would be able to hear his rapidly beating heart.

The back door behind Greg from across the kitchen began to rattle as someone tried to open the locked door. The back door stopped shaking after a few seconds and was followed by an equally noisy attempt to open the front door. Greg slowly stood up and started creeping up the stairs to wake the others.

***

Joseph suppressed a terrified scream when he woke to the sight of the tall man known as Greg standing at the foot of his bed.

"What the hell is wrong with you? What're you doing?" Joseph hissed in a hushed tone so as not to wake the others.

"Keep your voice down!" Greg whispered back. "Someone is trying to get in."

Joseph turned a sickly shade of grey, but the room was far too dark for Greg to notice.

"I'll go wake Hillary. Go get William," Greg ordered.

Joseph nodded, a gesture that was barely visible, and quickly got up. He made sure to retrieve his revolver from the wobbly nightstand beside his child-sized bed before he tiptoed down the hallway towards William's room, the aged floorboards creaking in protest with each step. Joseph opened the door and whispered, "William! William, wake up—someone's trying to break in downstairs."

William sat up and gave his head a confused shake.

"Okay…" he said groggily. "I'll be right there."

Joseph left the room and saw Greg and Hillary standing at the top of the stairs, squinting into the darkness below. Joseph crept over, almost giving Hillary a heart attack in the process.

"Well? Did they leave?" Joseph asked hopefully.

"We haven't heard anything yet…we're just listening," Hillary said in a hushed voice, holding a large machete with both hands.

The three of them just stood there in the dark listening for signs of intruders, and soon William joined to make it four. William held a vintage 1950s-era Thompson submachine gun that suited him in a strange way and prompted Joseph to wonder what the old man did for a living prior to this whole nightmare. Joseph felt that even his breathing would be too loud and began to hold his breath like a child about to be caught while playing a game of hide-and-seek. Just as Joseph was about to suggest that perhaps whoever had tried to open the door had moved on, both the downstairs doors began to violently shake at the same time. It was apparent that there were at least two entities outside trying to enter the once picturesque farmhouse. The doors abruptly stopped shaking and the house fell silent once more.

"We should say something. Maybe they need help," William suggested nervously, exposing his empathetic heart.

"No, let's just wait and—" Greg was cut off by the sound of shattering glass in the living room only a few feet away from the bottom of the staircase. Everyone instinctively readied their weapons. Joseph, Greg, and William aimed in the direction of the shattered glass, still unable to see anything clearly, and Hillary gripped her machete tightly while watching behind them. Even though they were on the second floor of the two-storey house, it didn't hurt to have someone watch their back.

"Whoever you are, we don't want any trouble! We don't have enough room for you, and there is nothing worth fighting for inside!" Greg shouted into the dark.

"That sounds like fresh meat!" something horrible snarled from the bottom of the stairs. There was no denying that it was an Orville. A mutant. A freak. A sicko. Whatever the going name was. What was yet to be known, however, was just how many there were.

Greg blindly fired two shots towards where the voice had come from, the second bullet finding its mark. The Orville let out a blood-curdling shriek and fell to the floor with a loud thud. Its body was then dragged back out through the broken window and onto the porch where more Orvilles could be heard tearing into their wounded, not willing to pass up an opportunity to feast. It screamed in agony as fellow pack-mates tore the flesh from its bones, consuming the fallen alive. The agonized scream was finally silenced by a forceful bite to the throat.

Everyone's eyes had adjusted enough to make out faint silhouettes in the darkness. Three Orvilles jumped through the broken window one after the other in rapid succession and started sprinting up the stairs. They had nothing left to lose — to most of them death was a welcome means of escaping their deranged state of mind. The Orvilles often had an edge when it came to seeing in the dark, as they spent most of their waking hours at night or holed up somewhere dark during the day to protect their ruined skin from the sunlight. William ripped off a burst from his Thompson, tearing through the three assailants with ease. The first two were killed instantly and the Orville at the rear was severely injured. The trio of bloodthirsty monsters tumbled down the wooden staircase into a heap. William kept his gun aimed at the bottom of the stairs, showing no signs of panic.

Hillary, on the other hand, was hyperventilating but remained vigilant. For a minute that seemed closer to five, nothing happened. The third Orville that was shot but not killed had stopped squirming around in the body pile at the bottom of the stairs, presumably having lost consciousness or finally succumbing to its injuries. There was a rapid thumping coming from above the group. Everyone looked up but there was no third floor — the Orvilles had somehow managed to climb onto the roof. Joseph spun around, immediately worrying about the upstairs windows. The master bedroom where William had slept had a very small terrace that could be accessible to someone jumping down from the roof.

The sound of broken glass could be heard again, this time coming from William's room. Joseph's fears had been confirmed. William's half-open door was torn wide open and three more

Orvilles ran down the hallway on all fours like starving dogs towards the group. At the same time, two more climbed through the shattered downstairs window again. Joseph flinched and fired his high-powered revolver at The Sick who were running down the hall in an unnatural manner, the recoil sending a sharp pain into his wrist. The lead Orville collapsed, tripping the other two. Joseph fired off four more shots, finishing off the trio of Orvilles and effectively sending a rush of tingles up his forearm.

Greg and William made quick work of the two on the main floor, not allowing them to get even halfway up the stairs. Greg and William both had to reload and Greg realized that the rest of his ammo was downstairs, still sitting beside the couch. William's ammo remained in his room, which now was hosting four more uninvited guests standing in the doorframe. Joseph was struggling to reload in the dark and another group of Orvilles hopped through the downstairs window. Hillary was holding her machete like a baseball bat and still hadn't had to take a swing yet.

"Shit! There's too many of them!" Greg shouted as he started to back away from the stairs.

"We're outta ammo, Joseph!" William exclaimed.

"In here!" Joseph yelled as the Orvilles began to converge on them once more.

The four darted into the nearest room, which was Joseph's, and slammed the door shut. It was immediately rocked with violent force as the seven remaining Orvilles attempted to break through while Greg and Joseph held the door shut. William and Hillary started to push a large oak wardrobe over to the door to act as a protective barricade. They slid it into place and the four stepped back and watched in horror as the door continued to be bombarded, shaking even the cumbersome wardrobe.

Joseph ran over to his window, which overlooked the front of the house. It was only a 15-foot drop at most, maybe less if they hung from the windowsill first. Joseph's resourceful escape plan was thwarted when he saw a group of six more Orvilles crowded underneath the window looking up at him, their eager jaws excitedly snapping at the air like ravenous wolves. Although the Orvilles had lost most of their ability to rationalize and work through complex problems, they had become excellent hunters of humans over the past two years. They were relentless and they were effective.

Hillary started to scream, her anxiety finally getting the better of her. William was trying to calm her down and Greg was leaning his large body against the wardrobe to buy them some extra time. Joseph had successfully reloaded by now, having a full six shots but nothing left to reload with afterwards. This was by far the largest pack of Orvilles Joseph had ever encountered, although the raids at the settlement that he had been forced to flee from a few months prior had gotten pretty large as well. The snarls from the Orvilles outside the door were increasing in volume as they became more and more frustrated. Some of them could be heard swearing and threatening Joseph and his companions, whereas others made what could only be explained as tortured animal noises. Joseph was beginning to lose all hope and was starting to tremble, when there was a sudden explosion of gunfire from somewhere outside in the night.

Everyone except for Greg, who didn't dare to stop putting his weight against the wardrobe, hurried over to the window and saw that the six Orvilles that had been snapping their hungry jaws just moments prior were now crumpled together on the ground. They all squinted into the darkness but could not see any signs of the shooters. The pounding on the bedroom door stopped; the remaining Orvilles had heard the gunfire as well and were now listening for the approaching threat. Everyone in the house was silent and for a couple of minutes the only sound was the laboured breathing of The Sick outside Joseph's bedroom door.

The silence was shattered by a massive explosion that came from downstairs. Joseph could hear something splintering into tiny pieces, presumably the frail wooden front door. Seconds later, Joseph and his companions could hear the Orvilles shrieking with fright and a series of gunshots that proceeded to silence their guttural screams. Joseph gripped his revolver tightly while aiming at the door, not sure if whoever just killed the Orvilles would do the same to him and his newfound acquaintances for the clothes off their backs.

"First floor clear!" an unidentified voice from downstairs shouted.

Someone tried to open Joseph's bedroom door, just as unsuccessfully as the group of Orvilles. There was a pounding knock and then a loud voice hollered, "Anybody in there?"

At first no one knew how to respond. It was Hillary who had the courage to eventually answer.

"Yes, we're here! Is it safe? Who are you?"

"We're the guys who just saved your life. Now open up." The voice was a gruff no-nonsense kind of voice.

Another voice from down the hall hollered "Second floor clear!"

"How do we know you're not going to kill us and steal our stuff?" Hillary asked, seeking some kind of assurance.

"We've got no reason to kill you folks," the no-nonsense kind of man responded. "Besides, if we wanted you dead you would be."

Everyone in the room whispered frantically, trying to figure out what to do. To Joseph, it didn't seem like they had much of a choice. Everyone agreed to open up except for Greg, but it was a three-to-one vote.

"This is your last chance," the voice from behind the door warned.

"Okay, okay, hang on," Joseph replied quickly.

"And if you have any weapons it would be best to set them on the ground," the stern voice advised from beyond the door.

Joseph looked down to his right hand, his knuckles white from clenching the grip of his pistol so hard out of fear. He shakily and slowly placed the gun down on the ground. His companions also set down their weapons before William and Greg began to scooch the heavy wardrobe away from the bedroom door, undoubtedly scratching the hardwood floor. Once the door was fully revealed, it could be seen that the relentless Orvilles had managed to smash a jagged hole right in the centre. All anyone could see through that hole was blackness.

William stepped back and Greg unlocked the door with an audible click. The door burst open with tremendous speed, almost striking Greg. Five men, all dressed in black, rushed into the room with automatic rifles at the ready. Joseph, Greg, William, and Hillary all raised their hands and stumbled backwards towards the far wall at the foot of the astronaut bed by the window.

"Don't move—and stay against the wall!" the familiar voice that had spoken to them from behind the door barked. "Wolf, Ghost, and Beetle, set a perimeter around the house. Rex, stay with me," he continued to order. The man was clearly the one in charge as the four other men obeyed his command without hesitation.

Both the men remaining in the room were dressed almost identically from head to toe. They wore black combat boots that matched their urban camouflage pants and dark tactical jackets. They had black gloves on and sported thin backpacks that possessed unknown contents. They were dressed as dark as the lightless night itself. The man on Joseph's left that had been identified as 'Rex' had on an inky-coloured balaclava that covered his entire face minus a small slit for his eyes. His eyes, however, were concealed by night-vision goggles that allowed him to defy the laws of nature and see perfectly in the dark. The man in charge wore the same night-vision goggles but the rest of his face was exposed, revealing a bushy black beard that could've put the notorious pirate by the name of Black Beard to shame. There was one more commonality between the two men. On the left side of their chests were three dark-red letters that read: PAR. Both of the PAR members kept their rifles aimed at Joseph and his new companions.

Joseph was dumbfounded at the timely coincidence. He had gone his entire life never hearing a word about this PAR association until the day prior. Now, not only had he been informed of the existence of PAR but he was also standing face to face with members of the organization. Well-armed members. This only strengthened Joseph's belief that Outpost Zulu would still be alive and well. If anything, staring down the barrel of these two men's rifles only gave Joseph more hope in a backwards sort of way.

"Please, we're not a threat. Lower your weapons," William assured the PAR operatives.

"Relax, you'll all be fine if everyone just cooperates," the bearded man replied calmly. "Rex, check their radiation levels."

"Yes, Sir," Rex replied. The man following orders slipped his backpack off and retrieved what looked like a finger prick used for diabetics, only a few sizes larger. He stepped up to Hillary first.

"Hey, what is that?" Greg demanded to know protectively.

"We're just checking your blood levels. Making sure you four aren't infected," the bearded man answered.

"And if we are?" Greg enquired.

"I doubt you are. Let's just hope that you're not." It was Rex who answered.

Rex pricked Hillary's finger and looked at his device for a moment. After a few seconds he nodded and repeated this process with the remaining three, finishing with Joseph. Joseph had always been slightly squeamish when it came to needles, so he was none too pleased to have his finger pricked.

"Radiation levels are high but acceptable," Rex reported to the bearded leader.

"Good," he said as he lowered his gun and Rex tucked the device back into his backpack.

"You're PAR," Hillary blurted out, also noticing the patches on their jackets.

"Yes," the bearded man responded without much emotion. "You folks heading somewhere in particular?"

"Yeah, we heard the broadcast about the outpost on the north side of Hathbury," William promptly answered.

"Ah yes, Outpost Zulu. Smart group of people, I see. The rest of the road should be relatively quiet, but exercise caution when entering the main city."

"What's so dangerous about the city, other than the usual stuff?" Hillary asked.

"Bandits like to wait for newcomers who are heading up to Outpost Zulu," the man said as he retrieved a fat cigar from his upper chest pocket and lit it. "There are lots of places to hide in a city that big."

"Can you take us to Zulu? You know, so like, we can get there safely?" Hillary sounded hopeful, like a child asking Santa for a special Christmas present.

The man shook his head and took a long drag on his cigar. "We've got important work to do. The population of the infected is continuing to increase and they are moving closer to the outpost. We've been tracking this horde that was attacking you lot for a few days. They had been making a beeline straight for the city—it was only a matter of time until they reached Outpost Zulu. It's like they can smell folks out, like bloodhounds."

"You think they can *smell* survivors now? Track them?" Joseph asked incredulously. The very thought sent a chill down his spine.

The man with the beard blew out a puff of smoke.

"Yeah, we're starting to think so. Better be careful out there," he warned, but it came across more like a threat due to his imposing demeanour.

"Anyways," he continued, "the sun will start to rise soon and you folks should get a move on if you want to reach the outpost before nightfall. I'd strongly advise you don't spend the night in the city outside of Zulu."

"Right!" William said, clapping his hands together. "Let's get a move on, gang!"

William made his way past the two soldiers with a slight bounce in his step and went to his room to quickly gather up his things. Greg and Hillary also departed to prepare for the long journey ahead, leaving Joseph alone with the two PAR operatives in his room. Rex had made himself at home, lying on Joseph's bed with his hands behind his head. Rex had removed his headgear. He looked to be around Joseph's age but in very good health. His colour was healthy and his short blond hair was neat. His canteen was sitting on the nightstand beside him where Joseph had kept his revolver as he slept. Joseph's revolver was currently still resting on the hardwood floor.

"You got a name?" the man asked, flicking the small butt of his cigar onto the ground.

"Joseph."

"You look like shit, Joseph," the man smirked beneath his beard.

"Yeah, thanks," Joseph replied sarcastically as he walked over to the far side of the room to collect his bag.

"What did you do before all this?" the bearded man asked, seeming genuinely interested.

"What?" Joseph responded, not really paying much attention to the man as he made sure all of his belongings were accounted for.

"Your job. What did you do?" he repeated.

"I was a lawyer," Joseph answered as he zipped up his backpack.

The man laughed.

"What's so funny?" Joseph asked, slightly offended.

"How's it feel to be a lawyer in a lawless world?"

Before Joseph had a chance to respond, the bearded man's walkie-talkie went off.

"Reaper, there's nothing out here, man. Permission to break perimeter and come back?" the voice on the walkie-talkie asked.

Reaper pinched the button on the walkie-talkie that was located on his left shoulder. "Yeah, get your asses back inside and take some R and R time."

"Reaper," Joseph repeated. "How'd you get that name?"

"Take a guess." Reaper winked, his night-vision apparatus now resting on top of his head, which was covered by a black toque.

Joseph had gathered all of his belongings except for his revolver. He walked over to it and picked it up, stuffing it into the waistband of his dirty jeans. The extra width from the revolver actually made Joseph's pants fit a little better—they usually sagged even with his belt due to his unplanned weight-loss programme.

"You should get a holster for that. Gonna shoot your foot off," Reaper warned.

"Yeah, well, if you've got a spare one…" Joseph began to say before Reaper shook his head.

Joseph began making his way to the door and paused, turning to Reaper. Rex appeared to be fast asleep now.

"So Outpost Zulu is real then—it's survived all this time?" Joseph asked, wanting to be reassured one more time.

"Yeah, she survived alright," Reaper informed Joseph. "It's safe there. The only danger is getting there in one piece."

Joseph nodded, feeling reassured by the straight answer.

"You coming, Joseph?" Greg hollered from downstairs.

"Yeah, be right there," Joseph shouted back.

"Thanks for saving our skins," Joseph said.

Reaper shrugged and simply replied, "It's what we do."

Joseph left the room and made his way downstairs to join the others. The three men who had been sent to secure a perimeter were sitting around the kitchen table playing cards and were dressed similarly to Reaper and Rex. Their headgear was also off and they all looked to be around their late twenties or early thirties. Similarly to Rex and even Reaper, they all looked healthy and well groomed. Reaper had been the only one with any type of facial hair and appeared to be the oldest of the bunch, floating somewhere in his late thirties or early forties.

Greg, William, and Hillary were waiting for Joseph by the front door. Greg had a massive green hiking pack on his back and William had his green duffel bag slung over his right shoulder. He looked very uncomfortable and Joseph felt bad that the old man had such an awkwardly shaped bag. Hillary had two reusable grocery bags, both overflowing with blankets and bulging with supplies underneath.

The quartet headed out the front door as the soldiers at the kitchen table watched them depart. Reaper and Rex observed them from the upstairs window in Joseph's room. The four began trudging through the sloppy field towards the highway where they would continue their journey to the promised land known as Outpost Zulu.

Chapter 4

Into the City

The group of four had been travelling down the highway for a few hours now and they had not encountered a single soul. Greg and Joseph took up the rear, allowing William and Hillary to set a comfortable pace. Everyone had been taking turns carrying Hillary's and William's bags, as they were the least physically capable of the group and their bags were awkward to carry. They weren't far from the south side of Hathbury, and the countryside that previously consisted primarily of farmland had now given way to off-ramps that led to the subdivisions below.

These subdivisions were a sorry sight. From what the group of travel companions could see from the highway above, most of the houses that were still standing had been broken into and the streets were littered with debris and corpses in various stages of decay. The highway had now expanded into four lanes that went both north and south and were separated by a concrete divider. There was an abundance of abandoned cars of all makes and models. This had been slowing their progress down tremendously as it forced the group to weave in and out of the wrecks in a single-file line like an extended snake weaving through long grass. The outline of high-rises and skyscrapers had become visible as the quartet got closer to the main part of the city. The group came to an abrupt halt as William spotted a lone figure ahead of them sitting with their back against the remains of a pick-up truck that was resting on four flat tyres.

"Look over there," William whispered as he pointed out the man sitting alone ahead of them.

"He doesn't look sick to me," Hillary commented.

"Yeah, but what if it's a trap? He could have a bunch of his bandit buddies waiting to pounce," Joseph warned, and Greg nodded in agreement.

"Regardless, we're going to have to get past him anyways. Just stay alert," William instructed as he unslung his duffel bag and took out the Thompson submachine gun. He only had one drum mag remaining, but it was full and already loaded into the gun. Joseph and Greg readied their handguns and Hillary remained unarmed, having to use two hands for her bags, the handle of her machete sticking out of the top of the reusable grocery bag in her left hand.

"Stay in between Joseph and myself," Greg protectively told Hillary.

The group began cautiously approaching the unknown man. As they got closer to the stranger it became apparent that he wasn't sick. He wasn't showing many signs of life either, barely moving, and his eyes were tightly squeezed shut. He was dressed similarly to Joseph, but instead of a tattered leather jacket he wore an equally battered red hoodie with the name 'HARVARD' plastered to the front of it. He was a long way from Massachusetts, Joseph thought. The young man cracked open his eyes and looked up at William, who had taken the lead.

"Help me," he said weakly, his eyes red and wet.

Joseph looked down and realized that the man was sitting in a small pool of congealed blood which had stained his faded blue denim jeans beyond repair. It was impossible to identify exactly where the blackish red leak was coming from—the man's entire lower half appeared to be drenched in blood. Joseph tasted the iron in the air when he inhaled, just like he had back at the gas station the day before.

"What happened?" William asked sympathetically as he crouched down to the wounded man's eye level.

"Bandits...they shot me last night...took everything," the man managed to say. Every word that escaped his parched lips was a struggle.

Hillary looked away from the man, deeply saddened by the situation.

"How many?" Joseph asked, more concerned about his own well-being as he scanned their surroundings for any potential threats.

The wounded man held up a shaky hand and signalled the number five. He then lifted his sweater to reveal three bullet holes around his waist. It was a miracle that he was even still alive, especially after he had spilt such a copious amount of blood onto the highway. If anything, it was unlucky; it only prolonged his suffering and inevitable demise.

"Can you...can you help me?" the man asked again, his voice barely a whisper.

Joseph and his companions exchange worried glances. Joseph only had a box of drugstore Band-Aids that he had been using for blisters and a couple of painkillers. Hillary had a bottle of rubbing alcohol that could help ward off infection, but by now the man was past the point of any possible recovery. William began to take out a wad of gauze from his duffel bag so that he could at least wrap the wounds. The injured man shook his head and pointed at William's gun; it was clear what kind of help he wanted.

"I'm dead anyways..." the man said, his voice now hardly audible. He did not look scared, not like the bandit that Joseph had executed yesterday. He just looked tired, tired of all the pain he had had to endure for the last two years. William stepped back, mortified at the request. Hillary was trying not to listen while she sat on the concrete divider facing the other side of the highway. Joseph's heartbeat was accelerating. He knew it was the humane thing to do, but he wanted to believe that there was an alternative.

"Okay," Greg spoke up.

Everyone looked at him, even Hillary, who had to look back over her shoulder.

"You three go on ahead—I'll catch up," Greg sombrely said.

Nobody argued; they were all thankful that it wasn't them having to put the man out of his misery. Joseph, William, and Hillary walked about 30 feet up the highway and waited. There was a loud pop as a lone gunshot reverberated into the voiceless air. Shortly afterwards Greg solemnly rejoined the group and they continued moving onward towards the city. Nobody said a word.

**

Reaper and Rex had joined the other three PAR operatives downstairs at the pinewood kitchen table. Everyone was eating their MRE rations, and a large map of the region lay unfolded across the table. The sun had started to rise and the dining room was temporarily filled with a soft orange light. In less than an hour, the sun would rise above the clouds and the world would resume its ghastly grey ambience.

"Beetle," Reaper said while digging into his MRE that consisted of a mixture of pork and rice, "what's our kill count at now?"

Beetle wore a pair of ballistic glasses with prescription inserts that gave his eyes a buggy appearance, hence his characteristic codename. He retrieved a small notepad from his chest pocket and flipped through it.

"After last night's skirmish we're sitting around forty, give or take," he informed his leader.

"Good," Reaper nodded. "How many civilian casualties?"

"Seven, although if I recall correctly, a few of those so-called 'casualties' were shooting at us," Beetle scoffed as he recalled the trio of bandits that they had neutralized a few days earlier.

"Alright, not bad at all," Reaper remarked. "How are we for ammo, Wolf?"

"Low but not out. We have enough for one more day, two if things are quiet," Wolf replied in a loud matter-of-fact kind of voice.

Reaper stood up to get a better view of the map, which was covered in pencil marks.

"Ghost, explain these markings to me," he commanded as he squinted at the tarnished map.

Ghost sighed and stood up as well, pointing and explaining the markings that he had made.

"These are the major hot spots of infected populations I've scouted over the last few operations. I marked them like you asked me to. As predicted, they're getting closer to Hathbury with each mission we go on," he informed Reaper.

The group of PAR operatives, nicknamed Alpha Squad, had been sent on a series of 'waste management' missions for the last couple of months. It was the Commander's euphemism for eliminating pockets of the infected. The population of the infected proceeded to grow and their packs continued to migrate towards the city where there was more food to scavenge and people to prey on. Alpha Squad had been ordered to eliminate a minimum of 30 infected per mission and to keep track of their migration trends. Reaper suspected that these missions were just an excuse to keep his unit battle hardened, like field training. Outpost Zulu was well fortified and he doubted that the infected would pose a significant threat. Regardless of whether or not the threat to Outpost Zulu was consequential, Reaper enjoyed working with his unit and loved any excuse to pull a trigger.

"Good news, boys," Reaper said with a smirk, "I think we've earned some R and R back at HQ. We've hit our kill count as per usual and Ghost's markings confirm the suspected migration trends that the infected have been following for the last couple of months. It's time to head home."

Everyone cheered. Alpha Squad's current mission had kept them in the field for almost two weeks. Everyone in the unit was more than happy to head back to base and switch off for a few days. Reaper personally couldn't wait to take a hot shower and eliminate the perpetual smell of death that seemed to linger deep within the fabric of his uniform. The battle-hardened death squad was all smiles now. Reaper took out a sleek black tracking device from his backpack and turned it on. Alpha Squad sat at the kitchen table eating, laughing, and waiting for their ride home.

***

The silence that followed Greg's return to the group had dragged on for a long while. Despite the awkward silence, nobody blamed him for what he had done. It had been the merciful thing to do. It was just an unwelcome stark reminder of the brutal world that they were now forced to be a part of. They were approaching the edge of the main city now and had an important decision to make. They could either continue on their current route along the congested four by four-lane highway, or take an off-ramp that led to the city streets below. They were all stopped at the off-ramp deliberating about what to do next. The overpass would be less direct and take much longer, but it would also most likely be safer. Cutting directly through the city would be much faster and provide opportunity to gather loot, but it would also be substantially more dangerous. Joseph was keen on risking it through the city; the quicker they made it to Outpost Zulu the better, and his supplies were beginning to dwindle.

"It's safer if we stick to the highway. We'll be able to replenish our supplies at the outpost," William said to Greg. The two of them had been arguing about what the next best course of action was for a couple of minutes now.

"No, we'd be sitting ducks up here! The entire city could see us walking around and it would be way too easy for a group of bandits to set up an ambush," Greg countered.

Hillary was exhausted and just wanted to get to the outpost as quickly as possible so that she could rest; she didn't really care which route they took at the moment.

"Which way is the fastest?" she asked no one in particular.

Greg and William were too fixated on their argument to notice her.

"The highway is safer, but slower," Joseph answered Hillary. "I agree with Greg—I think we should go through the city. We might find supplies that we could trade at the outpost or even keep for ourselves."

Greg and William stopped arguing and looked over at Joseph.

"There, see? Two against one, old man," Greg sneered.

William scowled, making his old face seem even more aged.

"Don't I get a say in the matter?" Hillary chimed in as she made up her mind. "I say we take the highway—better safe than sorry."

William nodded in approval.

"It would seem we are at an impasse," William declared.

Joseph sighed. They were wasting time. It was late in the afternoon and they would have to make it through the entire city in a matter of hours if they wanted to make it to the outpost before nightfall.

"Does anyone happen to have a coin? We could flip on it," Joseph suggested.

Nobody had a coin—there was no use for conventional currency any more. Before the bombs dropped almost everyone paid for commodities virtually anyway; physical currency had become a rarity.

"Here," Joseph said as he unscrewed the cap of his water bottle. "If it lands upright we travel through the city. Upside down we take the highway. Deal?"

Everyone nodded; it seemed like a reasonable solution. Only it wasn't a reasonable solution and Joseph knew it. About a month ago, he had been holed up in an abandoned house for two days taking shelter from a ferocious storm that had no end in sight. He had spent his time thinking, sewing his battered clothes, and trying to get his bottle cap to land upside down. It never did. Joseph flipped the bottle cap, and as predicted, it faithfully landed upright yet again.

"Ha! Through the city it is!" Greg exclaimed.

"This is a bad idea," William groaned.

Hillary simply sighed, too tired to argue any more. The four started to head down the exit ramp, traversing around more car wrecks. When they got to the bottom of the ramp, everyone stood still and listened for a while. There was an exchange of gunfire in the distance, although it was hard to tell how far and in which direction the gunshots came from as they echoed around the concrete jungle. No one would know if The Sick had a strong presence here or not. For all they knew, the surrounding buildings could be packed with Orvilles waiting for the shroud of darkness to strike.

The group began moving through the city streets in the same direction that the highway overpass had been heading: north. They had been walking for half an hour when Joseph spotted a promising corner store that seemed to be in relatively good condition. The quartet entered the store in search of supplies. It had been picked clean for the most part, but Joseph found a can of beans that had rolled under the counter and had been forgotten about. Other than the lone surviving can of baked beans, the store had been looted entirely, just as so many other stores had been. A single can of baked beans could last Joseph several days and provide a temporary lull in the perpetual hunger pains he constantly dealt with.

They continued on their journey. For the most part, they followed the overpass. It was going north towards the outpost and it would be far too easy to get turned around in such a big city if they ventured away from the overpass. There was another burst of gunfire, this time much closer and accompanied by maniacal laughter. Joseph could tell that the noise disturbance was just down the street, the exact source concealed by debris and overturned cars. Everyone froze and listened to the nearby laughter.

"That sounds close," Greg said as he peered down the litter-ridden street in the direction of the laughter.

"Yeah, what's the plan?" Joseph asked.

He still had his revolver and six shots. Greg had his Glock with two mags and William had his one 50-round drum mag for his Thompson submachine gun. Hillary had her machete. In other words, the group was surprisingly well armed. Still, getting into a firefight wasn't particularly high on anyone's daily to-do list. Greg pointed at a huge building that used to contain offices for corporate employees to slave away in. Everyone hurried into the corporate office building in order to stay concealed from whoever had been just down the street in front of them. It was dark inside, as most places were these days, and there was a skeleton propped up behind the reception desk waiting to greet them.

"Gross," Hillary said with a look of disgust on her face. To the left of the desk was a large lounge that was used at one point as a waiting room for clients who would come to see the higher-level executives. To the right was a set of bathrooms, and behind the receptionist was a flight of stairs and an elevator that was no longer in service. The group darted into the lounge and took cover behind a long red sofa that looked to still be in good condition. If someone were to sit in the black leather chairs that lined the large glass window on the opposite side of the room, they would see four faces peeking up from behind the couch with wide eyes. Joseph, Greg, William and Hillary all remained quiet and attentively watched the street beyond the window.

"This was a bad idea!" William hissed in a hushed voice.

"Just relax—no one is going to know we're here," Greg whispered back.

Joseph held his revolver in his sweaty right hand. Everyone's weapons were out, including Hillary's machete. They could start to hear voices, a lot of them. A large group became visible on the far side of the street. Joseph thought there were about ten, but it was difficult to know for certain. There was a male and a female near the back with their hands bound by zip ties; two men kept pistols aimed at the back of their heads as they walked. The group turned and began crossing the street towards the office building. Everybody ducked down, waiting for the group to pass. Only they didn't pass and the broken glass door could be heard opening, accompanied by the sound of broken glass crunching under heavy footsteps. Joseph got on his side and peered out at the main lobby from underneath the couch; it was dim enough inside to ensure his concealment. He could see a freakishly tall man, wearing a long dark-blue trench coat with unruly blond hair that was down to his shoulders, approaching the front desk.

"Susan, honey! I'm back, did you miss me?" the man in the trench coat hollered at the skeleton working the receptionist desk. The rest of his entourage was shuffling into the lobby now and more shards of glass crunched beneath their assortment of footwear. The tall man caressed the skeleton's face, bits of flesh still clinging to the bones.

"I hope you didn't find someone else while I was gone." The man swooned while he smiled from ear to ear, gazing into the empty sockets of the skeleton where eyes would have once been.

"Hey, boss, what do you want us to do with these two?" someone asked the unhinged man as they shoved the two captives forward. The man spun around, his trench coat trailing like a cape.

"What do you think I want you to do?" the tall man bellowed as he looked down at a man in a baggy hoodie and cargo pants. The shorter man nodded and began shoving the captives towards the stairs. The two captives pleaded desperately as they were marched up the stairs, and several other men and women followed. That left only the man in the trench coat and his four remaining companions.

"Come," he said to them, "take a seat with me."

The group of five entered the lounge and Joseph could feel his chest begin to tighten. The long-haired man sat in the black leather chair across from the couch. Three of the men sat on the red couch and the last man stood in the corner by the entrance, holding some kind of assault rifle. The room was so quiet that you could've heard a pin drop. Nobody was uttering a single word. Joseph looked at his friends; they all looked just as terrified as he felt. Except for Greg. Greg looked like he was ready to be the hero and save the day. The silence was interrupted by a series of shrill shrieks coming from one of the upper levels. It was the scream of a woman at first, but soon the tortured screams of a man accompanied her. Greg made eye contact with Joseph and pointed to his gun, indicating that he wanted to spring up and take the element of surprise. Joseph shook his head and put a finger to his lips. Greg scowled and the quartet remained silent. Joseph was in no rush to get into a firefight, especially when there was a man with an assault rifle looking directly at the three men on the couch that he was hiding behind.

The screams continued to echo through the building, but still nothing was said. A few full minutes passed before an unstable voice that seemed to switch octaves mid-sentence finally spoke. The voice of the tall man in the trench coat.

"So," he said, "you three would like to join my family."

It was a statement, not a question. Instead of replying, the three men simply nodded, a gesture Joseph and his partners could not see.

"I always welcome new brothers and sisters with open arms," the trench coat man said, smiling widely.

"We've heard so much about you—we heard that you can cure The Sick!" a new voice from the couch exclaimed.

"I can do many things, as I am the chosen one. You shall address me as Overseer, for I oversee my brothers and sisters. I take care of my own." Overseer twirled his long hair around one finger, one leg resting on top of the other. Joseph and company were becoming increasingly uncomfortable.

Another person from the couch spoke.

"So, now what?" asked a very young voice that sounded about 14 or so.

"Now, little one, you must prove your loyalty to me. All three of you must. Remove your itsy-bitsy left pinky finger and show me that you are one of my people," Overseer declared.

"You're crazy! I'm not cuttin' my finger off for you!" the third voice said.

Overseer's smile vanished entirely.

"Get out," he demanded.

"What?" the man replied incredulously.

"Did I stutter, you ignorant pig? Get. Out."

Overseer drew a snub-nosed revolver and aimed it at the defiant man. The man slowly raised his hands and began backing out of the room. The guard at the door stepped aside and the man took off running down the street, melting into the city once more. Overseer put his gun back into his trench coat and continued to smile as if nothing had happened.

"Now, who's first?" he asked.

Greg had made eye contact with Joseph again, trying to encourage him to jump up. Joseph continued to shake his head. Hillary looked terrified and William was just staring straight ahead at the wall behind them. The young voice volunteered first and walked over to Overseer. There was a small wooden table beside him where a lamp had once stood. Overseer handed him a large hunting knife and patted him on the back. The young boy did not hesitate and started furiously sawing away at the base of his pinky finger. The boy was eager to demonstrate his loyalty and become a part of some kind of twisted post-apocalyptic family, also known as a cult. Within a matter of seconds, the finger had been sawn off entirely and the young boy let out an animalistic howl of pain as the nub that was now his pinky began to squirt blood. Overseer stood and embraced him in a hug.

"Welcome to my family," he said as he kissed the boy on the head. "Now go on upstairs—join your brothers and sisters. They will take care of you."

The boy eagerly ran into the lobby and up the stairs while he clutched at where his finger had once been, skipping every second step as he left small splatters of blood in his wake.

"I guess it's my turn," the remaining man said without enthusiasm. He went over to the table beside Overseer and begrudgingly hacked his pinky finger off with the same knife that the boy had used moments ago. He cursed in pain and looked down in horror at his finger that was now resting next to the young boy's finger in a small, communal pool of blood.

"Welcome to my family," Overseer repeated, embracing the man and kissing the top of his head as well.

"Now hold this," Overseer demanded as he handed the man another handgun that had been hidden within his jacket. The man confusedly took the gun and stood there awkwardly as he tried to press his amputation wound against his grimy shirt in order to slow the bleeding. Joseph wondered how many people actually survived this bizarre initiation test without succumbing to infection. He supposed that it was a sadistic yet effective way of weaning out the weak.

"Now, would my friends behind the couch like to join us?" Overseer asked with a grin as he observed Hillary's bag that was just barely sticking out at the end of the couch.

Joseph's heart skipped a beat. Surely he didn't just hear what he thought he heard. Greg jumped to his feet, aiming his gun directly at Overseer. Joseph followed his lead and aimed his gun at the man in the corner guarding the entrance to the lobby, who was now aiming his assault rifle at Greg. Overseer pointed his revolver at Joseph as the recently indoctrinated man aimed back and forth between Joseph and Greg. William was struggling to stand up as he battled his arthritic knees, and when he finally did manage to get to his feet he held his Thompson loosely by his artificial hip. Hillary remained behind the couch, out of site, with her machete.

"Easy, friends, is that anyway to treat your host? Eavesdropping and popping up with your guns out?" Overseer asked while still smiling.

"We were just leaving," Joseph carefully replied as he shifted his focus to the unnaturally tall man who identified himself as Overseer.

"Oh? That hurts my feelings. You sneak into my castle and you don't even stay for dinner? Tisk tisk," Oversee replied as his eerie smile was beginning to diminish.

"Look, I'm sorry. We didn't know anyone lived here. We'll see ourselves out," Joseph said, turning for the exit. Two more men were now standing behind the man toting the assault rifle who had been guarding the door; they too were armed with similar weapons. Joseph had no idea where they had been lurking seconds earlier, but they were here now and looking for a fight.

"Listen, buddy, just call your goon squad off and no one gets hurt!" Greg shouted, taking a much more aggressive approach than Joseph.

Overseer's face was now completely void of any emotion.

"You, my friend," he said, "are outgunned. Do you really want to die over a dinner invitation?"

William lowered his weapon.

"Okay. Let's just all be civil about this," he said calmly.

Overseer rose to his feet, the tallest one in the room by several inches. Even Greg appeared short by comparison.

"Yes, splendid! Yes, you *can* be reasonable, can't you?" Overseer said excitedly and did a little jump of joy. "Now I'm going to have to ask you all to set your little toys on the ground, so we can all be friends again."

William, Greg, and Joseph reluctantly placed their weapons down on the dusty floor. Not even Greg thought that they could survive a firefight in this small room and outgunned as they were. Hillary finally revealed herself from behind the couch, still clutching her machete tightly with both hands. The two men who had seemingly appeared out of thin air by the doorway entered the room and collected the guns that had been placed on the floor, also gathering up everyone's bags. Overseer smiled and walked over to Hillary. He stood an intimidating 6 foot 7 and Hillary was a mere 5 feet even. He peered down at her. "Hi, sweetheart," he said warmly.

For a moment Joseph thought she was going to take a swing at him. She was certainly thinking about it. Overseer crouched down to her eye level.

"Why don't you put that down, okay? Wouldn't want you to hurt yourself."

"Nah, I think I'll hang on to this," Hillary said with fire in her defiant brown eyes.

Overseer rose back to his full height and grabbed her wrists with tremendous strength for such a slender-looking man. Hillary cried out and dropped the machete with a loud clang on the broken-tiled floor. He threw her to the ground at the feet of Greg, who lost his temper and charged at Overseer. The recently indoctrinated man who was still suffering from his self-inflicted wound took this opportunity to shine and tackled Greg around the legs. The man who was originally guarding the door helped restrain Greg and zip tie his hands. William helped Hillary to her feet and held her protectively. Joseph felt utterly useless, but he knew he'd only make his situation worse by trying to intervene. Once Greg was restrained, he was yanked to his feet by the two men.

"Civility is a fleeting mannerism today. I graciously invite you for dinner, and this is how you respond?" Overseer said, making eye contact with an infuriated Greg. "There are consequences for every action."

"He was trying to protect Hillary, and rightfully so!" William raised his voice, something Joseph had not yet seen from the elderly man.

"Ah, yes. The arrogant girl. I thought she could protect herself?" Overseer jeered, now focusing his dark-brown, almost black eyes on Hillary.

"I can! I just...I wasn't ready is all!" she claimed as she rubbed her left wrist, which Overseer had grabbed particularly hard.

"Okay, okay, okay!" Joseph blurted out. "Let's all just take it easy, alright?"

Overseer slowly walked over to Joseph and looked down at him, saying nothing for a moment. Joseph could feel his hands tremble as adrenaline pumped through his veins. Overseer suddenly burst out into a hysterical fit of laughter.

"Yes, yes! Let's take it easy, alright? Absolutely! You're all probably just hungry! Hangry even!" he exclaimed, wiping tears from his eyes as a result of laughing too hard. "Come, come. Let us go upstairs now. I can't wait to have you four for dinner. We'll have a feast!"

Overseer confidently led the way out of the room and up the concrete flight of stairs, blowing a kiss to Susan the skeleton on his way past her. Joseph, Greg, William, and Hillary followed while being escorted by his four armed disciples. Truth be told, Joseph did have a rumble in his stomach and could use a good meal, even if it came from such a deeply disturbed man.

Chapter 5

Dinner Party

Alpha Squad had been picked up by a state-of-the-art military cargo carrier that had been produced about a decade prior to nuclear Armageddon. The aircraft was jet black and had been fitted with rotatable thrusters which gave the ship the ability to hover in a stationary position just like a helicopter. In fact, the production of this particular model practically made helicopters obsolete. The aircraft was faster than most common planes and more manoeuvrable than helicopters. The cargo ship, CS50 for short, could land on almost any surface and could reach upwards of Mach 1, travelling at a top speed of 1,234 kilometres per hour. The CS50 was revolutionary for the military during its nearly ten years of regular use as it allowed for the transportation of troops and supplies to be accelerated exponentially.

Now the once mighty ship held only seven occupants — Alpha Squad and the two pilots up front. The interior was not quite as wondrous as the technological capabilities the ship possessed. The cargo bay for troops and supplies was windowless and had a large empty steel floor with hooks strategically placed for strapping down various items. On both the port and starboard sides of the ship were rows of seats equipped with harnesses for soldiers who were being transported. The entirety of Alpha Squad was sitting on the port side of the carrier, strapped into a handful of these seats and bantering back and forth. The two pilots were the only people with a view outside of the aircraft, but there wasn't much to see during the day anyway. Below the aircraft was an endless sea of black clouds that did their best to block out the sun from the land below. The air itself above the clouds carried a sickly orange haze. Alpha Squad wasn't missing out on any kind of sightseeing.

The CS50 began descending through the thick cloud coverage. Once below the clouds, the pilots could take in the entirety of the bleak and lifeless earth below. They were currently flying over a vast skeletal forest that showed very little signs of life. Even the running river below was an unnatural shade of grey as it reflected the ominous cloud coverage that never broke apart. The plane began to approach a bit of a clearing, where long yellow grass and a few patches of bright purple flowers blossomed. The vibrant purple wildflowers were a stark contrast to the otherwise defoliated wasteland and could've been viewed as an inspirational demonstration of the world's natural resolve to survive. Unknown to the eye of the beholder, these flowers were not a demonstration of Mother Nature's resilience as they did not blossom naturally. They were planted and carefully maintained to act as a discreet landing marker for PAR airships. The CS50 slowed to a complete halt as the state-of-the-art thrusters traversed to face the ground and allowed the aircraft to gently hover 50 feet in the air.

"This is CS50 Bravo Echo Whiskey Whiskey, requesting authorization to land. Clearance code four, two, two, four," stated the main pilot over a headset that transmitted into the hidden base below.

"Cleared for landing," an anonymous voice replied through the headsets, audible only to the two pilots.

The patch of land decorated with artificially sustained violet flowers began to retract, revealing a long and narrow vertical steel tunnel that was lined with red, green and white guidance lights. The aircraft began to slowly descend into the shaft as the plot of land above began closing to conceal the tunnel once more. It took a couple of minutes to reach the bottom as the narrow vertical shaft required careful patience by the pilots to manoeuvre. It was almost a perfect fit, making descending without scraping the edges of the aircraft no easy task. Eventually the CS50 made it to the end of the vertical tunnel, entering a spacious and brightly lit hangar that contained a handful of military aircrafts. There were only four other aircrafts in the hangar, a small but versatile collection available to be used by PAR at any given moment in a world where so little technology remained. The aircraft landed in its designated spot next to the only other CS50 in the hangar, and the two pilots high-fived each other for not scratching up their ride yet again.

The dim red glow in the cargo bay turned bright green and the large loading ramp began to open. Alpha Squad started to unbuckle their harnesses and stretch their legs as the door began to slowly reveal the hangar.

"Welcome home, ladies!" Reaper said cheerfully as he gave his neck a good crack.

"Man, I can't wait to take a hot shower," Rex said.

"Oh yeah, or use an actual bathroom!" Wolf exclaimed.

The entire unit laughed as the loading ramp fully opened with a loud thud of metal on metal as it slammed onto the hangar floor. A very muscular man dressed in a painfully tight suit was waiting at the end of the ramp, holding a clipboard. The man's fashionable suit looked on the verge of ripping at the seams as his immense muscular frame fought to be released from the fabric prison. This physical specimen of a man was clean-shaven, and his tidy white undershirt beamed in comparison to his smooth dark complexion.

"Welcome back…" The oversized man paused and squinted at his clipboard, which seemed impossibly small for his large hands to grasp: "…Alpha Squad."

Reaper strutted down the metal ramp, his heavy footsteps echoing through the hangar as his combat boots pounded the ramp. With his rifle slung on his back he extended a hand to the big man and said, "The name's Reaper. I haven't seen you around, but then again we've been gone for a while. You are…?"

"Yes, I know who you are—Sergeant Andrew Rodriguez, codename Reaper. My name is Klein. Nice to meet you," Klein replied as he firmly shook Reaper's hand with enough force to make Reaper suppress a wince.

Klein took a sleek black pen out from his chest pocket and counted the members of Alpha Squad.

"Looks like everyone is accounted for. Excellent."

"Damn straight. Ain't nothing tougher than us," Ghost said, still in the cargo ship with the rest of Alpha Squad minus Reaper.

"You all must be starving. The mess is open for another four hours. The special today is..." Klein paused again, referring to his clipboard once more: "...meatloaf."

"At least it's not more MREs," Beetle joked.

The rest of the squad disembarked from the aircraft and joined Reaper. They were all eager to get some grub and began to head towards the mess, a room not so easy to find in this underground labyrinth. As Reaper was turning to join them, Klein called for his attention once more.

"Reaper, hang on just a moment, please."

Reaper turned back to Klein, the rest of the unit stopping as well to wait for their leader.

"It's alright, boys, I'll catch up. Save me a seat, yeah?" Reaper told his faithful crew.

"Absolutely, Mr Boss Man Sir!" Wolf replied with a fake salute. The unit laughed and continued to exit the hangar, their growling stomachs encouraging their fatigued bodies to move quickly towards the mess.

"So what's up? I can't even begin to tell you how hungry I am," Reaper said impatiently as his stomach rumbled on cue.

"As soon as you are done eating, you are to report to Commander Ventress's office," Klein said matter-of-factly.

"I see. And what for?" Reaper enquired somewhat nervously. One-on-one time with the Commander was often less than pleasurable.

"She didn't say, but I'd imagine she just wants a debriefing on your mission. Nothing to stress over," Klein assured Reaper.

"Oh, right. That makes sense," Reaper replied, trying to suppress the uneasy feeling in his stomach that could have been caused by nerves, hunger, or both.

Klein and Reaper shook hands once more before separating. Klein went to inspect the CS50 and speak with the pilots while Reaper hurried to catch up with his ravenous unit. Right now the only thing that mattered to Reaper was getting the biggest slice of meatloaf he'd ever had.

***

The makeshift dining room had been constructed on the tenth floor, a place that once had been bustling with disgruntled office workers. The cubicles had been cleared out and an assortment of various tables had been brought in to fill the empty space. The padded office chairs on wheels had been saved and were now spread out among the mismatching tables. Since power no longer existed without generators, which were hard to come by, the entire floor was illuminated by candles and lanterns, casting a soothing orange glow throughout the room. Joseph was shocked to see almost two dozen people helping themselves to a large table of food that had been laid out similarly to a buffet. Joseph was beginning to understand why some people were willing to cut off their finger for the deranged man with the long blond hair. Through him they had access to food and shelter; they had salvation.

The table of food consisted of various canned goods such as peaches, pears, beans, and other miscellaneous items. There was also a variety of sweets such as chocolates and candies for dessert. The main course was a massive roast, covered in a mouthwatering zesty sauce; Joseph couldn't even begin to guess what ingredients it consisted of or where they came from. Everyone in the room, except for Joseph, Greg, William, Hillary, and oddly enough Overseer, was missing their pinky fingers.

Joseph's stomach growled and he could tell his companions were also mesmerized by the sight and smell of food. This was the most people Joseph had ever seen in one place since the bombs dropped, even more than the settlement he had resided in temporarily a few months back.

"Oh that smell. Delicious, isn't it?" Overseer boasted.

"Yeah, it actually is," Joseph said, feeling a little awestruck.

"Can I at least have these undone now?" Greg annoyedly asked, indicating his wrist restraints.

"Do you promise to be a good boy?" Overseer replied with an arrogant smirk.

"Yes," Greg growled.

Overseer waved a hand and one of the men cut the ties off of Greg's wrists. Greg rubbed his bloody wrists; the restraints had been outrageously tight, which had no doubt been deliberate. Overseer motioned for Joseph and his three companions to follow him to an oakwood table that would have looked more at home in a medieval castle. The royal table was equipped with six office chairs that varied in degrees of luxury, and paper plates had been set on the table along with plastic utensils. There was a seventh seat at the head of the table. It was more of a throne than a seat, a large purple-cushioned chair with handcrafted wooden armrests, fit for a king. The dishes and utensils in front of this seat were tasteful and elegant, none of that paper crap. Overseer was king around here.

"You will dine with me tonight, my beautiful friends. Take a plate and help yourself to the food!" Overseer exclaimed as he grabbed his own plate and began to head up to the provisional buffet table.

"Should we make a run for it?" Greg whispered to Joseph.

"Not yet. Let's at least get a free meal—I'm starving," Joseph whispered in return as his stomach audibly growled. "Just play along and we'll leave when the time is right."

Joseph grabbed his plate and made a beeline for the buffet line. Greg, Hillary, and William waited behind Joseph in that order. Joseph couldn't help but notice the untrusting glances that were thrown his way from the other people in the room, the other people who were all missing their left pinky fingers. The line inched along and Joseph helped himself to a huge serving of everything available; there was plenty to go around. The roast fell apart like butter when Joseph cut into it, and his stomach eagerly growled once more. Joseph took his mountain of food back to the table, beating his friends and joining Overseer, who had an equally large plate and a bottle of red wine.

"Care for a drink?" Overseer offered politely.

"Yeah, sure. Thank you," Joseph replied, as Overseer filled Joseph's paper cup to the brim.

Joseph took a sip and closed his eyes in pure bliss as dry crimson liquid travelled down his throat and warmed his stomach. He hadn't had much luck finding alcohol as of late. It was perhaps the most valuable commodity nowadays and no bottle went to waste. Joseph's companions joined the table but were not offered anything to drink. Everyone had a gluttonous amount of food on their plate, except for Hillary. She had very minuscule portions of everything; she was sceptical of the whole situation. Something didn't quite feel right to her, but she couldn't quite place her finger on what. Perhaps that was it — most people were missing a finger due to some kind of twisted indoctrination ritual. The envious amount of food had failed to seduce Hillary and she kept her wits about her. She knew that the sooner they left, the better.

Overseer, Joseph, and Greg had no trouble eating whatsoever. Joseph was absolutely devouring the roast and had already drunk most of his wine. William was careful to not forget his manners and ate quite slowly, a gentleman to the core. Hillary more or less just poked at her food and couldn't stop thinking about the screams they had heard coming from upstairs while they were hiding behind the couch earlier. What had happened to the two captives that they saw being marched up the stairs with their hands bound? Overseer reached over and topped up Joseph's cup without asking.

"You gonna share that, Joseph?" Greg asked, nudging him with his elbow.

Joseph was about to pour some into Greg's cup when he was abruptly halted by Overseer's outburst.

"No! Absolutely not! I have given *you* my wine! You! No one else! Don't you dare disrespect me," he roared.

Everyone seated at the royal table flinched and the entire room fell silent. Joseph looked down at his cup and sipped it quietly, avoiding eye contact.

"Go back to your meals, everyone!" Overseer declared to his disciples. "Just a misunderstanding with our lovely friends—nothing to worry about."

The normal buzz of people talking returned throughout the room and everyone resumed their indulgent behaviour.

"This roast is delicious," William remarked, trying to ease the tension. "But I just can't seem to figure out what it is. Some kind of pork roast?"

Overseer giggled like a schoolgirl and answered with, "Oh yes, a pork roast! Two particularly noisy piggies at that."

Everyone lost their appetite and put down their plastic utensils, except for Joseph who was buzzed off of his second glass of wine and continued to munch away.

"You have...livestock? Like, living pigs?" Hillary enquired suspiciously.

"Oh yes, oh yes! Would you like to see later?" Overseer replied with his usual excited demeanour.

"No, that's quite alright, sir. We've probably overstayed our welcome anyways," William said timidly.

"Nonsense! You are my friends, my special dinner guests. Plus it's almost nightfall. You four should spend the night here."

"We've got to get to the outpost—" Greg began to say.

"I wasn't asking," Overseer interrupted, his disposition becoming ice cold in an instant.

Joseph threw back the last splash of his second glass of wine, not clueing into the disturbing revelation that his friends were beginning to have about the savoury roast he had just consumed.

"Well, it would seem that everyone is finished eating," Overseer said, despite everyone still having a considerable amount of food remaining on their flimsy paper plates. "I'll have you brought to your rooms. Except for you." Overseer pointed at Joseph.

"Me? I'm kind of tired too," Joseph said, not wanting to be separated from his companions.

"You will endure," Overseer said simply as he motioned for two of his guards that had been lurking by the stairwell to come to the table. "Take these three to the guest rooms on floor twelve."

The two guards nodded and ushered Greg, William, and Hillary out of their seats. They all looked back over their shoulders at Joseph like terrified puppies that were being ripped away from their mother. Soon they were out of sight and were being led up the stairs. Now it was just Overseer and Joseph, Joseph sobering up quickly from his crippling anxiety that had been induced by having his recently acquired friends taken away from his side.

"Now that those buzzkills are out of our way," Overseer said, while taking his first sip of wine of the night, "tell me about yourself."

"I want to know where you're taking my friends first," Joseph demanded.

"They'll be fine. You'll see them later tonight, I promise. Now, tell me about yourself," Overseer said, dismissing Joseph's concern.

Joseph wasn't sure what to do or say. He figured that his best chance of survival, and his best shot at saving his friends, would be to play along for the time being. The room was starting to clear out and the once steady buzz of conversations had diminished to inaudible whispers. Those who had finished eating began to head up to higher floors, presumably to retire for the night.

"Well...I used to be a lawyer before all this," Joseph answered hesitantly.

"Look at you, Mr Fancy Pants! What kind of lawyer?" Overseer replied as he polished off the last of his meal.

"Criminal defence."

"Defending the bad guys! You certainly are an interesting one, Joseph. Tell me, why defend criminals?"

Joseph had to think about that for a moment. He had initially pursued law for the money and because he had a knack for it. People had told him that he would make a good lawyer and it turned out they were right, so he rolled with it. Joseph had never been particularly passionate about law, but the pay was excellent and it allowed him to do something that he was actually good at. For some reason, however, Joseph did not think that this would be an answer that Overseer would approve of. So he did what he often did in court. He lied.

"I think, or thought, that laws were...unfair. Restrictive. Punishing someone for something that had already happened didn't seem to make much sense and maybe if we didn't have so many restrictive laws we wouldn't have had as much crime."

Joseph leaned back in his chair, satisfied with his answer. He didn't believe a single word that he had just said, but he was hoping to appeal to the vanity of Overseer. He succeeded.

"I knew you were different from the others, I just knew it! Polite and reasonable, not to mention cute too!" Overseer clapped his hands excitedly before continuing. "Isn't the world so much better now? Nobody can tell anyone what to do—we are as free as birds!"

Overseer's eyes had opened excessively and he was leaning in closer to Joseph, his long blond hair falling onto his plate. Joseph forced a smile, which took a tremendous amount of willpower.

"Yeah," Joseph said agreeably, "absolutely."

Overseer leaned back in his throne and was pleased with Joseph's response.

"Now if only your friends could share your vision and etiquette. The old one was kind of nice, but he was wrinkled and ugly," Overseer muttered.

"They do! They were just nervous—they're usually much more talkative and grateful. You have to give them a chance to open up," Joseph insisted.

"I see," Overseer said while frowning. "Would they join my family? More importantly, would you join my family, Joseph?"

"Of course," Joseph lied without hesitation, "and I'm sure my friends would too if you would let me talk to them so that I could help them understand what a great guy you are."

Overseer was silent for a while, tapping his long fingers on the table as he thought. Joseph could hardly breathe; it was impossible to know when Overseer's emotional pendulum would swing from ecstasy to unexplainable fury.

"Okay, I'll make you a deal," Overseer said after a few moments of mental deliberation. "If you can convince your friends to join my family, all will be forgiven and we will proceed with the welcoming ritual in the morning."

"Perfect, I'll make sure that they do," Joseph said with a huge sigh of relief.

"I will take you to them now. Come," Overseer said as he got up abruptly.

Joseph followed Overseer across the now almost empty dining room. The savoury aroma wafting throughout the room seemed to tug at the back of Joseph's jacket in an effort to pull him back towards delicious fleshy sustenance. Joseph resisted the primitive urge to eat and continued to follow Overseer into the stairwell. The stairwell had no source of light and both men had to take cautious steps in order not to trip. They ascended to floor 12, the same floor to which Joseph's companions had been escorted. Floor 12 seemed to be one stupendously long hallway with private offices lining both sides of the hall. This is where the big shots had worked, the ones that reeled in visitors who would wait in the stylish lobby on the main floor for their appointments to kiss ass. The hallway was dimly lit with a handful of candles that were dangerously close to burning themselves out. The third office on the right had two armed guards standing watch outside. Overseer led Joseph over to the armed duo.

"Nathan and Billy. Leave us and go to bed," Overseer ordered.

"But Overseer! What if they try to escape?" Nathan protested.

"They are our guests! And soon they will be our family. Now go to bed—my patience has worn thin," Overseer instructed the two men sternly.

The two guards hurried off down the hall like a couple of children that had just been scolded by an angry parent. Overseer turned to Joseph, towering almost a full foot above him.

"I don't know why, but I trust you, Joseph. I trust that you will keep your word and that you won't try to leave us."

"Of course. My word is my bond." Joseph extended a hand for a handshake.

Instead of shaking his hand, Overseer embraced Joseph in a bone-crushing hug and whispered into his ear, "I'm looking forward to welcoming you to my family tomorrow. We're going to get really, really, really close."

Overseer ended the uncalled-for embrace but not before kissing Joseph on the cheek. Joseph suppressed a surge of nausea. Overseer turned abruptly, his trench coat trailing behind him, and promptly walked back down the hall towards the staircase. Overseer ascended to the higher floors and disappeared from sight. Joseph quickly entered the room to find all three of his companions completely unharmed and illuminated by a lone lantern on the floor. The room was exactly what one might expect a hotshot executive's office to look like. A massive hardwood desk to go along with an inflated ego, a bookshelf that lined the entirety of the left wall filled with sophisticated books that had never been cracked open, and the canvases that polluted the right wall were of stock nature images with thoughtless inspirational quotes scrawled across the bottom in an obnoxious font. The only thing out of the ordinary was the three terrified people huddling together on one big dirty mattress that had been carelessly tossed into the middle of the room.

"Joseph!" Hillary exclaimed, jumping up to hug him. Joseph returned the hug and it was much less awkward than the embrace he had just had with Overseer.

"Hey guys," Joseph said sheepishly.

"What the hell happened down there?" Greg wanted to know.

"I used my old law-school charm." Joseph winked, trying to make light of the situation.

"Very funny," William said unamused, "but what actually happened?"

"Well," Joseph began to explain, "I just said what Overseer wanted to hear. I told him that I thought the world was better now that laws didn't exist and I insisted that you all would join his...family."

"Shit, he bought all that?" Greg asked in disbelief.

"Honestly, the guy is a nutcase. I think he just believes whatever he wants to believe and he's taken a strange liking to me. I think he's into me," Joseph said with a shudder.

"Good. Well, not good that he has some kind of perverted crush on you, but good that he believed your story," Greg said as he started to get up. "Now let's get the hell outta here."

"Hang on," Joseph said, holding up a hand. "I want to get out of here as much as you do, but I think it would be smart if we at least waited a few more hours."

"He's right," William agreed. "We should wait for the candles to die out and for everyone to fall asleep."

"Alright, fine, that's not a bad idea," Greg reluctantly admitted.

Greg sat back down on the dirty mattress with Hillary and William. Joseph joined them and they discussed what their next course of action should be once they escaped from the building; it would be night-time by then after all. Their planning was interrupted by a tortured scream coming from the floor above. Joseph's blood turned to ice and everyone sat and waited for the blood-curdling scream to stop. Only the screaming didn't stop. In fact, the screaming was amplified as more tortured souls began to cry out in hysterical harmony. The entire building was filled with the sound of pain and terror; it was as if a gathering of banshees had congregated on the floor above. Joseph and his petrified companions all turned as white as banshees themselves. Several excruciating minutes passed before the screams finally trailed off and all was silent again. Hillary was in tears and Joseph wasn't far from it either.

"Those poor people!" Hillary sobbed. "What are they doing to them?"

William shook his head in shock.

"As soon as this lantern burns out, we're leaving," Greg said; even his voice was a little shaky.

Everyone nodded in agreement. Nobody spoke as they all watched the dwindling flame within the lantern cast dancing shadows around the once illustrious office. Demons. That's what Joseph thought the shadows looked like, demons provocatively dancing to the sounds of terror.

***

Ivan was a burly man who had immigrated from Ukraine when he was in his early twenties in order to escape Russian expansion. His mother had passed away during childbirth and his father was non-existent; he had no brothers or sisters. Ivan wasn't leaving anything behind when he immigrated other than his small-scale butcher shop that was frequently empty of both livestock and patrons. When he landed in the West, he turned to the only thing he was good at: cutting meat. Ivan opened a downtown butcher shop that soon generated a steady flow of loyal customers and, more importantly, income. When Ivan encountered Overseer shortly after the beginning of the end of the world, they had immediately clicked. Ivan's cold and stoic demeanor was contrasted with Overseer's eccentric and animated personality. Maybe opposites really do attract. In the time that followed their encounter, Ivan had learned that butchering a human was not much different than butchering a pig. If anything it was easier—there was much less fat to slash through.

Ivan was currently standing in the doorway to the thirteenth floor, admiring his work. The thirteenth floor had formerly been used primarily for storage and was dimly lit just like the rest of the building, now illuminated only by a variety of scented candles that masked the smell of blood that hung in the air. Ivan's new meat shop was much different than his prior shops in his other life. His produce no longer consisted of homegrown beef and pork; it was made up of a selection of unfortunate souls Overseer deemed to be undesirable. Half a dozen people were securely fastened to unneeded desks by duct tape and rope. The humane thing to do would have been to put these tortured souls out of their misery before harvesting their flesh. Unfortunately, if Ivan were to do that then the meat would spoil. His livestock needed to be kept alive so that he could selectively butcher his human pigs while preserving the rest of their flesh for later. Refrigeration was a concept of the past now and Ivan had to improvise. He didn't mind; he had never been too fond of people anyway. Ivan stood there with his bloodstained apron and his bald head glistening with sweat when he heard footsteps rushing up the stairs behind him. He spun around, a large butcher knife held lightly in his right hand.

"My sweet Ivan!" Overseer exclaimed as he came up the final few steps to stand face to face with Ivan. Ivan was a stocky man and the lanky Overseer towered above the butcher.

"Overseer!" Ivan's voice had a strong Ukrainian accent. "To what do I owe the pleasure of your company?"

"Well, my brother, I have come to ask you a favour."

"A favour? Of course! Anything you wish," Ivan replied warmly.

"Splendid! I need you to make your piggies squeal. They need to be loud," Overseer informed him with a grin so wide that it looked as if his face was about to split open.

"I was under the impression we had guests downstairs, yes?" Ivan asked quizzically.

Overseer nodded his head with rapid speed, his long hair flailing around wildly.

"Oh yes, we do indeed!" he said. "Which is why these piggies must squeal! I must test their faith in me, you see?"

"Ah, I see. Then these little piggies will squeal all the way home, I promise," Ivan assured Overseer.

"Oh good! 'Wee wee' they will say! Now I'd love to watch, but I promised my wife that we would have a date night tonight.

Toodles!" Overseer winked and began running back down the stairs before Ivan could ask about his supposed wife, whom he had never heard of until now.

Ivan turned back around and continued to admire his new shop with dead blue eyes that were as cold as the sleepless nights he endured as a boy, huddled by the fireplace of the orphanage that he grew up in. He would make them squeal, but it wouldn't be for nothing. Meat should never be wasted; that was something Ivan was certain of. He hadn't known the feeling of a full belly until he was almost 30. Every morsel of food was sacred. Ivan began to whistle an old Ukrainian folklore song and fired up a small Coleman grill. His livestock began to cry out in terror as they knew what would come next. Ivan smiled, something the emotionally jaded man didn't do often, and began to sharpen his knife.

***

The choir of banshees had begun to sing their haunting songs once more and the stubborn flame of the lantern illuminating the swanky office refused to burn out. Joseph watched the devilish demons continue to dance across the supposedly inspirational canvases that covered the wall in front of him. The prancing demons were mocking him and anyone else who dared to dream, the shrieks of pain emboldening their sadistic dance of pleasure.

"Okay, that's long enough, let's get the hell out of here!" Greg demanded, finally reaching his breaking point.

"What about our bags?" Hillary asked. No one had seen their belongings since Overseer's disciples had collected them in the lobby.

"We're gonna just have to tough it out. We're not far from Outpost Zulu and we can hopefully replenish there, or even on the way," William said.

"Yeah," Joseph agreed, "they could be anywhere in this building. I just want to get out of here."

Hillary nodded and the quartet quietly made their way over to the door; any sound they did make was drowned out by the persistent screams coming from the floor above. Greg led the pack and took a deep breath before he slowly opened the door, peeking out into the hallway. It was pitch black now; the candles that lined the hallway had burnt themselves out or perhaps they had been blown out. Greg motioned to follow him and the group slowly crept out into the hall. Joseph was focusing on Greg's back and trying not to lose him in the dark. They made it to the stairwell without a problem and began to quietly descend. The stairs were made of metal and a heavy footfall could easily alert vigilant ears of their escape attempt. Joseph was suppressing an overwhelming feeling of nausea as he began to realize what he had just consumed for dinner. He couldn't think about that now — he had to keep moving. They reached the bottom of the stairwell after several suspenseful minutes without encountering anyone. The only noise Joseph had heard was the perpetual screams that slowly receded as they made it down each floor. Joseph could faintly make out the front door that led back to the main street as they entered the lobby once more.

"We made it," Joseph declared with an audible sigh of relief.

Everyone began to quickly make their way towards the exit when a battery-operated lantern was switched on behind them. The group spun around to see Overseer sitting behind the receptionist desk with the skeleton propped up on his lap.

"Where do you think you're going, my sweethearts?" It was Overseer who was speaking but he sounded like a woman as he put on a convincing ventriloquist act with Susan the skeleton, his wife. Everyone turned to run, but there was a group of half a dozen men standing just outside the doorway with machetes, their lanterns now switched on as well, revealing their presence in the night.

"We were just—" Joseph began to lie.

"Save your lies. Boys who lie aren't friends of mine," Susan scoffed as Overseer wiggled her lifeless jaw with his hand.

Overseer stood up and placed Susan gently back down in her seat with a kiss on her skull before turning to face Joseph.

"I knew it would come to this, Joseph! I knew I couldn't trust you, I just knew it!" he said, seeming panicked.

"I'm sorry, I—"

"Silence!" Overseer roared. "You think me to be a fool! You will learn that every action has a consequence!"

Overseer took a deep breath before continuing in a much more relaxed tone.

"But I do like you, Joseph," he said. "So that is why you and your filthy friends will have a twenty-second head start."

"A head start from what?" Greg demanded to know.

Overseer answered while still looking Joseph in the eye. "Six of my best hunters are armed only with machetes. You will have thirty seconds before they hunt you down. Your time starts... now," Overseer told the group while tapping his Casio watch, which was shattered and no longer functional. Nobody moved for a couple of precious seconds and then they all exploded into a sprint out of the building past the eager men with machetes.

"Run, little piggies, run!" Overseer screamed from inside the building before unleashing a maniacal laugh.

The group ran down the cluttered city street and Joseph's heart was pounding. The darkness that consumed the world at night was like a thick veil; it was impossible to see more than a few feet ahead. Despite the lack of visibility, the quartet had to run. They had no choice and it was abundantly clear that William would not be able to keep up. The old man was already wheezing like an asthmatic and Greg was trying to haul him along like an old dog reluctant to go for a walk. Joseph and Hillary were both running blindly down the street side by side when Hillary suddenly vanished from existence. Joseph didn't notice at first; he had tunnel vision like a petrified wildebeest attempting to outrun a pack of starving lionesses. Hillary had tripped over the corpse of an Orville that had succumbed to starvation and she was sprawled out in the middle of the road. Joseph slid to a stop, almost falling himself, and called out for Hillary. She was too scared to respond and, instead of Hillary's voice, Joseph heard Greg call out from several feet back the way that he had just come from.

"Joseph!" Greg screamed hysterically and uncharacteristically. "Help me!"

Joseph stumbled towards Greg's voice and found him supporting William like a wounded war veteran. Joseph grabbed William's other arm and helped Greg keep the geriatric man moving forwards.

"Where's Hillary?" William asked between laboured breaths.

"I don't know! She fell in the dark and she won't answer!" Joseph replied frantically.

"Hillary?" Greg called out into the night.

The bright battery-powered lanterns began to bob up and down in the dark as Overseer's men began their hunt. Joseph and his friends' head start was over—the savage hunters were on the prowl. Hillary appeared out of thin air and slammed into the back of Joseph with a startled scream. Joseph grabbed her hand and steadied her, also making sure not to lose her again. The four moved as fast as they could, tripping over debris constantly. Behind them the hunting parting was laughing and hollering as they began charging towards the sound of scuffled footsteps that rang out in the night. Joseph, William, Greg, and Hillary were only 50 feet or so away, barely out of range of their lights. William swore and collapsed as he twisted his ankle in a pothole near the side of the road, a hole that had existed long before the bombs were dropped.

"Come on, old man, get up!" Greg hissed.

"My ankle! I think it's broken!" William cried out.

Joseph and Greg tried to lift him up as they were caught in the ray of light from the lanterns that were rapidly approaching.

"There! Get 'em!" a voice hollered as the pack began to converge on the wounded prey.

Joseph let go of William and yanked Hillary away. Greg also let go of William's soft liver-spotted hand and choked on the swelling lump in his throat as he followed Joseph and Hillary back into the dark.

"No! Please! Please don't leave me!" William screamed as tears streamed down his weathered face. Joseph, Hillary, and Greg did not look back as they darted down a nearby alley just out of range of the lanterns. They ducked into a service entrance to a local shop that was left ajar and paused in the doorway. They could still hear William crying out. By now the pack of feral hunters had reached William and he was a blubbering mess, begging for his life.

"Please don't do this!" he pleaded. "Please, I don't want to die! I'm so scared..."

One of the men began to laugh uncontrollably and began hacking at William's leg with his machete. William's pleas of terror transformed into screams of pain as the rest of the group began to join in and hack away at his extremities. His death would not be quick. Joseph slowly closed the door, which only slightly muffled the savagery taking place around the corner. The service tunnel was pitch black and Joseph couldn't even see his own hand in front of his face. Joseph led the way anyway, sliding his hand across the cold concrete wall to guide his path. Hillary placed a trembling hand on Joseph's shoulder and Greg rested a sweaty palm on Hillary's shoulder as the group of newly formed friends, which was now a trio, made their way through the dark. They were approaching the end of the service tunnel and Joseph could see a soft glow coming from inside the main shop. Everyone stopped and listened for signs of life or imminent death.

Joseph could hear a familiar wet slurping sound accompanied by a series of crunches. The same audible hell he had heard days prior in the abandoned gas station. Orvilles. Joseph knew that they couldn't turn back now; at any second the back service door was bound to burst open and a bunch of psychopaths wielding machetes would storm down the hall. Joseph summoned every ounce of courage he had left and jumped into the main room of the shop, which appeared to formerly be a posh fashion boutique. Five Orvilles were crouched around two corpses; by the looks of the carcasses, they were almost done with their meal. A dwindling flame was burning in a garbage can situated in the back corner of the once elegant shop. All five Orvilles sprung to their feet and snarled, their lips curled back in an inhuman way.

"Wait, wait, wait!" Joseph held up his hands. "People are coming! A lot of people! Unarmed, unsuspecting, and well fed!"

Joseph's hunters were indeed armed, but these radiation-cooked abominations didn't need to know that. Joseph thought that the image of their cannibalistic pursuers being eaten alive was incredibly ironic and a fitting end to their reign of terror.

The Orvilles looked at one another and one managed to say, "So? You're here now", in a guttural-sounding voice.

"Yeah, and we won't go down without a fight. But they might, if they don't see you coming. Put out your fire, take them by surprise. An easy six-course meal," Joseph said in a hurried voice, trying to ensure safe passage before they were caught between ravenous Orvilles and psychotic machete-wielding maniacs.

The Orville who spoke nodded and pointed to the front door, miraculously seeing Joseph's logic. Joseph motioned for his friends to follow and they ran outside and were swallowed up by the dark night once again. The small pack of Orvilles snuffed out the fire by smothering the flames with the corpses, blood sizzling as it dripped onto the hot coals. Just as the final flame flickered out, the service door swung open and the six psychopaths entered the hall covered in William's blood. They scraped their blades along the concrete walls as they arrogantly strutted down the service hall.

"Here, piggy, piggy, piggy!" one of them called out.

The hunters were approaching the end of the hall, completely unaware of their impending doom. The five Orvilles tore around the corner and began running down the hall toward the unsuspecting men on all fours, their presence being revealed by the sickly green light shining from the lanterns. The men readied their machetes and the Orvilles lunged forward, jaws snapping and untrimmed fingernails slashing. The two equally deranged parties clashed, and blood painted the once white concrete walls a vibrant crimson red. Overseer's men put up a valiant fight, but were overwhelmed in the end. They were unable to swing their machetes effectively at such close range and fell victim to the powerful mutated jaws of The Sick. When it was all said and done, only two Orvilles remained, both grievously injured. That did not stop either of them from indulging in one last meal as they dug into their fresh kills and enjoyed their second dinner of the night.

Chapter 6

Outpost Zulu

Reaper was seated alongside his fellow Alpha Squad members at a white cafeteria table that was bolted to the floor. The meatloaf had actually been quite good and he was currently digging into his second hefty slice that was smothered in a mushroom sauce. The cooking crew stationed at the PAR base ate their own culinary creations, which incentivized them to cook meals that were as flavourful as possible given the limited ingredients available. The entire cafeteria was white. White floors, white tables, and a white ceiling lined with fluorescent white lights. The only splash of colour was the dark-green plastic trays that people ate off. The cafeteria was empty with the exception of Alpha Squad and three other military personnel sitting at a table near the entrance. It was often quiet around the base and Reaper preferred it that way; it gave him time to decompress after missions.

"What did that guy with the clipboard have to say?" Rex asked with a mouthful of food.

"I've got to meet with the Commander when I'm done eating. Debriefing," Reaper replied with an eye-roll.

"Yikes. She might steal your soul. Be careful, boss." Rex laughed and then gulped down his entire glass of purified water.

Reaper let out a gruff laugh that sounded more like a grunt and continued to eat. Reaper wasn't fond of the Commander, but he respected her authority. Over a decade of military experience prior to nuclear Armageddon had conditioned him to never question the chain of command. He had grown fond of taking orders; it kept things simple. Shoot this, do that, go here, eat this, sleep now. In a way it alleviated a lot of sources of stress.

Despite his obedience to authority, he found the Commander to be somewhat abrasive. She refused to listen to the advice of others and demonstrated little regard for those who served her. Her accelerated rise to power after Reznoff's untimely suicide, the former leader and founder of PAR, had only inflated her ego and sense of self-worth. Still, she was his commander and Reaper knew his place within the hierarchy. Reaper finished the last of his meatloaf and looked longingly at his now empty tray. He could go for thirds, but he also wanted to get this debriefing out of the way so that he could finally take a shower and shut his eyes.

"Alright, boys, I'm off. I'll catch you guys later," Reaper said as he stood with a sigh.

"It was nice knowing you!" Ghost joked, prompting the table to laugh.

"Guys, relax. It's just a debriefing," Reaper replied, not joining in on the wisecracks.

"Oh sure, right. I bet you'll be fine—she's a real charmer," Wolf remarked with a sarcastic grin.

"Yeah, I appreciate the enthusiasm," Reaper said unenthusiastically as he began to head out of the almost deserted cafeteria. The rest of his squad went back to their meals and routine banter as their leader departed.

Reaper had been to the Commander's office a couple of times before, so he knew the way. He took a left upon exiting the bleak cafeteria and travelled down an equally depressing hallway that was void of all colour. The polished ceramic tiles reflected the obnoxiously bright fluorescent lights directly into Reaper's deep-set brown eyes. He would have benefited tremendously from a pair of sunglasses as he involuntarily began to squint. The hallway abruptly came to a halt with a dead end and the Commander's office was the last door on the right. It was a reinforced steel door with a black plaque bolted onto the center that read: Commander Ventress. Reaper felt as if he had just been sent to the principal's office and he took a deep breath before knocking, his knuckles pounding against the cold steel, creating a metallic clang that echoed down the barren hallway.

"Come in," a faraway voice responded irritably as if he had just interrupted an artist on the verge of creating a masterpiece.

Reaper turned the silver handle and pushed the cumbersome door open, entering the office. Commander Ventress's office was spacious and immaculately organized. There were two large oakwood bookshelves on the right wall that housed a plethora of different books ranging from medical logs to works of fiction. On the left-hand side of the office there was a slew of abstract paintings that were open to interpretation. For some reason these paintings never failed to make Reaper feel uneasy. The room was painted a dark shade of burgundy and was illuminated only by a handful of tall vintage lamps that were spread throughout the room. The lamps looked like they would be more at home collecting dust in a family-owned antique shop rather than in the office of the leader of a sophisticated Post-Apocalyptic Republic. Reaper stood in the doorway looking over at Ventress's desk. It was a huge walnut desk with a gold letter 'V' engraved into the front. Reaper could only see the very top of Ventress's head as her high-backed black office chair faced the window lining the far side of her office, overlooking an indoor vegetable garden similar to the kind found on a spaceship. She swivelled her chair to face Reaper.

"Close the door and take a seat," Ventress instructed him.

Reaper did as he was told and sat in one of the two uncomfortable metal chairs that had been placed in front of Ventress's grand desk. Ventress sat there and looked Reaper over as she clicked a red pen that she held loosely in her right hand. Ventress had jet-black hair that went down past her shoulders and breathtaking emerald-green eyes that were intoxicating to gaze into. She was currently wearing a long black leather trench coat with the top buttons undone to reveal a thick bulletproof vest beneath. On the left side of her chest was a gold letter 'V' stitched into her jacket that was nearly identical to the one on her desk. Her fair skin sharply contrasted with the black jacket and gave her an almost haunting appearance, yet she remained exquisite and alluring. She continued to closely examine Reaper, all while subconsciously clicking away at that red pen. After what felt to Reaper like several minutes, but in reality was only a handful of seconds, Ventress finally broke the deafening silence.

"Your mission was successful, I presume?" she enquired. She spoke with confidence and clarity.

"Yeah, the 'waste management' went smoothly. Unfortunately, as you predicted, the infected continue to move towards Hathbury," Reaper informed his commander.

"That's fine," Ventress replied, showing very little interest. The awkward silence returned and Reaper could hear the automatic sprinklers engage in the garden below the window.

"What's to be done to deter the infected from Outpost Zulu?" Reaper finally asked.

Ventress stopped clicking her red pen and carefully set it back down on her desk.

"The infected are the least of my concerns right now. There is a much more pressing internal threat that needs to be dealt with," Ventress replied, studying Reaper's facial expressions very closely before continuing. "The head of security at Outpost Zulu, Captain Andor, has informed me that some particularly compromising photos from our R&D facility have made it into circulation. Photos that are undermining the positive reputation that we have meticulously constructed with survivors."

The Research and Design facility was located east of the base, built into the nearby mountains. Only the hoity-toity scientists had access to the facility to conduct their research and experiments. Most of the work conducted within the R&D facility focused on reversing the effects of radiation sickness, improving horticultural techniques, and advancing medical capabilities. Reaper had never been to the facility himself. In fact, no one here had been to the facility other than the handful of on-base doctors who rotated back and forth from R&D, and of course the Commander herself.

"Photos of what?" Reaper asked curiously.

Ventress hesitated, unsure of just how much information to divulge.

"Our work," she finally replied after a few moments of deliberation.

"Which is?" Reaper probed.

"Which is classified," Ventress replied sternly.

Reaper remained silent and decided not to push his luck, prompting Ventress to continue.

"We have had great success in the R&D department, but success rarely comes without sacrifice. Those pictures seem to have been taken at our worst of times. They've got the people at Zulu in a frenzy. We are on the verge of losing years of carefully forged public relations, and in turn losing the outpost, all because of some disgruntled scientist."

"So where do I come in?" Reaper enquired, realizing that this wasn't just a routine debriefing after all.

"I will be travelling to Outpost Zulu to deliver a speech that will hopefully put their minds at ease," she informed Reaper. "Your unit will accompany me for security purposes. Captain Andor's security force is lacklustre to say the least, another matter I will have to deal with when I get there."

"Business as usual then," Reaper said in a tone indicating that he had heard all that he needed to hear.

"Not quite," Ventress replied sharply. "I believe you've met Klein?"

Reaper nodded.

"Good. You two will be entering the outpost undercover. I need you to locate these pictures and deliver them back to me immediately. I'll be having a little chat with the outpost doctor while I'm there. I suspect that he can point me towards our mole." Ventress flashed her gleaming white teeth in a brief smile before crossing her hands on top of her desk and finishing with, "Any questions?"

Reaper leaned back in his stiff chair and crossed his arms stubbornly. Outpost Zulu could be a rough place at the best of times and he wasn't so sure Klein would be an adequate partner. The man looked more suitable to be a high-school gym teacher than an undercover operative.

"Let me take one of my guys instead. I've got no rapport with Klein. I need someone who I can trust," Reaper demanded.

Ventress scowled and leaned forward, the tips of her long black hair resting on the table.

"I also need someone that I can trust. Klein will go with you. End of discussion," she replied coldly as her smile vanished.

"You can trust me, Ma'am," Reaper assured her.

"We shall see. The implications of these photos may be more severe than you realize. Klein will provide a unique skill set that is invaluable to the mission. You are dismissed, Sergeant."

Ventress spoke sternly and her dazzling green eyes made contact with Reaper's dark-brown eyes. Her mesmerizing glare tempted Reaper to continue to argue his point in a convoluted form of reverse psychology, but he knew better than to fall victim to her seductive trap. She loved to fight, whether it be verbally or physically. She was a dangerous woman and Reaper was well aware of that. He continued to maintain eye contact with Ventress in a brief moment of defiance before finally breaking his gaze.

"Yes, Ma'am," he said, a phrase all too familiar to his tongue.

Reaper politely saw himself out of the room and began to walk briskly down the hall, his combat boots echoing along the empty corridor. He was none too pleased being assigned to work a mission with a complete stranger. Alpha Squad's track record was impeccable—there was no need for Klein. He continued to walk quickly down the hall towards the barracks and contemplated what the photos could have possibly captured that had the ability to send an entire outpost into a frenzy. The R&D facility that was tucked away in the eastern mountains had always been shrouded in secrecy; this new assignment only added to Reaper's curiosity. He contemplated how he'd be able to track down these photos if he didn't know what they were of. Perhaps that's where Klein came in. Regardless, Outpost Zulu was relatively small and word travelled fast there. Paying the loose-lipped bartender a visit was a surefire way to learn the latest gossip and maybe get a free drink if he was feeling particularly social. As Reaper approached the barracks he gave his head a shake—he couldn't stop thinking about what the photos could entail. He told himself that it didn't matter, that he had received his orders and that he had a job to do. A good soldier follows orders and Reaper was a damn good soldier.

***

Joseph slowly opened his eyes. He was staring at an overturned stool behind a counter that a convenience store employee had once sat on as they checked out customers purchasing a variety of goods such as chips, pop, or even power bars. The trio had taken refuge in the convenience store, which had been picked clean ages ago and the windows were void of all glass. A damp autumn breeze blew through the store that made Joseph shiver before he slowly sat up and rubbed his shoulder which he had been lying on for most of the night. Sleep had not come easily. When Joseph wasn't listening to distant gunshots or inhuman screeches that rang out into the night, he was haunted by William's disturbing demise. Joseph hadn't known William for long, merely two days in fact, but he had quickly grown fond of the kind-hearted old man. William had a grandfatherly demeanour that comforted Joseph and now he was gone just like Joseph's biological grandparents. Joseph thought that it was relatively lucky that he had only known William for a couple of days, otherwise his death likely would have been much more traumatic. Hillary had seemed to be the most distraught about losing William.

Joseph had listened to Hillary's gentle sobbing that perpetually endured through most of the night. She had been close with William; the two of them had been travelling together for over a month before they had stumbled into Greg while looting an abandoned warehouse that used to ship packaged goods to nearby cities. Greg had also grown quite fond of the elderly man, but he did a much better job at concealing his emotions. Greg had somehow managed to fall asleep sitting upright while leaning against the bottom of the counter. A lone stick of gum was on the shelf beside his head, the wrapper frayed and exposing the peppermint delight within. Joseph slowly reached for the stick of gum, careful not to wake Greg. His mission was a success and he popped it into his mouth. Stale and hard as a rock, yet with some effort, Joseph managed to chew the stick gum enough to be able to taste the refreshing flavour of peppermint filling his mouth. He imagined it was the equivalent of brushing his teeth. It's the little things that he would often find himself missing the most, like using a toothbrush or getting a haircut. He made eye contact with Greg, who was now apparently awake. No words needed to be spoken—they both felt the heaviness in the air. Greg gently shook Hillary awake, and she continued to carry on where she had left off with the tears.

"Those bastards..." Greg muttered as he slowly rose to his feet.

"Yeah," Joseph murmured as he gently helped Hillary get up.

The trio just stood there in silence for a while as they tried to loosen their stiff muscles with a few light stretches. Hillary stopped audibly crying, but tears continued to trickle down her rosy cheeks as they escaped from her enormous chocolate-coloured eyes.

"We can't be much further from the outpost," Joseph finally said, although it was like he was talking to himself. Greg looked like a dog that had lost its bark after years of abuse and Hillary was seemingly on autopilot. Joseph clapped his hands together as he attempted to break their trance-like state.

"We have to keep moving," Joseph insisted. "We're not safe here and we won't last long without our supplies."

Greg nodded and Hillary wiped her wet eyes, the two of them ready to hit the road once more. Joseph led the way out of the convenience store and cautiously stepped through one of the shattered windows, his hiking boot crunching on an empty bag of chips partially pinned beneath a corroded hubcap that had found its way onto the sidewalk. The street was quiet and a light misty drizzle caressed his face. It was refreshing, but the water carried a rotten taste, a taste of death. Joseph wondered how much longer it would be until he started to lose his once luscious hair. They carefully crept through the streets in the direction of supposed nirvana, of Outpost Zulu. They would stop often, listening for sounds of life or imminent death. Any lurking Orvilles would likely be holed up deep within the unlit buildings that lined the streets. It was unusual for them to attack during the day, but not entirely unheard of. Bandits and other malicious folks that wandered the wasteland were just another reason to continue exercising caution.

The group had been travelling for almost 30 minutes and had been completely unbothered. The only life that the trio had seen was a mangy-looking mutt bouncing down the street and proudly carrying a severed human arm in its jaws. Although no one said it out loud, everyone had wondered if the arm had once belonged to their former companion. Joseph was at the front of the line, followed by Hillary and then Greg. Joseph slowed his pace when he saw a body lying next to an abandoned car. He slowly approached the body and nudged it with his boot. No response. Hillary and Greg came up behind him, also taking note of the body.

"Poor guy. Better off in our hands, I guess," Greg said as he crouched down, removing the backpack from the body. As he removed the bag he also unintentionally rolled the body over.

The deceased person, now identifiable as a young woman, didn't appear to have been dead for long. Her face gave the impression that she was peacefully sleeping, but the pool of blood that she lay in as opposed to a bed argued otherwise. As Greg examined the contents of the backpack, Joseph searched the body for anything else of use. He was in luck as he found a pistol that was stuffed into the waistband of her filthy blue jeans. He removed the gun, examining it closely. It was a Colt 1911, but to Joseph it was just a pistol. He had never used a gun prior to the end of the world and now he felt naked without one. Joseph checked that the pistol was loaded, which it was, and then he found one more clip of ammo in the front right pocket of the blue jeans.

"Anything good?" Joseph asked Greg who was rummaging through the black backpack.

The backpack contained a large hunting knife, which Greg took, half a bottle of water, some Cheez-Its, and two packs of unopened smokes. The three friends sat down next to the body, sharing the small amount of water and eating the Cheez-Its. Joseph only felt more hungry and thirsty when they were done, as if the cheesy snack only reminded his body of how malnourished he really was. Their feast from the night prior had filled Joseph up temporarily, but the familiar cramps of hunger had returned with a vengeance. They sat there for a while, unfazed by the body lying next to them.

"How much further?" Hillary asked as she rubbed her bloody feet, her tattered designer sneakers on the sidewalk beside her. Joseph and Greg looked at each other before they both simultaneously shrugged.

"Can't be too much further. We're already downtown," Joseph said.

"Yeah, we'll be there soon," Greg assured her.

The trio of weary travellers could hear shouting a few blocks over, which was followed by a flurry of gunshots, a not-so-subtle reminder that sitting in the middle of the street was a gamble. The gentle drizzle had increased to a light rain and Joseph shivered again, his body absent of any insulating fat. Greg was admiring the enormous buildings that surrounded them. Hathbury had held up relatively well against the bombs. Although a big city, it hadn't contained anything worth targeting, other than people. It had been a very trendy place; most employment was linked to pop-culture, social media, and anything else internet related. Despite being spared from the worst of the blast, neglect and violence had forced people to flee the city. Between rioters, looters, bandits, and now Orvilles, there wasn't much incentive to remain there anyway. Until now, that is—until Outpost Zulu.

It was time to proceed with their journey and the trio continued onwards deeper into the city. Their pace was slow as they stopped frequently to listen for approaching threats, the occasional gunshot or yelp of pain forcing the trio slightly off course. They briefly encountered another traveller toting a hunting rifle and heading in the opposite direction. The lone wanderer paid them little attention and no words were exchanged, just nods of mutual acknowledgement as the two separate parties continued in their respective directions. Joseph kept checking back over his shoulder to make sure that his companions were keeping pace and that they weren't being followed. A few skirmishes on the main street had sent the trio down a multitude of side roads, contributing to their slow pace. They eventually worked their way back to the main street after each detour and resumed their route north. The trio had been walking for a couple of hours and daylight seemed to be slipping away. Joseph had no idea what time it was, but he was not pleased with the growing dimness in the streets. Just as he was beginning to think that they would have to spend another night in the city, Joseph abruptly came to a halt, sending Greg bumping into him, followed by Hillary colliding with Greg. What Joseph saw forced him to smile from ear to ear. A red arrow had been spray-painted onto the sidewalk and below it in the same paint was one word: Zulu.

"Check it out!" Joseph exclaimed as his companions shuffled around him to see what had caused their pile-up.

They all let out a whoop of triumph and dished out a series of hugs. That crudely drawn indicator had been their first tangible sign of the outpost since listening to the archaic radio back at the farmhouse. Joseph continued to lead the way, resuming their travels north and keeping an eye out for more signs. Everyone had a bounce to their step now and their spirits were high. About 20 minutes later the group found a second arrow and they let out another quick triumphant whoop. The trio continued to follow the arrows, which began popping up more frequently, and as they did they began to encounter travellers also heading towards Outpost Zulu. Joseph and company began to feel less nervous as there was an inherent safety in numbers. Not far ahead of them was a group of three, two women and a small child, all of which appeared to be unarmed. Joseph knew that looks could often be deceiving; there was no chance that the trio ahead of him had made it this far without a means of defence. Behind Joseph, Greg, and Hillary was a duo that had also been following the marked path—two teenage boys. One was carrying a shotgun that looked disproportionately large in comparison to his frail body.

The growing herd of people continued to follow the arrows, each group keeping to themselves. Hillary periodically looked over her shoulder at the two teens behind them. They were uninterested in everyone else as they loudly chatted to each other, their occasional laugh echoing through the streets. Joseph watched the group ahead of them and was careful not to get too close.

The rain had finally tapered off but not before thoroughly soaking through all of Joseph's clothes. He longed for a hot shower, something that he had realized he would likely never experience again. The group in front of Joseph turned right as an arrow had indicated and disappeared from sight. Joseph eventually arrived at the same street corner and also hung a right. Joseph froze. At the end of the once busy city street was a massive wall that was nearly 40 feet tall. The towering wall had been constructed out of a variety of wooden planks and scrap metal. It was Frankenstein-esque, but was remarkably impressive nonetheless. The words 'Outpost Zulu' had been spray-painted in large red letters along the front of the wall in the same paint that had been used to guide people on the final leg of the journey. The wall extended deeper back into the city and seamlessly merged with the surrounding infrastructure. Joseph couldn't help but wonder how long it must have taken to create such a barrier, especially with the constant threats that were prevalent within the city. He was more curious, however, about what he would find on the other side of the wall.

"So it *is* real!" Hillary exclaimed.

"Well, I'll be damned," Greg murmured to himself.

The three of them stood there for a while taking it all in, and the two young boys who had been following them quickly hurried by. At the base of the wall was a makeshift chain-link gate guarded by four soldiers dressed head to toe in green camouflage. The first group of three were admitted into the outpost rather quickly, but the pair of teens had a much longer conversation with the guards before having their shotgun taken prior to entry. Joseph subconsciously touched the pistol that was concealed within his jacket as he started to lead his companions over to the gate. As they began to get closer to the guards, Joseph could see that their uniforms were all mismatching. In fact, one guard wasn't even wearing camouflage at all; he simply wore green cargo pants and a dark-green sports hoodie. The only consistency among the guards was a little black and red PAR patch over their left chest that looked like one of those 'Hello my name is…" name tags. The guards looked substantially less qualified than the five operatives dressed in black that Joseph had encountered two nights prior. They did, however, carry matching M16 assault rifles, but that did little to hide their sloppy apparel and unshaven faces. One particularly unkempt guard halted Joseph's group as they approached.

"Any guns or other weapons?" the scruffy guard lazily asked.

Everyone shook their head, including Joseph who could feel his pulse throbbing in the side of his neck. He wasn't quite sure why he lied about the pistol hidden within his brown leather jacket, but he had a feeling that it would be best to stay armed even if they were in a guarded outpost. A second guard took the backpack from Greg and examined the contents. He briefly looked at the hunting knife before dropping it back into the bag, clearly not concerned.

"Good enough," the scruffy guard declared as he nodded at two other guards standing by the flimsy chain-link gate.

The guards opened the gate and stepped aside, motioning for the trio to enter. Joseph, Greg, and Hillary passed through the gate and entered Outpost Zulu.

Chapter 7

Beneath the Surface

Outpost Zulu was significantly larger than Joseph had anticipated and he thought that the word 'outpost' was somewhat misleading. Then again, he had only previously seen makeshift settlements that were home to no more than a dozen folks at a time. The protective wall that surrounded Outpost Zulu stretched almost a kilometre deep into the city before joining at the back behind an old courthouse, one that was similar to where Joseph had gone to defend his clients in his former life.

The days were becoming shorter as the city transitioned from summer to winter, and the sun was beginning to dip below the clouds, setting the sky on fire. Joseph and his travelling companions were standing just inside the gate in the middle of the street, a street that appeared to have once been a main strip. Both sides of the road were lined with neglected buildings that used to be bustling city shops. Most of these shops remained in ruins, along with the hopes and dreams of opportunistic business owners.

A few of these shops, however, had been restored and seemed to be open for post-apocalyptic business. Fresh coats of paint had been applied to a handful of these shops that brought a splash of colour to the otherwise grey outpost. The paint was poorly applied, clearly not a professional job, but the bright whites, soothing blues and warming reds were a welcome sight to Joseph nonetheless. The shops had crudely painted names that covered up whatever the stores had formerly been called such as BAR, SHOP, TOOLS, and STORE. Joseph wondered what the difference between a 'shop' and a 'store' was. Greg was already eyeing up BAR and Hillary was silently taking it all in. At the very end of the main strip sat the old courthouse that used to be a necessity in a world full of laws. Such a symbol of justice seemed out of place now, an ancient relic of a forgotten civilization. Joseph could faintly make out the wall just behind the courthouse that wrapped around the outpost, protecting it from Orvilles and bandits. There were side streets that jutted off from the main strip and Joseph wondered if there were more storefronts just out of sight. The street was eerily empty and the stores seemed void of all business with the exception of BAR. A couple of drunken guards were stumbling out of the bar and laughing loudly as they carelessly swung their rifles around. An elderly man had just exited SHOP, tightly clutching a can of peach slices as if it were about to grow wings and fly away. Joseph's stomach growled for food and he could feel himself salivating.

"Well...here we are," Joseph said in awe as everyone continued to take it all in.

"Yeah, here we are," Greg repeated absentmindedly after a few moments.

"It's a lot bigger than I expected," Hillary remarked.

"Yeah, me too," Joseph agreed. "We should check out one of the stores for supplies. What do we have to barter with?"

Greg rummaged through the backpack and retrieved the two packs of smokes, which were no doubt a precious commodity. Joseph and Hillary didn't have anything of use, although Joseph's concealed pistol held intrinsic value for their own protection. The trio figured that the two packs of smokes could go a long way when it came to bartering; addiction was a timeless ailment and smoking had not yet gone out of style. The group headed over to STORE and crossed the desolate street. Joseph entered first and they all stopped dead in their tracks, gawking in astonishment. The shop was remarkably well stocked and resembled an ordinary convenience store that would have existed prior to the war. There were three shelving units filled with canned goods, bottled liquids, and miscellaneous items such as knives, can openers, and yes, smokes.

The rest of STORE looked to be as expected in a post-apocalyptic outpost. The refrigerators were emptied out, as power had been lost long ago, and the remaining shelving units were cleared out as well. Remnants of broken glass sprinkled the hard-to-reach corners of the store and the windows had been boarded up, which gave the shop a dingy ambience. None of this fazed Joseph, Greg or Hillary as their eyes fixated on the three fully stocked shelves. They felt like they were kids at Disneyland, or more accurately, starving dogs who had just found a pile of meaty bones. Greg and Hillary hurried over to the fully stocked shelves; meanwhile Joseph took a direct route to the shop owner instead. The man who was sitting on a stool behind the counter had an amused look on his face. He was very thin, gaunt even, and wore a jean jacket that looked far too big for him with a grey T-shirt underneath. Joseph was pretty sure that the T-shirt used to be white once upon a time.

"First time?" he asked Joseph with a smirk.

"What?" Joseph replied.

The man rolled his eyes and clarified, "First time in the outpost?"

"Oh, yeah. How'd you get all this stuff?" Joseph asked, still in disbelief.

"Those PAR fellas keep us well stocked. Some folks don't like 'em, but as long as they keep bringing in supplies they're fine by me," he answered with a lazy southern drawl.

"Why wouldn't people like PAR?" Joseph asked curiously.

"Listen, if you want to gossip and hear rumours, go talk to Big Mike over at the bar. He'll chew your ear off. Now, you buying or just window shopping?" the shopkeeper replied irritably.

"What can a cigarette get me?" Joseph asked.

The man shrugged. "Depends on what you want. Usually not much. Two or three cigarettes can maybe get you a can of something if I like ya enough."

Joseph nodded and rejoined his companions who were combing through the shop's inventory with wide child-like eyes filled with wonder.

"It's about three cigarettes for a can of food, so we should be able to get a good amount if we trade one full carton," Joseph excitedly informed his friends as he began to fully appreciate the inventory with them.

The trio of companions took their time deciding what items to select. They decided that it would be best to gather a moderate amount of supplies now and then restock later on once they had a plan for accumulating more goods to trade with. Joseph figured that if two to three cigarettes could get them a full can of food, they'd probably be able to get enough for a few days' bartering with one full pack of 20 cigarettes. When their shopping spree came to an end, the once almost-empty backpack contained one can of baked beans, two cans of tuna, two bottles of water, and one glorious can of mouthwatering sliced peaches. Joseph figured that their selection would be a fair trade for an unopened pack of smokes, but then again bottled water was a hot commodity nowadays. Joseph led his friends to the front of the store and emptied the contents of the bag onto the counter. The shopkeeper whistled at the grand selection of goods and Joseph produced the pristine pack of cigarettes. The shopkeeper studied the trade carefully before finally shaking his head disapprovingly.

"Too much," he said after a while. "Put a bottle of water back and a can too."

"Come on," Joseph protested. "People would kill for a cigarette these days, let alone an entire pack!"

"I ain't met a smoker these days who'd give up a sip of water for a ciggy," the shopkeeper stubbornly insisted.

"Then you haven't met many smokers," Joseph grumbled as he opened the second pack of cigarettes and placed six more individual smokes onto the counter.

After a few moments of deliberation, the shopkeeper finally agreed to the trade and Greg began to pack the goods back into the black bag.

"How do people usually afford this stuff?" Joseph enquired.

"Well," the shopkeeper replied, "a lot of folks don't got much to trade. So they offer to work for PAR. They'll do scavenger runs in the city, and PAR lets them keep a large portion of what they find. Dangerous work—some people never come back—but you gotta do what you gotta do."

"Why wouldn't they just keep everything they find instead?" Joseph asked with a mischievous grin.

"They'll get booted from the outpost," the shopkeeper answered matter-of-factly. "PAR has a good little system. Play the game, get the prize. Which in this case is food, shelter, and protection."

"I guess that makes sense," Greg chimed in as he slung the bag over his shoulder, "but what about you? How'd you end up running this place?"

"I've been here a real long time. As long as I continue to make fair trades I get the room in the back and I can help myself to the inventory within reason. Pretty good gig, if I do say so myself." The shopkeeper winked, clearly proud of being a dystopian store owner.

"Yeah, not a bad gig at all," Greg said with envy in his voice before asking, "Where do people sleep around here?"

"If you have the goods to trade," the shopkeeper paused, indicating their food supply that they had just traded for moments ago, "I'll let you stay here in the back. Or, there's an inn just up the road on the right."

"We'll check the inn out first, but thanks for the offer," Joseph interjected. He was excited about prospectively staying at an inn and was in no hurry to share a room with a loafing shopkeeper whom they had just met.

"Suit yourself," the shopkeeper replied with another sluggish shrug.

The group exited the store and Greg was happy to feel the weight of their newly acquired supplies on his shoulders. The sun that had once transformed the endlessly grey cloud coverage into magnificent hues of fiery oranges and vibrant purples was beginning to dip below the horizon, taking the spectacular colours away with it. There were a few lanterns that had been lit along the main road hanging from makeshift hooks. None of the shops appeared to have any kind of lighting with the exception of BAR. A gentle orange glow flickered from inside and Joseph could make out the outline of thirsty patrons lining the booths along the large glass window that overlooked the main street. Joseph was definitely interested in speaking to Big Mike and getting a rundown on the outpost, but right now he was exhausted and eager to find the inn. The trio began walking down the street and passed a group of people sleeping on the sidewalk covered with tarps, blankets, and even sleeping bags for the more fortunate drifters. Joseph led his friends across a couple of side streets that intersected with the main strip; these streets were without lanterns, and darkness consumed whatever they led to. After a short five-minute stroll under lantern light, the trio arrived at the inn and to everyone's surprise the inn was actually an inn. In fact, it still had its original lettering on the front: 'Courtview Hotel'. The pre-war hotel was ten storeys tall and therapeutic orange candlelight shone through a handful of windows, indicating that those rooms were occupied. In front of the large oakwood doors that led inside to the main lobby were two lanterns that illuminated the entrance. With Joseph at the helm, the trio entered Courtview Hotel.

It was dim inside the hotel but certainly not dark. A variety of scented candles had been lit strategically throughout the lobby, filling the room with the aroma of springtime flowers and the distinct smell of lavender. Joseph could tell that this inn had been quite luxurious before the war; even now the lobby still maintained an aura of sophistication and class. Tasteful maroon-coloured leather chairs and couches that had once provided a comfortable place for guests to wait for taxis were spread throughout the lobby. Several gorgeous vases with intricate stained-glass patterns were placed on otherwise empty shelves but were void of any signs of life. Despite the handful of candles that brightened the room there was a rustic fireplace ironically unlit. Joseph thought that perhaps it was an electric fireplace like the Napoleon fireplace he had back home, when he still had a home. The front desk was curiously unattended and there was a note nailed to the bright-red reception counter. The note had been messily written with a black marker and it read as follows:

Take a key if available. Return key upon departure. Maximum 3 day stay. Enjoy!

Joseph, Greg, and Hillary simultaneously read the note while they all gently bumped heads, having to lean in close and squint to make out the dark writing. Behind the desk was a cork board full of hooks. Some of these hooks had keys; others did not.

"I wonder how they enforce that three-day stay policy," Hillary thought out loud.

Greg shrugged and went behind the counter to select a key.

"We could all have our own room on the same floor," he suggested.

"Yes!" Hillary shouted enthusiastically before softening her tone. "It's just that...well...listen, no offence, Greg, but you snore like an ox!"

Greg chuckled and grabbed three keys that were close together on the board.

"You good with that, Joseph? Or do you need me to tuck you in?" Greg joked.

"You're hilarious, Greg," Joseph sarcastically replied with a smirk on his face as he took a key from him.

It was nice to see his friends cracking a couple of jokes. It was no secret that they were all still grieving the loss of William. Joseph had learned that it was best not to dwell on the past. With all that he had lost, Joseph had found that reminiscing about things that once were or could've been was enough to make him lose his mind and contemplate ending his persistent suffering once and for all. Needless to say, remaining in the present and having a few laughs when it was possible to do so was the best remedy for his grief. Joseph looked down at the key in his hand and was surprised by the weight of the little gold object. Their room keys were actual keys, not keycards that most modern hotels used to have. The keys that the trio had selected were tagged with the numbers 306, 308, and 314. There was a trail of dwindling candles that led to a stairwell and the metal door was propped open with a wooden plank. Greg led Joseph and Hillary into the stairwell and they began to ascend towards the third floor, taking great care not to miss any steps in the dark along the way. Once the trio had made it to their level, they entered the hallway, which was illuminated only by a lone lantern that had been placed on the red carpeted floor. Joseph picked up the lantern and cast its soft glow onto the doors as they searched for their rooms. Hillary's room was 306, which they found first. She inserted her key, unlocked the door, and shoved it open. It was impossible to see anything without a light, so Joseph pushed ahead of Hillary with the lantern and pierced through the veil of darkness.

Joseph and company thoroughly inspected the tiny room, making sure that there weren't any monsters lurking in the shadows. Housekeeping evidently no longer remained at the Courtview Hotel, but the place looked relatively well maintained considering the circumstances. There was a double-bed mattress with a single pillow pushed into the back corner. No sheets, no blankets, no pillowcase. Just a mattress and a pillow, but that itself was a modern-day luxury. It would surely be more comfortable than the previous night that Hillary and her peers had spent lying on a cold concrete floor in the middle of a treacherous city while she wept over the loss of her dear friend William. There was also a large dresser at the foot of the bed and a useless lamp resting on top of a lopsided nightstand. Joseph opened the door to the bathroom, although his hopes weren't high. The toilet seat had been taped shut and a tin bucket in desperate need of being emptied had been placed beside the inoperable lavatory. Joseph suppressed an overwhelming urge to empty his stomach onto the floor and quickly closed the bathroom door. Hillary had already flopped onto the bed and was sprawled out like a kid who had been tuckered out from a family vacation.

"This is the most comfortable bed I've ever laid on. Like ever. Of all time," she declared with pure bliss radiating from her voice.

"We should be safe here," Greg said with an approving nod.

"Yeah, for three days," Hillary laughed.

"I'm right next door if you need me," Greg told her in a paternalistic tone.

"I'll be fine," Hillary replied with an eye-roll, although she appreciated Greg's assurance.

Joseph and Greg said goodnight to Hillary before making their way out into the hall, the light fading from her room as Joseph carried the lantern out. Hillary didn't care about the overwhelming darkness — she was already drifting off to sleep. Joseph and Greg stood outside room 308 for a moment, Greg's room.

"This place is almost too good to be true," Greg remarked sceptically.

"Yeah, I know what you mean. I'm just happy to finally be somewhere safe," Joseph replied, the relief in his voice noticeable. "I want to talk to that Big Mike fella at the bar tomorrow. See what he has to say."

"Fine by me, I could use a good drink," Greg replied with a hearty chuckle.

"It's a plan then, we'll head over first thing tomorrow," Joseph said.

"Sounds good, buddy," Greg agreed before unlocking his door.

Joseph followed Greg into his room with the lantern and after a brief inspection the two weather-beaten men said their goodnights and Joseph left. Greg's room had been almost identical to Hillary's, although unfortunately for Greg, there was no pillow on his stained lumpy mattress. Joseph continued down the hall towards room 314, the last room on the left. Before he could even insert his key into the lock, the door to room 315 opened directly behind him. Joseph spun around, rightfully startled. They hadn't seen, let alone heard, anyone since entering the hotel. Joseph could faintly make out the figure standing in the doorway thanks to the communal lantern that he was still holding. The man standing in front of Joseph was broad, his shoulders taking up almost the entire doorframe. Although broad-shouldered, the man wasn't very tall and stood around Joseph's height.

"Richard?" the man in 315 asked quizzically with a thick Hispanic accent as he squinted to see who was holding the lantern.

"Uh…no. Joseph," Joseph cautiously replied.

The two stood there awkwardly for a moment before 315 finally spoke again.

"Sorry, thought you were a friend. I'm Aaron, you new around here?"

Joseph could see now that the man had short curly black hair and a dark complexion. He seemed to be around Joseph's age, although it was hard to say for sure as the glare from the lantern altered Aaron's face.

"Yeah, just got here today," Joseph replied with an unintentional yawn—he was eager to climb into bed and close his heavy eyelids.

"Right, well, keep your wits about you," Aaron said while nervously glancing down the dark hallway.

"My wits? This place seems safe enough, isn't it?" Joseph asked, suddenly waking up a bit.

The man in room 315 seemed hesitant to say anything more. He poked his head out and looked down the hallway once again.

"Come inside," Aaron urged.

"Hey, listen, I don't even know you and—" Joseph began to say before Aaron cut him off.

"The more you know, the safer you'll be. Haven't you wondered why it's so damn quiet around here?"

"It's getting dark," Joseph answered with uncertainty, "plus that bar seemed pretty busy."

"Of course the bar was busy, it's the only safe place in this outpost," Aaron quickly replied.

"Safe from what?" Joseph asked as the increasingly familiar wave of nausea returned.

"From…" Aaron hesitated before whispering, "From PAR."

"From PAR?" Joseph repeated, not matching Aaron's hushed tone.

"Yes and we shouldn't even be talking out here, you never know who's listening. Come in, I have something that you might want to see," Aaron insisted as he opened the door a little wider. Joseph began to instinctively reach for his concealed weapon before he caught himself and dropped his hand back down to his side.

"I'm unarmed," Aaron continued. "I know you don't know me, but trust me on this. Everything isn't as it seems here. Just come in, I'll show you what I mean."

Aaron stepped aside and continued to hold the door open. The light from Joseph's lantern flooded into the room and he could see that the young Hispanic man was alone. Joseph was comforted by the hard steel Colt 1911 that was pressing against his hip bone beneath his jacket and by the fact that his two companions were just across the hall. For some reason Joseph felt like he could trust this unfamiliar face who supposedly had a secret to share. There was something intrinsically genuine about the way that Aaron spoke.

"Fine," Joseph said after a few moments of careful consideration.

Aaron gestured once more for Joseph to enter room 315. Joseph took a deep breath as he stepped inside the room, and the heavy wooden door slammed shut behind him.

***

Commander Ventress, Klein, Reaper, and the remainder of Alpha Squad sat in the back of the abundantly spacious CS50. Ventress sat with her back against the wall that separated the pilots from the cargo and the troops, facing the rest of her PAR associates. She hadn't said a single word since boarding the aircraft and her subordinates mimicked her silence. Her very presence demanded respect and she would occasionally cast a domineering glare around the cargo bay as she evaluated her soldiers in a rather judgmental manner. Ventress was dressed as dark as night itself. Black combat boots, black cargo pants, and that same black leather trench coat with the gold letter 'V' stitched onto the left side of her chest that Reaper had seen her wear in her office the day before. Reaper thought that his codename almost suited Ventress better as she currently had the demeanor of the Grim Reaper herself.

Alpha Squad, with the exception of Reaper, had their iconic black combat gear on and looked ready to jump into a battlefield with weapons blazing. Both Reaper and Klein were dressed for their special undercover occasion. Reaper had donned a pair of filthy blue jeans that were more grey now than blue and a faded black hoodie that used to say 'ACDC', but now just said 'A C' as the cheaply laminated lettering had begun to peel away. His short black hair was covered by a bright-blue baseball cap and his dark bushy beard gave him the appearance of a real homeless drifter, which was the hottest fashion in this post-apocalyptic wasteland. Klein, even undercover, appeared to be well maintained with his freshly shaven face that matched his shiny hairless head. He too wore an old pair of jeans and a hoodie. His hoodie, however, wasn't terribly worn out and had a well-preserved football logo on the front which had presumably been his favourite team. The seams of his extra large sweater looked at risk of tearing apart as they strained to contain Klein's muscular torso. The behemoth of a man had a terrible time finding properly fitting clothes both before and after the nuclear fallout.

Reaper and Klein were to be dropped off just outside the city, far enough away from Outpost Zulu to ensure that no one could see their affiliation with the flashy PAR aircraft. Once they had been dropped off, Ventress and Alpha Squad would continue on directly to Outpost Zulu.

The CS50 had slowed to a complete stop. The grinding of oil-starved gears was audible as the thrusters shifted in order to allow the aircraft to steadily hover in the sky before beginning its gradual descent. Reaper and Klein made brief eye contact from opposite sides of the cargo bay, a silent acknowledgement that their mission was about to commence. The aircraft came to a halt before making direct contact with the ground as it continued to levitate and the large cargo door began to lower. Reaper and Klein pulled their rifles out of the wall mounts and began walking towards the now open cargo bay door that was allowing a rush of sickly grey light to fill up the back of the aircraft. The duo stocked up on ammunition and grabbed a pair of headlamps prior to departing the CS50—it would be dark well before they entered the core of Hathbury. Once they were sufficiently equipped, both men simultaneously jumped off the ramp as the aircraft continued to hover a few feet above the desolate highway. Almost as soon as their strategically unimpressive sneakers made contact with the cracked pavement, the CS50 began its ascent and the cargo door began to close once again. Within mere seconds the airship was back on track and slicing through the clouds towards Outpost Zulu.

Reaper and Klein began walking down the highway, manoeuvring around, over, and sometimes through, abandoned cars of all makes and models. Every move that Klein made was calculated and smooth—he would have had the physique of a gymnast if he wasn't so immensely tall. Reaper also navigated the maze of wreckages with relative ease, but he moved much less gracefully than his irritatingly athletic counterpart. He moved just as you would expect a man on the north side of 35 who had known only a life of combat since he was 18. The two travelled down the lonely highway in silence for the most part. It wasn't long until Reaper noticed the familiar farmhouse coming up on their right, the one where he and Alpha Squad had rescued that ragtag group of survivors a couple of days earlier.

"You don't suppose she could've dropped us off a little closer to the city, eh?" Reaper scoffed as the farmhouse was now directly to their right, about a mile away on the other side of the neglected muddy field that was once home to a grand corn crop.

"It's imperative that our cover is not blown and that we are not recognized as members of PAR," Klein replied matter-of-factly as he deliberately avoided a large pile of glass shards.

"Yeah, yeah," Reaper said, already annoyed by Klein's teacher's pet act. "What's your story anyways?"

"My story?" Klein repeated, as the two made it onto a relatively clear stretch of the highway.

"Yeah, your story. I've never seen you around the base and then here you are walking the highway to hell with me undercover."

Klein didn't reply immediately. In fact, Reaper almost thought that he was ignoring the question entirely.

"I was transferred specifically for this mission," Klein finally answered.

"Transferred from where?" Reaper probed at his assigned partner.

"R and D," Klein replied.

Reaper's usual one-track mind was uncharacteristically flooded with questions. He knew that it shouldn't matter, but he desperately wanted to know what was going on at the R&D facility and why these photos were of such a high importance. Klein was carrying his rifle loosely with one hand on the foregrip while keeping the muzzle pointed at the ground. Reaper carried his death stick more conventionally, with two hands like a proper soldier. They were beginning to enter the outskirts of Hathbury and the farmlands were gradually giving way to suburban sprawls on either side of the highway. The distant silhouettes of skyscrapers loomed ahead of them as the daylight was rapidly deteriorating.

"What are we looking for, Klein? What are the pictures of?" Reaper asked, as his curiosity got the better of his discipline.

"It's classified," Klein replied without breaking stride, the same answer that the Commander had given Reaper.

"Enough of this 'classified' bullshit. Give me something to work with, give me a reason to trust you," Reaper demanded as he stopped walking.

Klein also stopped and turned to face Reaper, both men partaking in an intense stare-down. Reaper believed that he had a right to know what they were looking for; he had done nothing but obey orders his entire time working for PAR. If he were to carry out yet another successful mission, he needed more intel than what he had been given. In the event that Klein suffered an untimely demise while travelling through the city, Reaper would be waltzing into Outpost Zulu blindly looking for…well, that's just it, isn't it? He had no idea what he was looking for.

"You want answers, Sergeant? Then give me your knife," Klein ordered.

"Why?" Reaper asked sceptically.

"I will show you exactly what you want to know," Klein replied firmly.

Reaper reluctantly handed Klein his combat knife that had been secured in its sheath on the waistband of Reaper's faded blue jeans. Klein rolled up his sweater sleeve and then immediately plunged the blade into his forearm.

"What the hell are you doing?" Reaper asked in horror.

"Just watch," Klein answered calmly.

Klein made one horizontal incision and two vertical incisions that took on the shape of a blocky lowercase letter 'n'. He then handed the knife back to Reaper, who could hardly comprehend what he was witnessing. No blood. Not a single drop. Klein peeled the flap of skin back with his massive fingers. To both Reaper's amazement and terror, beneath the layer of artificial flesh was a plethora of steel and wires. No blood, no bones, no veins; simply metal and circuitry. Klein folded the chunk of skin back into place and the surrounding tissue seamlessly reconnected to it, sealing up the wound entirely.

"This is what we've been doing. Harmoniously merging man and machine, cybernetic enhancements," Klein said as he studied Reaper's horrified expression.

"How much of you is"—Reaper paused as he fumbled for words—"that?"

"Both of my arms and legs. As a result, I am faster, stronger, and more accurate than any ordinary man," Klein replied as he rolled his sleeve back down. "As you can see, we have made tremendous progress, but there have also been significant tribulations."

"And pictures of those tribulations," Reaper said.

"Yes," Klein responded.

"How bad are they?" Reaper asked, only partially wanting an answer.

"Bad. You were going to find out eventually; better now when you can see the end result at work. When you can see me at work," Klein informed him as he turned and began walking down the barren highway once more.

Reaper followed Klein towards the city center of Hathbury as his mind continued to race. Now he knew. Klein's cybernetic enhancements were no doubt impressive, but Reaper couldn't help but feel uneasy about this newly acquired information. It all felt wrong, unnatural. He couldn't even begin to imagine what kind of tribulations the R&D facility had encountered along the way. Medical science didn't have the luxury of experimenting on animals any more since most of the natural world had been decimated by nuclear warfare. Reaper felt sick to his stomach. For the first time in his professional life he was contemplating the implications that his mission might have and the bigger picture of it all.

Chapter 8

A Night to Remember

Aaron's hotel room was nearly identical to Hillary's and Greg's respective rooms, although it was slightly more spacious and the bed was queen-sized rather than twin-sized. Joseph noted that the bathroom door was also closed, likely to contain a grotesque scene festering within that was similar to what Joseph had witnessed in Hillary's bathroom. Joseph had set his lantern down on the floor and Aaron had lit a few candles which brightened up the room quite nicely. Joseph was more thankful for the comforting aroma of cedar that the candles emitted than for the light itself. The scent soothed his constantly churning stomach that consistently encouraged Joseph to empty his gut, despite it already being void of food more often than not. There wasn't anywhere to sit other than the queen-sized bed or the floor, and Aaron decided to stand awkwardly by the window that was reflecting the glimmer of candlelight, with his hands shoved deeply into his pockets. There was, however, a dark-blue leather chair in the corner of the room, but it was currently occupied by a beige duffel bag, which prompted Joseph to stand as well, as he continued to lurk near the front door.

"Listen," Aaron began, "this place, this outpost, it isn't safe."

"I don't understand. The guards and the walls seem to keep the bandits and Orvilles out," Joseph replied.

"The what?" Aaron asked, visibly confused.

"Sorry," Joseph said almost with a chuckle, "the uh... mutants? Ghouls? Zombies? Whatever you call them."

"Oh yeah, the Zonks!" Aaron exclaimed.

"Zonks? Why do you call them that?" Joseph asked.

"'Cause they're always all zonked out in the head. I heard a couple of guys mention it a few months back while I was on the road and it just kind of stuck. Why do you call them Orvilles?"

"Their skin is covered in blisters that look ready to pop, just like popcorn," Joseph answered while he sheepishly rubbed the back of his head.

"Gross," Aaron said, making a face of disgust.

"Yeah," Joseph replied.

"Okay, well anyways," Aaron continued, "it's not the bandits or the Zonks, or Orvilles as you say, that you need to worry about. It's the soldiers. It's PAR."

"That's the part I don't understand. This place is like a little slice of nirvana—what's not to like about PAR?" Joseph asked with a hint of scepticism in his voice.

"I'll show you."

Aaron took a few steps over to the beige duffel bag that was currently occupying the only chair in the room. The duffel bag was once military issued and someone's name that had previously been written on the side in black permanent marker was now scratched out. Aaron unzipped the hefty bag and began rummaging around. It was difficult to tell due to the limited lighting, but Joseph thought that he saw a gun in the bag, as something metallic reflected a brief glint from the nearest candle that was lit beside the bed on the nightstand. Aaron pulled out a large orange water-stained envelope and turned back to face Joseph.

"What did you say your name was again?" Aaron asked shakily.

"Joseph."

"Right, right. Okay, well listen, Joseph. People have been vanishing from the outpost."

"Vanishing?" Joseph's eyes fell to the envelope that Aaron was white-knuckling.

"Yeah, and this has been going on for months. Familiar faces that have been here for weeks disappearing from the outpost overnight, and scavenger parties vanishing beyond the walls without a trace. At first we had thought that these people were just heading to greener pastures"—Aaron took a moment to compose himself—"but now we know the truth."

Aaron extended his hand, offering Joseph the envelope. Joseph took the battered envelope and folded back the sticky seal, retrieving three photographs from within. It was still too dark to make anything out and Joseph was visibly straining to see what he was even looking at. He moved closer to a candle on a dresser. On the wall above the dresser was a prominent outline where a television used to be mounted, presumably stolen by looters during the days that followed nuclear Armageddon.

"Careful!" Aaron shouted with wide eyes. "Don't get too close to the candle..."

Joseph nodded and proceeded with caution, ensuring that he kept the flickering flame away from the edges of the photographs. He examined the first photo. It was a poorly taken picture; half of the photograph was covered by something, presumably a clumsy photographer's thumb. What wasn't covered by a graceless thumb, however, was crystal clear. Joseph could make out a man lying on a blood-soaked hospital bed in a great deal of visible pain. All of his limbs were missing and a surgeon was observing the man from the background with an apparent lack of empathy. Joseph carefully flipped to the second of the three photos, which still possessed a photobombing thumb. It appeared to be the same man, although in this picture he had grown two new arms. At least that's what it looked like at first glance, before Joseph examined the picture more closely. A mix of steel and wires had been shoved into the man's shoulder sockets like some kind of enhanced prosthetic limbs. Joseph flipped to the final picture, feeling increasingly disturbed. There was no obstruction this time, although the picture itself was relatively blurry as if the photographer had taken the picture mid-stride. To Joseph's horror, the camera had captured the image of eight other people who had all sprouted various mechanical appendages in place of their missing organic limbs. All of these tortured souls were wide awake and had their mouths ajar in silent screams that the picture could not record. There was a ninth person closest to the photographer, and this woman had all of her biological limbs. Despite her retention of the limbs that she was born with, she was not without suffering. The woman had wires running in and out of her head, and a blank expression erased any resemblance of emotion from her face, a stark contrast to the eight other patients who had their silent screams immortalized within the photograph. Joseph put the pictures back into the envelope, his hands shaking and his stomach doing somersaults.

"Where did..." Joseph cleared his throat. "Where did you get these?"

"I can't risk compromising his identity, but I received the pictures from someone who is a member of PAR," Aaron said, careful not to divulge too much information about his source.

As a lawyer, Joseph had been taught to be critical of everything. Even the smallest overlooked detail or omission could reveal when someone was lying.

"As disturbed as I am...how do you know that these are real? Or that they're the reason people have been disappearing from the outpost?" Joseph enquired.

"Because that man in the first two pictures was my friend, Tom," Aaron answered sombrely.

"Oh...I'm...I'm sorry," Joseph said, a little taken aback.

"It's not your fault, it's that wretched PAR. They try to snatch up loners or drunkards that nobody will miss, but they've become complacent, sloppy. Tom was a drunkard no doubt, but a lot of people knew Tom. I knew Tom."

"But why? Why would they do this?" Joseph asked, trying to make sense of it all.

"Well, according to my source, the Commander has focused all of her energy on military expansion. She's trying to create some kind of human-machine hybrids, like super-soldiers. I guess even now people still want to rule the world, even if it's a world of rubble and fleeting memories of what once was," Aaron replied as he uncomfortably shoved his hands back into his front pockets.

There was an awkward silence that followed for several moments. Joseph was still processing the atrocities that he had seen take place within the pictures. If what Aaron was saying was true, and if the photos were in fact real, then PAR was just another tyrannical organization on a quest for world domination. Joseph didn't want to believe it, but it also wouldn't surprise him. The free world that had existed before the catastrophic nuclear war was under constant duress. Nations that had once been faithful allies became disgruntled foes as the earth's natural resources continued to dwindle and each world superpower fought to become the only superpower. Greed, gluttony, and a lust for power were intrinsic human characteristics that world leaders did an exceptional job of exhibiting. Why would this new world of ruins and death be any different? Joseph thought that perhaps he was a fool for getting his hopes up in the first place, for believing that there was still an entity that was looking out for the best interests of survivors.

"I'm going to need that back," Aaron said, breaking Joseph's line of thought and pointing to the envelope that he held loosely at his side.

"Oh, right," Joseph said, as he handed Aaron the envelope of horrors.

"Why would your source tell you all this?" Joseph asked after a few more silent moments.

"Ethics," Aaron replied with a shrug. "Sometimes bad guys can also be good guys."

"Now there's a thought," Joseph said, reflecting on Aaron's words. "So what now? Are you going to get out of here?"

"Look, I've probably said too much already," Aaron replied with a brief shake of his head. "Big Mike, the local bartender, has no problem over-serving both drinks and information. You should talk to him. You should also probably get going before Richard gets back; he's much less welcoming towards newcomers than I am. Please, come back again tomorrow night and I can fill you in on what I plan to do next."

"Alright, I might. But you know what they say, right? 'Curiosity killed the cat,'" Joseph said somewhat humorously in an attempt to break the tension.

"Yeah, well, 'they' are probably all dead now. Besides, satisfaction brought the cat back," Aaron added, matching Joseph's attempt at humour.

A deep rumble began to reverberate throughout Joseph's body. At first he thought that it was his pesky stomach begging for food once more, but then he noticed the frenzy of shadows dancing across the walls. The flames of the candles had accelerated from a gentle flicker to a frantic flurry, and the rhythmic waltz of the shadows had increased their speed to an up-tempo tango.

"I hear it too," Aaron said.

"What *is* that?" Joseph asked nervously.

"I'm not sure…"

The rumble suddenly became a roar that shook the entire room like an earthquake. The candle flames continued to passionately burn and the shadows dancing around the room increased the speed of their lively jig. Joseph had flashbacks to when the bombs first dropped, when it felt like the earth itself was shaking in pain.

Just as suddenly as the late-night disturbance occurred, the noise receded and the room returned to normal.

"PAR," Aaron said, scowling.

"PAR?" Joseph asked, clearly confused as to what they just experienced.

"They have a landing pad behind that old courthouse. They use it to deliver supplies and fly in doctors. I haven't heard an aircraft quite like that, though," Aaron informed him.

"Do they usually fly in this late at night?" Joseph asked.

"Never," Aaron replied.

The two stood there for a few more moments listening into the silent night for any other disturbances. There were none. The night had returned to normal and the dancing shadows had continued their slow waltz once more.

"I should probably get going," Joseph said as he turned for the door and retrieved his lantern. "Maybe I'll swing by tomorrow night."

"Yeah, you should," Aaron insisted.

Joseph left Aaron's room and crossed the hall to his own room, 314. He did a brief inspection of the room with the communal lantern, this time skipping the bathroom check, and then placed the lantern back in the hall just outside of his door. Unfortunately for Joseph, his queen-sized bed did not have a sheet or even a pillow. Joseph didn't care—he was wiped and excited just to have a mattress. He took his jacket off and rolled it into a ball, putting it where his pillow should have been. He then yanked off his mud-crusted boots and placed his M1911 pistol on the bedside table. Joseph leaned back and rested his head on his makeshift pillow. As soon as he closed his eyes the pictures came rushing back into his mind. He wanted to know what else Aaron had to say and what he would do next. Joseph's body, however, wanted to sleep. Within a few minutes, despite the vivid imagery of unimaginable suffering that was imprinted into his consciousness, Joseph succumbed to the all-consuming embrace of slumber.

***

It was already pitch black by the time Reaper and Klein entered the main part of Hathbury. They had been dropped off as the sun was already setting and lately it seemed to get dark faster than the days before the bombs had dropped. The thick and permanent cloud coverage did not allow any penetration of light at night. When it was night, the lights were out and not a single soul on Earth had the privilege of gazing up at the stars. Klein and Reaper both had their headlamps on now as they had increased their pace to a light jog. Outpost Zulu was still quite a ways away and their objective was to arrive before sunrise so that there would be fewer prying eyes upon their entry. The major downside to arriving under the cover of darkness was the inevitable exposure to threats such as radiation-filled freak bags and bandits, two factors that would inevitably slow their progress. Reaper and Klein were well armed, both toting M4A1s with extended 50-round magazines. They also had an abundance of ammunition attached around their waist and in bandoliers. The plan was to ditch the weapons and ammo just before arriving at Outpost Zulu. Until then, it was weapons free on anything that stood between Reaper, Klein, and the outpost. It was going to be an eventful evening to say the least.

The duo continued to move swiftly, although their momentum had slowed to more of a light trot now than a jog. They kept their weapons at the ready and their heads on a swivel. Regardless of their vigilance and Reaper's extensive combat experience, the city was large and possessed many places for potential foes to lurk within the dark. If it wasn't for the inhuman war screech, Reaper likely wouldn't have been able to turn around in time. Three deranged mutants sprung out from the inside of an old U-Haul truck that was only a few feet away from Reaper. Although these humanoids resembled people, sometimes even speaking like people, they were more animal than human— their brains corrupted from radiation, their bodies mutated in a way that was advantageous to primitive forms of hunting.

Reaper's headlamp illuminated the trio of mutants barrelling towards him as they scrambled quickly on all fours. He managed to get a single shot off, incapacitating the creature furthest to his left. The middle mutant came crashing into Reaper, knocking him onto his back, his rifle falling to the ground with a clatter. Reaper held his forearm underneath the feral man's throat, trying to keep his snapping jaws at bay, the smell of rotting flesh unbearable. Two shots rang out, the second shot silencing the gnashing mouth filled with elongated incisors that were trying to tear a chunk out of Reaper. Hot sticky blood covered Reaper's face, and his eye twitched with disgust as he shoved the corpse off him. The carcass rolled to Reaper's right and came to a rest beside the third mutant, which Klein had also shot.

"You're welcome, Rodriguez," Klein said rather sarcastically as he extended a hand to help Reaper up.

"Don't call me that," Reaper said with disdain, slapping Klein's hand away and collecting his weapon.

"It's your name though, isn't it?" he asked rather innocently.

"Not any more," Reaper replied with a grunt, readjusting his now sideways headlamp.

More inhuman screeching rang out from a few blocks over, followed by a barrage of gunfire.

"We're in the middle of a feeding frenzy," Klein remarked as the two continued onwards into the night.

It took less than five minutes for Reaper and Klein to find trouble again. Seven feral mutants were looking for their first meal of the night. Three emerged from a dark alleyway and the remaining four came charging out from a doorway that led to some kind of antique shop. This time the two PAR operatives were ready for the confrontation and put the creatures down with ease as if they were a pack of starving dogs. The unlikely duo scanned their surroundings for any more signs of danger, their headlamps casting a bright-yellow circle onto everything they looked at.

"It's these damn headlamps!" Reaper cursed as he flipped his light off.

Klein did the same and they were plunged into unfathomable darkness. The kind of darkness that almost made you wonder if you'd gone blind due to an undiagnosed underlying condition. They could hear another flurry of gunfire in the distance. This time there was no screeching to accompany the gunfire, indicating that this noisy disturbance was likely a little bandit-on-bandit action.

"In here." Klein pointed to a nearby doorway, the gesture hardly visible. "We'll go inside and let our eyes adjust."

Klein moved confidently through the dark and Reaper struggled to match his pace, tripping several times over a variety of debris. The two entered the doorway, briefly flipping their lights back on in order to secure the room, which appeared to be more of a lobby. Propped behind what might have once been the desk for a receptionist was a skeleton leaning back lazily on a tall swivel chair. Reaper couldn't help but smirk at the macabre display. The rest of the lobby was empty and the duo turned their lights off once again. It would take about 20 minutes for their eyes to adjust to the dark and it would still be difficult to navigate, but it would be doable. Reaper and Klein stood in silence and listened to the chaos within the city, which was anything but silent. Gunshots, screams, screeches, the tinkling of broken glass. It all echoed through the night air. Reaper was thinking about how amazing it was that there was any glass left to break in this ill-treated city when another scream rang out, this one much closer than anything else they had previously heard.

"That sounded like it came from above us," Reaper whispered.

The isolated scream soon transformed into a choir of hysterical wailing as more and more tortured voices joined in on the chilling chorus. Klein and Reaper slowly turned to face the stairwell, right next to the now inoperable elevator, and listened to the screams bounce off the concrete walls. The deafening choir of shrieking drowned out any noises that came from outside of the damned building. After a few minutes that felt like a few hours, the screams finally trailed off and allowed for the rest of Hathbury's terror to be audibly appreciated.

"Let's pretend we never heard that," Klein said dismissively.

Reaper couldn't help but take note of Klein's dismissive tone and he briefly wondered what Klein might have been a part of at the R&D facility. He continued to contemplate what he would see when they recovered the photos, as they continued to wait for their eyes to adjust to the dark. Eventually he shook the worrisome thoughts from his head and they exited the building that was home to the haunting cries of nameless banshees. Their eyes had indeed adjusted to the lack of light, although great caution was still needed in order to traverse the cluttered roads. They moved as quickly as they could, trying to utilize a combination of speed and stealth. The two stuck as close to the middle of the street as the wrecked cars would allow. They wanted to stay as far away as possible from the dark doorways and sporadically placed alleyways that jutted in between neighbouring buildings, as these spots were a perfect place to ambush unsuspecting travellers. Another flurry of gunshots rang out, this time close enough for Reaper and Klein to catch a glimpse of the muzzle flashes.

The gunshots were coming from directly ahead of them, and a couple of bullets whizzed by Reaper's head as he slid for cover behind a police cruiser, the side panelling now covered only with the four letters 'P LI E'. He swore and aimed his rifle in the direction of the gunfire. He could hear the assailants let out a series of shouts before ripping off another barrage of projectiles, but this time the bullets came nowhere near Reaper or Klein. Reaper caught movement out of the corner of his eye to the right as two large, mutated dogs came flying down the sidewalk towards the gunshots.

"They're not shooting at us," Reaper quickly informed Klein.

Reaper could hear a man cry out in pain, followed by the high-pitched yelp of a dog. The gunfire ceased and was replaced by a series of hushed voices.

"Hey, hold your fire!" Reaper shouted from behind the police cruiser, careful not to expose himself.

"Who that?" a voice called out from the darkness in broken English.

"Guys with guns, just like you. We're trying to get to Zulu!" Reaper shouted back.

There was a brief pause in the exchange and for a moment the city, filled with turmoil, finally fell silent.

"Us too! C'mere!" the voice finally replied.

Reaper emerged from cover, his index finger caressing the trigger of his rifle. Klein kept his distance with his weapon at the ready, silently moving from car to car. Reaper could now faintly make out the outline of a man. A few more steps closer and he could see a group of three, four including one man lying on the ground clutching at the side of his neck. The man closest to Reaper, the man with the broken English, held a rustic hunting rifle. The man behind him held some kind of shotgun and looked nervously from side to side. The third figure in the dark, a woman, appeared to have some kind of old western-style revolver. She was now crouching over the man who was clutching his neck as he lay in a puddle of blood that was rapidly transforming into a pool of blood.

"I'm Clive. This is Jordan and Lucy," Clive said before he pointed at the now deceased man. "That there was Jonathan."

"Sorry for your loss," Reaper said without much empathy.

Clive shrugged. "It don't matter. Hardly knew him."

Klein finally revealed himself, walking over to join Reaper's side.

"Those some mighty big guns you got there," Clive said, nodding at Reaper's and Klein's assault rifles.

"Found a couple dead soldiers a few blocks over," Klein lied.

"We a little lost," Clive continued. "It's dark as a barrel full of oil out here."

"I know the way to the outpost. Follow us and stay close, we're safer if we stick together," Reaper said.

No one had any complaints and the now quintet hurried off towards Outpost Zulu. Reaper led the way and Klein strategically placed himself at the back of the group. Klein wanted to keep an eye on their new travelling companions and was none too pleased that they were tagging along. Regardless of Klein's disapproval, the group actually made relatively good progress as a result of their increased numbers. Despite their nearly liquified brains, the infected were usually still smart enough not to pick a fight with a bunch of gun-toting travellers; they did still have a survival instinct after all. That's not to say, however, that they would pass up a chance at a meal if the numbers were in their favour or if they were hungry enough to test their luck.

The newly formed group of Outpost Zulu seekers were heading straight towards a particularly large and hungry pack of Orvilles that were lurking in the shadows waiting to pounce. Reaper saw them first, but he only saw the four that were hunched over a corpse and elbows deep into their late-night snack. He quickly executed the four less-than-human creatures and thought nothing of it until a series of screeches rang out from what sounded like every direction. Within a matter of seconds there were countless Orvilles flooding out from doorways, alleyways, and the interiors of abandoned cars. In all of his time in the field, Reaper had never witnessed such a massive amount of infected gathered in one location. All of their intel had indicated that the infected had been converging on Hathbury, but not even in Reaper's wildest dreams could he have imagined just how many freak bags had already set up shop within the city. Everyone in the group began to fire at anything that moved in the dark.

"I think you woke the horde!" Klein shouted as he put down mutant after mutant with incredible accuracy and machine-like efficiency.

"Oh good, I was getting a little bored anyways!" Reaper hollered back as he began collecting what little souls remained of the savage creatures.

The trio of newcomers were much less enthusiastic about their impending doom than the undercover PAR operatives. Clive was a decent shot thanks to years of hunting with his father as a young boy and was holding his own. The man with the shotgun, Jordan, seemed at risk of tumbling to the ground with every powerful shot that he took. The woman, Lucy, seemed well versed with her pistol but was hindered by the fact that it held only six shots at a time. She was the first to go down as a result of her weapon's limited capacity. She had shot her sixth shot and stuffed her hand into her black winter parka, pulling out a fistful of bullets. It was next to impossible to insert each round into the small slots of the chamber while in the dark and under such high pressure. She fumbled with the bullets, dropping half of them. An Orville grabbed her by her tight ponytail and started to drag her away from the group. She cried out and Jordan clumsily shot at the Orville that was pulling Lucy away. The buckshot took off the bottom half of Lucy's face and only grazed the Orville's left thigh. Lucy's screams were silenced and replaced with the sickening gurgle of her choking on her own blood as she disappeared into the shadows. If there was one positive takeaway for Jordan, it was that his terribly placed shot had likely spared Lucy from a much more painful death.

"And then there were four!" Reaper shouted as the group continued to fight against the overwhelming odds.

The remaining four survivors were now back-to-back. It was difficult to tell how many more mutants were left, but it sounded like there were dozens more converging on the commotion.

"Make that two," Klein said callously.

Klein turned around and fired several rounds into the legs of Clive and Jordan, the bullets barely missing Reaper as they passed through their soft human tissue. The two crumpled to the ground, crying out in pain.

"Run!" Klein shouted.

Reaper popped off a few more rounds at the mutants in front of him so that he could clear a path before reloading his rifle in one swift motion. Reaper took off into the darkness, Klein trailing behind him firing shots off into the dark in an attempt to deter the mutants from pursuing. The shots weren't really needed—the remaining Orvilles were now fighting among themselves over the still-fresh bodies writhing around on the ground in agony. There were a lot of hungry mouths, but only the strongest mutants would get to eat tonight.

Klein caught up to Reaper effortlessly, his breathing rhythmic and deep. Even prior to his cybernetic enhancements, Klein had been physically dominant. That is precisely why he was chosen for the enhancements; his natural physical prowess combined with the strength, speed, and precision of the cybernetics made him a human cheat-code. Klein, unlike so many others, did not have to go through any painful procedures. That's what his predecessors were for. They had paved the way for a seamless combination of human and machine.

Reaper, who was also in fairly good shape, was struggling tremendously to keep up with Klein. It infuriated him and he became more focused on keeping pace with Klein than anything else as he attempted to demonstrate his own physical prowess. Eventually, much to Reaper's relief, Klein slowed his pace back down to a very gentle trot. The pack of mutants were long behind them now. Those not strong enough to fight for a scrap of food were already on the hunt again while the alphas dug into Clive, Jordan, and Lucy.

"That was cold as hell what you did back there," Reaper said, trying not to let Klein know that he was still struggling to catch his breath.

"It was calculated. We would not have survived without such a distraction," Klein replied, constantly surveying their surroundings as the duo moved through the night.

"Those new limbs are a good fit on you—they match your machine-like personality," Reaper said mockingly.

"So I've been told," Klein replied indifferently.

The lethal duo carried on quietly, using both their eyes and ears to search for any signs of danger. The remainder of their journey was relatively uneventful for the two highly trained men. A few sporadic Orville encounters encouraged them to resume executing The Sick, and the odd group of gunmen diverted Reaper and Klein from their desired course a couple of times. Most of the gunfire, screams, and screeches had started to occur behind them as they continued to distance themselves from the core of the city. They were occasionally forced to stop in order to gather their bearings. It was incredibly difficult to make out landmarks and street signs; the lack of stars or moonlight made it all too easy to miss the arrows leading to Zulu. Both PAR operatives knew precisely where Outpost Zulu was located, so these brief moments of disorientation proved to be nothing more than a slight nuisance.

Pure luck is what allowed Klein to spot the first Outpost Zulu sign. He had quite literally stumbled upon it when he tripped over some debris, an error that had caused Reaper to grin broadly. The innocent stumble exposed Klein as just another man. Sure, he was faster and stronger, but at the end of the day he was still just a man, full of human flaws. Reaper's inherently competitive nature made him enjoy this brief moment of vulnerability demonstrated by Klein. They followed the crudely spray-painted arrows for a long while. Their pace had become painfully slow but through no fault of Klein. Reaper was exhausted; they had been moving non-stop since they had first deployed. The sun was bound to break the horizon soon and if there were still any birds left on this forsaken planet, they would surely be singing their songs of dawn right about now.

They were close enough now that they would likely not need their weapons any more and it would be safe to stash their rifles out of sight. Their façade of being two nobodies, two drifters just trying to get by, would unravel if they were to waltz up to the front gate of Outpost Zulu parading around their military-grade weapons and ammunition. The duo quickly darted into a nearby alleyway that separated a bakery from a butcher's shop, a sharp contrast to say the least. Of course, it was still much too dark for Reaper or Klein to be able to clearly identify either building and so the ironic comparison of sweet fluffy treats and raw bloody meats was lost on them. Even if it was the middle of the day, the dilapidation had reduced both once successful downtown shops into unrecognizable structures of filth, decay, and shattered dreams. There was a dumpster tucked into the back of the alleyway; its once fluorescent green paint had long since flaked away to reveal the rusted steel body underneath.

Reaper threw back the lid. To the surprise of both men, there was no stench whatsoever. Perhaps it had been garbage-collection day just before the bombs dropped, or desperate scavengers had gone dumpster diving and picked the container clean. Reaper made sure that his rifle had its safety on before tossing it into the bin, creating a loud clang that seemed amplified in the now quiet morning air.

Both men flinched at the sound. Klein, also making sure that his rifle was on safety, gently lowered his weapon into the bin by the sling. The duo then stashed the rest of their gear away, including Reaper's combat knife that had been used to reveal Klein's mechanical secret. Now neither operative had anything with them other than the clothes on their backs.

"It isn't much further," Reaper declared. "We just need to take the next right and the outpost is at the end of the street."

Klein simply nodded in reply; he was fully aware of where the outpost was. The two made their way back down the alley and popped out onto the main street. They took extra care not to be seen now, armed only with their fists and fighting spirits. It was only a matter of minutes before the duo turned right and could see the outpost at the end of the road. The front of the towering makeshift wall was illuminated by several lanterns suspended by hooks that had been nailed into the wooden planks. The Frankenstein-esque wall, composed of a variety of wooden planks and tin sheets, lurched dangerously forward and looked as if a strong gust of wind would send the towering behemoth to its demise. Still, the wall had held strong for the last couple of years and no breaches had occurred. Or at least no breaches had been reported by the security force.

PAR didn't exactly assign their best operatives to security detail at Outpost Zulu. In fact, it was quite the opposite. Most of the soldiers assigned to Zulu, if you could even call them soldiers, couldn't hit the broadside of a barn with their rifles. The men and women had virtually zero hours of military experience prior to the nuclear devastation that wiped out billions of lives. Commander Ventress had taken Reaper's troops, Alpha Squad, as her personal security detail for this very reason. Outpost Zulu was never supposed to have a large military presence anyway. It was supposed to be a symbol of hope, a way to show survivors that PAR could be trusted and could be relied on to provide a slight resemblance of pre-war life, even if that resemblance was just shipping in booze and snacks. The guards weren't totally useless, however. On multiple occasions they had been able to fend off mutant attacks and even bandit raids. Not an overly admirable achievement when the guards had been armed with military-grade assault rifles and tasked with protecting only a single entrance, but a military success nonetheless.

Regardless of their admittedly successful track record, Reaper despised the soldiers who were deployed at Outpost Zulu. He saw them as soft, weak-minded fools with guns and over-inflated egos. Although he would never admit it, a part of Reaper envied them in a way. All they had to worry about was how to manage their hangovers when it was their shift to guard the entrance, and the popular remedy was a 'hair of the dog': more booze. Reaper and Klein were here on a mission, a mission that might not even exist if the guards had been more vigilant or even somewhat competent.

Reaper and Klein approached the guards protecting the gate. There were six in total, all currently armed with M16 assault rifles. Security was always increased at night; that's when most of the problems tended to occur. Sunrise was only a matter of minutes away and the guards were taking turns sleeping. Four of the six were completely racked out, their chins resting on their tactical vests as they caught some sleep while sitting in small metal chairs. The remaining two observed Reaper and Klein as they approached.

"Halt," one of the guards demanded, smelling of cheap liquor and cigarettes. "State your business."

"Just looking for refuge," Klein replied.

"Any weapons?" the guard asked, uninterested.

"None," Reaper answered.

The two guards simply looked Reaper and Klein up and down before motioning to the front gate, which had been left ajar.

"Go ahead—no funny business," the guard said dismissively.

"Wouldn't dream of it," Klein replied as they entered the outpost.

There were an abundance of lanterns lining the main street, most of which had burnt out by now. All the shops had long since closed for the night, including BAR which was known to occasionally remain open all night if the tips and gossip were enticing enough. Reaper and Klein sauntered down the road until they came to the entrance of the Courtview Hotel, uniquely named for its view of the architectural masterpiece that had once been a courthouse. They both went inside, and to the surprise of no one the lobby was empty. One lone candle continued to defiantly flicker on the front desk as it clung to life—its brethren had all burnt out long ago. Reaper carefully picked up the last remaining candle; neither of them had a lighter in the event that the little flame lost its will to live. He slowly moved across the lobby to a painting that had been hung above one of the maroon leather lounge chairs in the far corner.

It was a painting of a white and red lighthouse on an island of rocks. It was a stormy night, the waters dark and the waves white-capping. The little rock island that the lighthouse had been erected on looked at risk of being swallowed up by the frothing sea. The lighthouse shone its beacon defiantly into the stormy waters in an attempt to guide any ungodly soul brave enough or foolish enough to be out on the water amid such a ferocious storm. Reaper carefully removed the painting from the wall to reveal a reinforced steel safe. By the aid of candlelight, Reaper rotated the dial and popped the safe open. Inside rested a single key, a key that would unlock room 312. He retrieved the key and closed the safe as Klein re-hung the painting, which he had very little care for. Reaper, on the other hand, thoroughly enjoyed the painting. To him it was a symbol of strength and defying the odds. To Reaper, he was the captain of that ship braving the untamable sea—the ship that hadn't been painted yet, but the one that the lighthouse surely must have been guiding.

Reaper and Klein ascended the metal stairs, Reaper taking the candle with them. They made their way up to the third floor and down the hall to room 312, the secret room designated for PAR operatives. Reaper unlocked the door with the rusty gold key and entered first. The room was pitch black, but both men knew what was inside. Weapons, communication devices, food, water, and an assortment of PAR exclusive gadgetry. The two men stood in the doorway in silence as the candle in Reaper's hand continued to weakly flicker, doing very little to brighten up the room.

"We should catch a few hours of shut-eye before we start the day," Reaper said, as he could already see the beginning of what would surely be a beautiful sunrise. The permanent covering of radiation-filled clouds always made sure that the sunsets and sunrises were particularly memorable.

"I say we start at Big Mike's bar later today," Reaper continued. "I've heard that he knows everything about everyone around here."

"Hopefully not quite everything," Klein replied as he moved into the dark room and claimed the single-sized bed by the window.

Reaper eased himself into his bed near the door and every bone in his body seemed to ache all of a sudden. He lay there with his eyes open, thinking about their mission and its implications yet again. These photos—how bad could they possibly be? What exactly were they of? Who were they of? Who took them and why? His mind was filled with questions, but now it was time to rest. Reaper slowly closed his eyes, allowing his mind to wander freely. As he came closer to slipping into unconsciousness, his mind drifted back to the painting that hung over the maroon-coloured lounge chair in the lobby downstairs. He could see himself now, standing on the ship that hadn't been painted into the scene. The turbulent sea reflected purple lightning that danced across the black sky and it was as if he was sailing on an ocean of electricity. His ship rocked violently, coming dangerously close to capsizing. Andrew Rodriguez held steady as he blindly followed the beacon from the lighthouse.

He looked up to see that the sails of his ship were as black as the endless void of space. Suddenly a monstrous wave struck the side of his ship with ferocity, sending Rodriguez plunging into the black and purple waters. It was now completely dark, with the exception of the light from the lighthouse. Rodriguez started to swim towards the light, but the belligerent waves repeatedly forced him back underneath the surface. He was becoming tired of fighting the turbulent waters. So tired. His body began to fail, the little rock island seemed impossibly far, and his ship was no longer in sight. Rodriguez began to sink into the depths of the cold lonely waters as the ocean consumed his body and sleep engulfed Reaper's conflicted mind.

Chapter 9

Bottoms Up

Commander Ventress's trip to Outpost Zulu was uneventful and remarkably quick in comparison to Reaper and Klein's treacherous adventure. Immediately after the two undercover men had disembarked from the aircraft, the CS50 had ascended and resumed its trajectory towards the outpost. There was tension swirling around the interior of the flying mechanical wonder. Alpha Squad had never been particularly fond of the Commander. They saw her as unrealistic with her expectations and, quite frankly, a real pain in their side. She would constantly send them on mission after mission with little to no reprieve. Despite their lack of fondness towards her, they respected her authority. Although these soldiers that radiated bravado would never admit it, their respect stemmed from a place of fear. To Ventress, fear was the greatest motivator of all.

Not a word had been said between Ventress and Alpha Squad for the entirety of the flight. Alpha Squad was the best in the business. They had a mission to accomplish and that's what they would do; there was no need for small talk or pleasantries. They kept their heads down and focused on the task at hand: keeping the Commander alive and well while inside Outpost Zulu. Ventress was lost in her own thoughts during the brief duration of airtime. Her piercing green eyes gazed absently ahead like a beautiful curtain that concealed a hideous monster hiding just on the other side. She too thought about the mission at hand and what needed to be done. It was a delicate matter. Captain Andor had informed her of the breach, but no one quite knew what the pictures entailed. If they had somehow come from the R&D facility as she had been informed, it wasn't going to be anything pleasant and PAR's positive reputation could be dismantled entirely.

Ventress believed in the work that she had authorized at the R&D facility. To her, nothing worth achieving came without sacrifice and suffering. Although in this case she was the one reaping the rewards while others provided the sacrifices for her. Ventress's fixation with cybernetically enhanced soldiers went hand in hand with her passion for power. Her predecessors, the ones who were either replaced or had succumbed to untimely demises, pushed narratives that Ventress had no interest in. They believed that PAR could unite the remaining survivors under one banner and provide them with all the post-war necessities that they could ever possibly need. The foremost necessity being hope, an idea or belief that could bring people together. Foolery, Ventress had thought. Humanity had shown its true colours time and time again until it culminated in nuclear Armageddon. Ventress knew that peace could only be achieved through order, order that was maintained through power and fear.

If you give a man an inch, he'll take a mile. Ventress would give and take whatever the hell she wanted because she knew best. Her obsession with cybernetic enhancements for her soldiers was also linked to her philosophy of peace through power, or as most would see it, peace through oppression. She believed that if she could assemble an army of super-soldiers then no one would dare to defy her. She could forge this dystopian wasteland into something great, into a world worth living in again. She didn't exactly have any major threats either, so she emphasized quality over quantity. There had been rumours prior to the bombs that a small private sector in the far east of Russia had been working on their own post-apocalyptic army, but Russia now just seemed like a distant memory as they were decimated by the powerful nuclear arsenal that had been launched from the West.

The Research and Design facility was never intended to house cybernetic experimentation. It was originally meant to act as a lab for scientists to conduct horticultural experiments and radiation therapies. Those works of science had been remarkably successful. PAR now had a sustainable garden to produce fruits and vegetables, as well as effective anti-radiation pills that kept folks looking relatively healthy. All this was great, but Ventress had always had a militaristic mind. Even as a young girl she'd rather shoot a rifle and smell gunpowder instead of sniff roses or perfumes. To her, what she was doing was what should have been done prior to the war. If someone strong, someone like Ventress, had had control over the planet then this entire nightmare could have been avoided. Of course, now she had only a wasteland of pain and suffering to punch her stake into, but pain and suffering suited her just fine.

The aircraft had slowed to a stop, still a hundred feet or so up in the air. The pilots had the special privilege of seeing the moon and the stars above the cloud covering that never seemed to break apart. The stars sparkled across the lonely night sky like little dazzling beacons of hope. The full moon, peaceful and bright, illuminated the cockpit with a yellowish light. These two nameless pilots were perhaps the only people left on Earth who were able to take in the otherworldly beauty of outer space. The CS50 had begun its descent, breaking into the cloud coverage and plunging back into the world of darkness, sickness, and death. The change in trajectory snapped Ventress out of her own little world that only existed inside of her head. There was a slight jolt as the aircraft touched down in the field behind the old courthouse. The field, filled with various walking paths, used to be home to a beautiful array of wildflowers. Now it simply served as an impromptu landing pad for PAR.

The large back door slowly began to lower and Alpha Squad swiftly moved down the ramp with their guns at the ready. Commander Ventress walked purposefully down the ramp behind them, her dark trench coat billowing in the chilling evening wind. Alpha Squad escorted her over to the courthouse and were met by two local security guards waiting by the back door. The courthouse had been rigged with a tremendous number of generators and had an adequate supply of power to keep the lights on as a result. The building had been repurposed to house important members of PAR for when special occasions called for it. As of late, there had been very little reason for anyone of substantial worth to visit Outpost Zulu. Until now.

Ventress had been promptly escorted to her exclusive suite, which in reality was a well-preserved judge's chambers. Rex and Beetle stood guard outside of her door for half of the night, switching once with Wolf and Ghost. Ventress had no issue falling asleep on the leather couch that was situated in the middle of her chambers. It was just as comfy as any bed, and her room had already been warmed up with space heaters prior to her arrival. Her conscience was clear and sleep could not elude her.

***

Commander Ventress was currently looking out of the large window that overlooked the long-forgotten flower field with her hands loosely clasped behind her back. The sun was ascending towards the clouds, painting the sky various shades of purple and pink. There was frost on the lawn by the CS50; winter would arrive in the coming weeks and claim many lives. There was a quick knock on the chamber door, a knock that she had been expecting.

"Come in," she said quickly as she took a seat behind the late judge's desk. She had replaced the judge's plaque with a plaque of her own, a black one that read 'Co. VENTRESS' in gold. The large mahogany door slowly opened to reveal a tall slender man with military pants and an unmarked black hoodie. He had short well-kept hair and the slight emergence of a five o'clock shadow. He strutted confidently over to Commander Ventress's desk and took a seat. The chair that he sat on was a small, cushioned chair with metal armrests, whereas Ventress was seated on one of those high-backed La-Z-Boy-style chairs.

The man who sat in front of Commander Ventress was the head of security at Outpost Zulu, Captain Andor. Andor's security force was less than desirable, but Captain Andor himself had proven time and time again that he was loyal to PAR, that he was loyal to Ventress. In fact, he was the one that Ventress had put in charge of identifying potential R&D candidates and making them disappear. Once Captain Andor identified someone who seemed to be travelling alone, he'd entice them with scavenger missions that paid handsomely. He would send them to predetermined locations that he knew to be safe and would begin building a rapport. After a few successful scavenger runs, he would inform Ventress of their target and she would set up the location for the grand disappearing act. Captain Andor would then send his loner unknowingly to a location where Ventress would have her R&D operatives waiting to kidnap the unsuspecting soul and transport them back to the facility to undergo cybernetic experimentation. The entire operation had been running smoothly for almost a year until the photo leaks had surfaced.

"Looking as lovely as ever, Commander," Captain Andor said with sleazy schoolboy charm.

"Cut the small talk, Andor, you know why you're here," Ventress replied sharply.

"Yeah, I do," Andor said, pushing his personal feelings aside.

"And? Do you have any idea how these photos came into circulation, or more importantly, who took them?" Ventress asked as she unintentionally clicked a blue pen that her fingers happened to find on the corner of the desk.

Andor shook his head silently.

"Damn it, Andor, what the hell do you even do around here? Drink, drink, drink and smoke, smoke, smoke! Your security force is a joke and I'm starting to wonder if we should make you disappear next," Ventress derided the captain.

Ventress slammed the little blue pen down on the desk, taking a deep breath and running her hands through her long black hair. Captain Andor sat there with a solemn expression on his face as if he was being reprimanded by an abusive schoolteacher.

"I don't know who leaked the photos, but I have my suspicions as to where they might be now," Andor said quietly. Ventress only glared at him, prompting him to elaborate.

"There's been some shady comings and goings at the Courtview Hotel. Large groups of people will slip inside late at night, only to emerge an hour later. People who I've never seen associating with each other during the day."

"Strange indeed, but how does this relate to the pictures?" Ventress asked, not disregarding the possibility that these large gatherings were simply desperate wastelanders seeking to fulfil primitive urges together.

"There's been" — Andor paused briefly to gather his thoughts — "a lot of animosity directed at PAR from the locals and it's becoming more noticeable now. Even newcomers will cast us the evil eye. If the pictures are even still here, which I think they are, I'm sure they're inside the hotel. They've got to be. The large comings and goings late at night just don't add up, plus the entire outpost is on edge now."

"And tell me, Captain Andor, why haven't you acted on this? If you're so sure that the photographs, the source of this entire headache, are inside the hotel, why haven't you done something about it?" Ventress demanded to know in an accusing tone.

"I can't! I can't even rely on half my men to watch the front gate! They just wear the uniform for protection and they don't care about the photo leaks. I don't know who I can trust. Some of my guards share the same animosity that the locals have towards PAR," Captain Andor rambled.

"Keep your damn house in check, Andor. Perhaps your security farce needs more discipline," Ventress hissed.

"It's not my fault you send me the absolute bottom of the barrel! You expect too much! I can't make lemonade out of lemons if you're sending me oranges—it just won't work," Andor protested in defence.

Andor had a point. Ventress kept all of her more qualified soldiers away from Outpost Zulu and used them for more important matters. She didn't think that it was a hard job for guards armed with assault rifles to protect a single entrance from mutants and bandits, even if they weren't well trained. All that the guards really had to do was screen newcomers for weapons and try to create a positive name for PAR. It was well known among the other members of PAR that the troops stationed at Outpost Zulu were the lowest on the hierarchical scale. Those who remained at the outpost for an extended period of time while remaining loyal to PAR would eventually work their way up the ranks and escape the outpost.

"Focus on your subordinates. Security needs to be tightened. They answer to you and you answer to me. If you suspect that any of your guards are at risk of betraying us, I'll see to it that they are…replaced," Ventress said as she subconsciously started spinning the blue pen that was on her desk.

"What—now? Like, what about the photos?" Andor asked curiously.

"Leave that to me. I have operatives looking into that as we speak. Inform the locals that there will be a speech tomorrow at noon and all are to attend at the front of the courthouse. I am going to put this matter to bed," Ventress said dismissively.

Captain Andor nodded and left the room. Ventress remained at her desk for several minutes and continued to spin the little blue pen. She was not pleased, not pleased at all. She had come here to deal with the fallout from the pictures that were leaked, to smooth things over and salvage PAR's reputation. Now she was also concerned about the incompetent and potentially disloyal security force that was under Captain Andor's command. Stripping the current guards of their PAR affiliation and replacing them with better-trained soldiers seemed like a plausible solution for the future. She would have to deal with the lacklustre security situation later. For now she had a more pressing matter to attend to. Ventress abruptly shot to her feet and walked over to the little radio that had been set on a cleared-out bookshelf. She got on the radio and provided her undercover operatives with an update about the information that she had just received from Captain Andor regarding the potential whereabouts of the leaked photographs.

***

Joseph was awoken to a loud knock on his door. He forced his eyelids open and groggily looked around the room. It never seemed to matter how much or how little he slept these days, he always felt tired. A familiar bout of nausea forced him to squeeze his eyes closed again and take a deep breath. The knocking persisted, prompting Joseph to compose himself and finally get up.

"Joseph, it's Greg! You awake?" Greg shouted from the other side of the door.

"Yeah," Joseph croaked. "Be right there."

Joseph slowly sat up and swung his feet over the side of the bed and into his crusty boots. He brushed his long hair out of his eyes and yawned before shuffling over to the door. He opened it to reveal the big behemoth of a man Greg and the petite by any comparison Hillary.

"Boy, you look rough!' Hillary exclaimed chipperly.

"Thanks," Joseph replied sarcastically.

The two entered Joseph's room, Hillary moving towards Joseph's window, which had a great view of the old courthouse. A view that Joseph had not been aware of last night in his drowsy and distracted state of mind.

"Did you see the courthouse last night? It was all lit up! Like, with real lights! Not these candles and stuff," Hillary asked as she curiously stared out the window towards the courthouse.

"No, I was a little preoccupied," Joseph said as he sat back down on the edge of his bed. His nausea was persistent but manageable. It was just enough to make everything slightly unpleasant, but not enough to make Joseph mentally map out the quickest way to the bathroom.

"It was actually quite the sight," Greg remarked.

Greg was leaning on the old dresser at the foot of Joseph's bed, the one where a TV should have been. With Hillary looking eagerly out of the window, Joseph sitting on the edge of his bed, and Greg leaning on the dresser nonchalantly, it almost looked like a scene out of a family vacation. Joseph smiled at the thought, before another wave of nausea took the wind out of his sails.

"You do kind of look like crap," Greg jeered.

"Yeah, I feel like it too. Slept good though, as well as I have in recent memory. I bumped into a neighbour across the hall last night. Boy, was he interesting," Joseph said as he leaned back on the bed with his hands behind his head. This position helped with his nausea a bit and he felt relatively good now.

"Interesting how?" Hillary asked, finally turning away from the window.

"Well..." Joseph began to say as he filled his friends in on the encounter that he had with Aaron.

He told them everything he could remember. The disappearances around the outpost, the grotesque pictures that haunted his dreams last night, the Commander's alleged plan to create super-soldiers that were human-machine hybrids, and Aaron's request for him to return tonight so that he could fill him in on what his plans were, moving forwards. When Joseph was done telling his companions about his late-night encounter the room fell silent for several moments and Joseph could hardly believe his own outlandish tale. It was a lot of information to take in, information that if true could ruin the picturesque appeal of Outpost Zulu and PAR.

"I don't know if I buy it—it seems far-fetched. Super-soldiers merged with mechanical parts? Give me a break," Greg said sceptically.

"Yeah, and this place seems nice, like really nice," Hillary chimed in.

"I know, I know. I'm not sure if I believe it either, but the guy seemed genuine. I've dealt with a lot of liars before the war and this guy didn't strike me as one," Joseph said, slowly sitting back up.

"Maybe he believes what he's saying. It's not lying if you believe it's the truth, right?" Hillary asked with a smile.

Joseph couldn't help but think that perhaps Hillary could have made a good lawyer too. Maybe in another life.

"You're not wrong, kid. Those photos though, they got to me. I don't see how they could've been faked. Maybe Aaron didn't tell me the entire story, but those pictures certainly said a lot," Joseph said, getting goosebumps just thinking about it.

"Nothing a beer or three can't help you forget!" Greg said dismissively, not wanting to turn his back on the relative safe haven that they had finally found.

Joseph was not about to disregard any possibility about Outpost Zulu or PAR. The world was a dangerous wasteland now, filled with psychos and mutants. Overseer and his cannibalistic cult had only been a small glimpse of the horrors that were now a mundane part of everyday life. He didn't find the thought of a power-hungry dictator seeking to conquer what was left of the world with an army of cyborgs so hard to believe. Maybe he would have three years ago, but not any more. Still, having a few beers was an enticing idea. Joseph could use a good drink—they all could. Going to the bar would also give Joseph an excuse to pick Big Mike's brain, just as Aaron had suggested.

"Oh yeah, Big Mike. I wonder what he's all about," Joseph replied before looking over at Hillary. "But what about you? Aren't you a little young to be poisoning yourself?"

"Oh please, I'm almost seventeen! At least I *think* my birthday is coming up; it's hard to keep track of time lately. Besides, I used to go to all sorts of parties back in high school." Hillary's eyes glazed over for a moment as she remembered a life that used to be.

"Needless to say, I think we could all use a stress-free day," Greg said quietly as he shot Joseph a quick glare, clearly not thrilled about hearing Joseph's horror story.

Joseph nodded and the trio promptly left the room. Joseph wasn't entirely sure how many drinks they could afford, or even how much a drink would be, but he very much liked the thought of getting day-drunk. The group made their way down the stairs and through the lobby, happy to start the first full day of their twisted little family vacation at Outpost Zulu.

***

"Klein. Reaper. Do you copy?"

Reaper opened his bloodshot eyes at the sound of the sharp voice protruding from the radio that was set up across the room on the dresser. Klein was already on his feet and heading to respond. Reaper was not pleased to see that the sun had begun its inevitable ascent and was shining its invasive rays directly into his face. He rubbed his eyes and yawned. He had been asleep for less than an hour.

"This is Klein. Go ahead," Klein replied.

"I spoke with Captain Andor, head of security. His security force is pathetic to say the least, but he provided me with somewhat promising intel. He believes that the photos are somewhere inside the hotel, right where you two are. Stay vigilant. Supposedly there have been some unusual gatherings at night." Ventress spoke excessively loudly; the mouthpiece was far too close to her face.

"Copy that, Commander," Klein acknowledged.

"One more thing," she continued. "I'll be giving my speech tomorrow at noon. Ideally the two of you will have those pictures on my desk well before that time. Zulu is small—get it done."

"Of course, Commander," Klein replied as Ventress switched off her radio.

"That certainly accelerates our timeline," Klein said to Reaper.

"Yup," he replied, closing his eyes again.

"What're you doing? Are you sleeping?"

"Trying to."

"We have a job to do, or have you forgotten?" Klein said irritably.

"Relax, tough guy," Reaper said, opening his eyes once more. "We'll split up. I'll head to the bar and see if I can gather any intel from the locals, particularly that Big Mike fellow. You can stay here and keep an eye on the comings and goings."

"That's...a good idea actually," Klein admitted reluctantly.

"I know," Reaper replied as he closed his eyes yet again.

"Shouldn't we get to work?" Klein anxiously asked.

"It's the crack of dawn. The bar won't even be open and the ever-so-charming Commander Ventress said that the strange gatherings have been occurring at night anyways. Now let me sleep—I'll be sharper."

Reaper rolled over, putting an end to any further discussion. After a few moments of silent mental deliberation, Klein went back to his respective bed and opened the drawer of the nightstand. A book that no longer had a cover sat alone in the drawer. Klein picked it up and began to read.

***

It was almost midday by the time Joseph, Greg, and Hillary approached BAR. There was a damp autumn chill in the air that was strangely rejuvenating to Joseph. He had always been fond of cooler weather, although these days the cold was much less tolerable with an empty stomach and a lack of adequate shelter. It was abundantly clear that the outpost bar was indeed also a bar prior to the great war. The three-letter word 'BAR' was painted in red over the top of where the letters from the original establishment used to be. Whatever BAR had been named previously would remain a mystery, as the original lettering had long since faded as a result of neglect. Huge glass windows lined the side of the building looking out towards the main street which the trio was approaching from. Joseph couldn't get a good look inside — the daylight glare was reflecting off the glass and shining directly into his light-blue eyes.

Greg led the pack and pulled open the heavy iron door, which had a long vertical gold bar as a handle. He held the door open and Joseph entered first, followed by Hillary and then finally Greg. Joseph was shocked at how busy the bar was. In fact, it was a bustling hub of Outpost Zulu locals and looked to be just as busy as it had been the previous night when Joseph and his friends had first entered the outpost. It's the only safe place from PAR, Joseph thought as he remembered what Aaron had told him. The interior had been well maintained; the original tables and booths were still intact and in relatively good condition. The main bar itself was quiet, occupied only by two patrons at the far end who were engaged in a heated argument over two pints of beer.

There was a burly hulk of a man who dwarfed even Greg working the bar. He was drying glasses, very cliché, but an effective way to seem busy while eavesdropping on loose-lipped conversations. The colossal-sized man looked up at the newcomers approaching his bar and smiled, his immaculately white teeth contrasting with his dark complexion.

"Welcome, friends! What can I do you for?" he asked, smiling warmly the entire time.

"I'll take a whiskey on the rocks," Greg ordered promptly, no longer wanting a beer.

"Same thing, but not on the rocks. So, just a whiskey please," Joseph said, as he too wanted something a little stronger.

"And I'll have...a shot of tequila," Hillary ordered after a moment of consideration.

"Coming right up, folks!" the bartender exclaimed as he turned to prepare the drinks.

Joseph took a seat on the barstool closest to the entrance on the left, followed by Greg to his right and then Hillary. The black stools had begun to rip and the white padding beneath the fake black leather had been exposed. Despite their wear and tear, the seats were remarkably comfortable. Any time spent not walking or running was a blessing these days. The bartender turned back around and divvied up the beverages.

"How exactly do we pay for these? We don't have a whole lot," Joseph enquired as he eyed up the sacred liquid that sat inches away from his grasp.

"First one's free! I just like seeing some new faces around here. The name's Big Mike," the bartender replied cheerfully. Joseph thought that 'big' was an understatement to say the least. Perhaps 'humungous' or 'massive' would have been a more suitable name. Massive Mike. It had a nice ring to it.

"Thanks, Mike, we appreciate it!" Greg said, before enthusiastically taking a deep sip of his whiskey.

Joseph did the same—and Mike had poured generously. Even Hillary's tequila 'shot' had been poured into a glass; it was more like three shots. The golden liquid burned at first and then Joseph could feel the fluid travelling down to his empty belly and warming his innards. Joseph used to love drinking on the weekends, maybe even a little too much. Now drinks were a rarity; it was no wonder BAR was packed with people.

"So, what's everyone's story? You three sticking around for a while or just passing through?" Big Mike asked as he innocently dried glasses that had not been used in over an hour. The trio exchanged glances; it wasn't something they had discussed since arriving. It was Joseph who spoke up. His loquacious personality that had landed him a job in law complemented Big Mike's talkative persona.

"We're not entirely sure yet. I don't see a reason for us to leave any time soon though, not unless there's a hotel manager who kicks us out," he said jokingly as he tried to ignore his 'doom and gloom' thoughts regarding PAR. His companions nodded approvingly at his response.

"Stay a while! Not much outside of these walls other than freakazoids and guys with guns!" Big Mike exclaimed. "Besides, between us four, I don't think there's a manager on duty at the hotel weekdays or weekends."

Big Mike said that last part with a mischievous smirk and Joseph thought back to the sign on the front of the lobby desk instructing guests to return their keys after three nights.

"So, what's it like out there?" Mike asked. "Outside of the outpost?"

"Terrible." It was Hillary who spoke this time. "It seems like everything and everyone either wants to rob you or eat you."

She took a gulp of tequila, looking ten years older than she really was. Life had not been kind to her the last couple of years or even the years prior to the bombs.

"Yeah, I hear you. I've been here a year or so now. Not much reason to leave, but not everyone agrees." Big Mike set the glass down that he had been polishing, only to pick up another and continue the same pointless motion.

Joseph was building up his nerve to ask if Mike knew anything about Tom's supposed abduction as he thought back to his conversation the previous night with Aaron. He didn't feel that the time was right, so instead he kept things light.

"So what's your story, Mike? Like...before the bombs? What did you do?" Joseph asked, genuinely curious. It was always an interesting line of questioning these days. It was astounding what a local accountant was capable of doing just for a can of beans, or what the physically imposing construction worker was too squeamish to do. There seemed to be no correlation between those who could survive and those who perished.

"Well, believe it or not, I was a defensive lineman in the league," Big Mike said with great pride.

"Really? No kidding! I mean, you fit the profile and all, a big guy like you," Greg chimed in with excitement. He had been a big football fan growing up and played well in high school, but injuries had pushed him away from football in college.

"Yup! Was pretty good too. Was looking to make a real name for myself but...well...you know the story," Big Mike trailed off.

"Yeah," Greg said sombrely, taking another drink.

A man and a woman approached the bar, eager for a drink of their own. Big Mike walked over to serve them, leaving Joseph and his friends alone. It occurred to Joseph that he had not learned much about his own travelling companions yet. He had no idea who they were prior to the nuclear fallout. He knew who they were now though, and that's really all that mattered.

Two companions that he could trust to not stab him in the back over a bottle of water. But it was more than that. He had grown quite fond of the two. In a way, he could see them being close friends even if the circumstances weren't so dire. Joseph had liked William too; he had seemed like a kind-hearted man. Unfortunately, this unkind world had a tendency to eliminate those who had kind hearts. There were always exceptions, however. Like Greg and Hillary. Two kind souls that Joseph was grateful to have met.

"What did you do, Greg? Before all this?" Joseph finally asked. The question came as just as much a shock to Joseph as it did to Greg.

"Oh. I was a mechanic. Fixed all sorts of cars—been doing that all my life," Greg said as he reminisced. If only he could have fixed his marriage the same way that he could fix an engine. Joseph was about to ask Hillary the same question when Greg continued.

"And I was a father. My wife left me and took the kid; they moved down south. I still like to believe that they survived all this and that they're doing okay." Greg cleared the lump in his throat and polished off his drink as Hillary gave him a sympathetic pat on the back.

"Hey, if we've made it this far, why not them too?" Joseph said, trying to be optimistic. It was a miracle anyone was alive at all, including them. Sometimes he thought that those who had perished in the blast were the lucky ones.

"Yeah, why not?" Greg said, forcing a smile.

"What about you, young lady?" Joseph asked Hillary.

"Oh you know, just your typical high-school girl. I was planning to go to college to become a nurse, but oh well! Guess that ship has sailed." She seemed to have much less remorse than Greg, which relieved Joseph.

"I didn't really have much of a family and my dad left before I knew him. Mom was never around either. I didn't really lose anyone close. Lucky me, right?" she said with a sarcastic eye-roll.

Joseph wasn't sure what was worse, losing your loved ones or having no one to lose.

"What about you, Joseph? You mentioned something about...oh how did you put it...'law school charm'?" Hillary was quoting him from the dreadful night that they spent with Overseer.

"Yeah, I was a lawyer. I was still fairly new at it, but I was doing well and my career was going in the right direction." Joseph omitted his personal losses, like how he teared up almost every day thinking about his mother, who undoubtedly had passed away, and his small handful of close friends whom he would never see again. Fortunately, although he didn't think that it was fortunate at the time, Joseph did not have a partner to lose, or any kids for that matter.

"Well, look at us," Greg said, his normal demeanour returning. "The lawyer, the mechanic, and the aspiring nurse. What a trio!"

"What a trio!" Joseph and Hillary shouted in unison as the group of friends threw back their drinks.

"Mike! Big Mike! Another round, good sir!" Greg hollered across the bar.

"I might need to charge you this time," he said with a wink as he walked back over.

Greg reached into his backpack and produced three cigarettes. The carton was running dangerously low now, with 11 smokes remaining.

"I don't smoke, but the fella over at SHOP will appreciate the inventory and give a good trade!" Mike accepted the trade and filled their glasses to the brim.

"Good thing the hotel is just across the street," Joseph said with a laugh.

"Hey, cheers, guys," Greg said.

"Cheers to what?" Joseph asked. There was an awkward pause.

"To William," Hillary said with conviction.

"To William," Joseph and Greg repeated with a sombre nod.

The trio clinked their glasses together and took a drink. Drinking on an empty stomach was hitting the group particularly hard, so it was Greg's brilliant idea to open up one of their cans of tuna. The three companions received a variety of stares, some out of envy for food and others stemming from the perplexing combination of tuna and hard liquor. Joseph didn't care. In fact, nothing in the world could bother him right now and he had entirely forgotten about Aaron's ominous warning. This was the most fun he'd had since the world had been turned upside down. Everything he cared about that still existed was in this bar right here, right now. His two companions had become more than just people to travel with or friends—they had become family. Joseph was in a bar with his two favourite living people, a generous bartender, and a can of deliciously salty tuna that would inevitably come back to haunt him when the alcohol wore off. What more could a man want in a post-apocalyptic wasteland?

Chapter 10

Lab Coats and Lies

Joseph, Greg, and Hillary were finishing off the remainder of their drinks. It was late in the afternoon now and daylight was receding quickly. The days were becoming shorter as the season began its gradual transition from autumn to winter. Snow would arrive in the not-so-distant future, canvassing the wasteland in colourless shades of white and grey. The trio of companions were engaged in a drunken conversation filled with smiles and laughs. It wasn't a surprise that no one noticed the rough-looking man with a bushy beard wearing a baseball cap entering the bar. The man took a seat at the far end of the bar and discreetly waved down Big Mike, who proceeded to pour him a glass of bourbon in exchange for a pre-cooked package of rice. That package of rice would likely cover as many drinks as the man desired, but he wasn't here for the drinks.

Joseph threw back the last splash of his whiskey and slammed the glass down with more force than he had intended. The room was starting to spin and his stomach was churning.

"Hey Big Mike! What's the deal with that old courthouse? The one that was all lit up like a Christmas tree last night?" Hillary asked the burly bartender, who had just finished pouring the glass of bourbon for the man in the baseball cap.

"It's where the high-ranking members of PAR stay when they visit," Big Mike explained. "Although these days it's usually just used for the doctors that are stationed here."

"Oh, that's kind of lame!" Hillary remarked as if she was expecting a much more magical answer.

"Kind of. But you know what? There's a really big aircraft that landed there last night. I ain't ever seen one quite like it! It's still there too, parked out back," Big Mike said.

"Let's check it out!" Hillary exclaimed excitedly.

All Joseph wanted to do was go lie down for a bit. He had decided that he would follow up on Aaron's invitation; curiosity was eating him alive. No matter how hard he tried, he just couldn't quite ignore the uneasy feeling that he had in his gut, not the nausea but the feeling of dread. Like something wasn't quite right here.

"I don't know—I'm ready to call it a day. I wouldn't mind sobering up a bit before tonight." Joseph slurred slightly as he spoke.

"Oh come on, you're not seriously going to talk to that basket case again, are you?" Greg asked as he sarcastically rolled his eyes.

"Yeah! Curiosity killed the cat, you know!" Hillary chimed in.

"I know, I know. But satisfaction brought him back!" Joseph protested with a smirk.

"Alright, well I'll go with Hillary to sightsee the aircraft. We'll catch up with you tonight—we won't let someone steal your kidneys in a hotel bathtub." Greg laughed.

Everyone was in a good mood, courtesy of their delightful alcoholic refreshments. It had been a long time since anyone in the group had drunk alcohol and the effects made the trio feel invincible.

"Sounds good. Be careful out there," Joseph said.

Greg and Hillary hopped off their stools, and Greg briefly braced himself on the counter before trusting his legs to do their job. The two stumbled out the door and headed in the direction of the old courthouse. Joseph peered into his empty glass and licked his dry lips.

"Hey Mike, any chance you could spare a bit of water?" Joseph asked sheepishly.

"Y'know, water is more valuable than booze these days"—Mike reached under the counter and retrieved a half-empty bottle of water—"but you three have been a real pleasure to hang with."

Mike poured what was left of the water into Joseph's glass; the residual whiskey that was hiding in the crevices tinted the water a slight brown. Joseph greedily drank the refreshing liquid, finishing it all in a matter of seconds.

"Hey Mike, did you ever serve a guy named Tom?" The question just fell out of Joseph's mouth. He had been waiting for the right moment to ask and now seemed as good as any.

Mike put both of his meaty paws on the edge of the counter and leaned forwards.

"What do you know about Tom?" Big Mike's cheerful demeanour had shifted into an aura of seriousness. Joseph felt like he was a sailor at sea who had found himself in unexplainably turbulent waters.

"I heard he was a local here who just vanished one day," Joseph replied quickly, as he recalled Aaron labelling Tom as a drunkard.

"Yeah, that's true. He was a good kid too. Why're you asking?" Mike continued to lean forwards, his dark-brown eyes locking with Joseph's light-blue eyes. The man in the baseball cap listened while sipping bourbon. Joseph might have thought that he was talking quietly, but his previous alcohol consumption ensured otherwise.

"I met a guy last night staying across from me at the hotel. He said he was good friends with him and he showed me..." Joseph trailed off, not wanting to sound like a lunatic.

"Showed you what?" Mike probed. Now it was Joseph's turn to lean in.

"He showed me these pictures...some were supposedly of Tom. Pictures of experiments and such. Of PAR. He said that they've been snatching up loners and drunkards. Making them disappear," Joseph whispered.

Big Mike looked to his left and to his right, making sure that no one was listening. The bearded man at the far end of the bar was throwing back the rest of his bourbon. Big Mike knew everything about everyone around the outpost. He had seen the pictures that Aaron had, the pictures of Tom in distress. Most of the outpost had seen them by now, for that matter. The outpost was torn between those who believed the validity of the photos and those who were wilfully blind. Mike couldn't deny that the photos were of Tom and he had known the young man quite well. As a regular, Tom had a face that Big Mike had seen almost every day for a month before his abrupt disappearance.

"What else did Aaron tell you?" Mike quietly asked. Joseph was taken aback for a moment, hearing Mike name-drop Aaron, and he hesitated before replying.

"He told me that the Commander of PAR was trying to merge human and machine together. I know it sounds crazy, but the pictures really disturbed me and I don't think that they were fake. He wants me to meet up with him again tonight." Joseph paused for a moment before asking, "Do you know Aaron?"

Mike stopped leaning on the counter and reached for the bourbon so that he could top off the man at the end of the bar who had waved him down again.

"I know everyone! He's a real stand-up guy and it's in your best interest to listen to whatever he tells you," Big Mike answered with a broad smile as his cheerful demeanour returned. He lumbered over to refill the ragged man's glass and by the time he turned back around, Joseph was already gone.

***

Reaper watched Joseph through the bar window as he sipped on his second glass of bourbon. He did not recognize Joseph to be one of the people that his unit had rescued from a pack of ravenous mutants on the quaint little farm two nights ago.

Reaper had been too focused on listening to the conversation that he was trying to eavesdrop on without looking suspicious, and Joseph's unruly appearance did little to make him stand out from the crowd. It had been difficult to catch what he had been saying over the steady hum of patrons, but Reaper had heard enough. He could now see Joseph stumble into the Courtview Hotel and he couldn't resist the smile that crept across his face. All the pieces of the puzzle were coming together.

***

Dr Tellick was a nervous man. The kind of man who never used to drive above the speed limit and was promptly in bed by nine o'clock. He had never seen a scary movie and he had an irrational fear of the dark, a fear that had proven problematic in this new world that was constantly shrouded in darkness. Confrontation was something that he absolutely detested, which is why he was currently nervously chewing on the inside of his cheek as two PAR operatives, also known as Wolf and Ghost from Alpha Squad, escorted him to Commander Ventress's chambers. Despite his timidness, Dr Tellick was remarkably bright. He had a PhD in family medicine and he was well on his way to a second PhD in engineering before the nuclear Armageddon disrupted his plans. He knew precisely why he had been summoned. Wolf and Ghost opened the doors to the chambers and motioned for Dr Tellick to enter, which he did. The doors closed behind him and he could see that Commander Ventress was sifting through a file on her desk, presumably his file.

"Ah, Doctor Tellick. Come in, take a seat," she said without looking up.

He obliged without saying a word. He twiddled his thumbs as he watched Ventress's keen green eyes devour the information within his file. He doubted that there could really be any information of substantial intrigue. Perhaps his medical certificate, pre-war accomplishments, and his ongoing tech developments at the R&D facility. Dr Tellick had been the lead brain on designing the cybernetics. He had been under the impression that this state-of-the-art technology would be used to aid survivors who had suffered grievous injuries. That's what he had been told initially, but now things had gone too far. Ventress finally looked up from the file. There was a small ceramic teacup on the corner of her desk. She reached for it, took a sip, and then set it back down, all while studying Dr Tellick closely.

"Do you know why you're here?" she finally asked, clasping her hands together on top of the file.

"I have my suspicions," Dr Tellick carefully replied.

Ventress looked back down at the file once more, shuffling through a few papers.

"You've done great work for PAR, Tellick. For me." She examined a black and white sketch that Dr Tellick had drawn for his original prototype of a left arm. "Which is why I am so... disappointed."

The doctors that were stationed at Outpost Zulu followed a strict rotational schedule. Dr Tellick would spend one week per month at Outpost Zulu tending to the medical needs of the residents. There was a reasonably large medical tent down the street from the courthouse that locals in search of medical aid would come to. It wasn't as busy as one might think and it gave Dr Tellick a lot of free time during the day. Idle hands are the devil's playthings and he often found himself questioning whether or not his allegiance was misplaced.

"Loyalty is of utmost importance to me, Dr Tellick," Commander Ventress continued. "A knife in the back makes for a special kind of pain."

"I know where you're going with this, Ma'am, and I assure you that it wasn't me," Dr Tellick said as calmly as his nerves would allow him to. To his benefit, three other doctors rotated in and out of the outpost. Four doctors in total, one for each week of the month.

"I know it wasn't you," Ventress said with a charming smile. "You're much too spineless to put your own neck on the line."

Dr Tellick shifted in his chair uncomfortably before asking, "Then why am I here?"

"Because you know. You know who took those photos, don't you?"

Dr Tellick shook his head. "I don't. I'm sorry but I don't."

Ventress slowly reached into her black leather jacket and retrieved her golden .50 handgun, placing it on her desk. She then stood up and shrugged off her lengthy trench coat. This was one of the rare occasions when she did not have a bulletproof vest on. Instead, she wore a simple white woman's dress shirt with the sleeves rolled up. She clasped her hands behind her back and walked over to the window, turning her back on Dr Tellick and looking out towards her aircraft. Remnants of the breathtaking wildflower field that used to fill the yard behind the courthouse were visible, as a handful of flowers defied the laws of nature and continued to bloom.

"I have four doctors from Research and Design that come and go from this outpost. One of these doctors is the culprit. No one else has access to both the research facility and Outpost Zulu other than the four of you." She spoke with her back turned to Dr Tellick, who was now eyeing up the pistol sitting on the desk in front of him. "So if it wasn't you, which doctor was it, Tellick?"

"I told you, I don't know," he repeated.

Ventress turned back around and looked down at Dr Tellick, her hands still clasped behind her back.

"I may have underestimated you, Tellick. Perhaps you do have a backbone." She paused for a moment, took another sip of tea, and then continued. "I see the way that you doctors gravitate towards one another. How you all think that you are somehow superior. It's cultish."

She took one final sip of tea and then set the now empty cup back down on her desk. She placed both of her hands on the edge of her desk and looked Dr Tellick directly in the eye. The inherently nervous man proceeded to quickly break the uncomfortable eye contact.

"I hear the hushed whispers whenever I enter the lab. The change of mood. I know you know who did it, Tellick. Just tell me." Ventress spoke softly as if she were speaking to a child.

"All I know is that it wasn't me. I swear I don't know who took the photos." Dr Tellick was beginning to sound like a broken record and he could feel his pulse thumping in the side of his neck as his cheeks became flushed with colour.

Ventress let out a sigh and reached into her pocket, retrieving a small, serrated pocketknife.

"Ma'am, I don't know who did it!" Dr Tellick insisted, the fear in his voice clearly evident.

Ventress slowly moved around her desk like a lioness stalking her prey. Her intoxicating smile was genuine and sincere; she was going to enjoy what would come next. Without thinking, Dr Tellick grabbed the hefty handgun and sprung to his feet. For his entire life he had been pushed around and bullied into submission, even as a young boy in school. Something inside of him suddenly snapped; perhaps it was caused by the sheer terror that he felt. He aimed the gun at Ventress's chest with his trembling hands.

"Oh Dr Tellick," Ventress said amusedly, "you'd better not miss."

She continued to slowly advance towards her prey. Dr Tellick closed his eyes and squeezed the trigger. Click. He opened his bewildered eyes and pulled the trigger again. Click. Ventress was now a foot away, the barrel of the .50 pressed against her sternum. She gently took the gun away from Dr Tellick and his entire body shook with fear. With tremendous speed and aggression, Ventress struck the doctor in the face with the unloaded pistol, which sent him crashing to the ground. He cried out, holding his now broken nose that was gushing a vibrant red stream of blood onto his once pristine white lab coat. He attempted to scramble to his feet but caught a heavy boot to his side, sending him sprawling onto his stomach. Ventress put her knee behind Dr Tellick's neck, effectively pinning him to the ground.

"Now, doctor, you will tell me which one of your friends is responsible for this thorn in my side. Otherwise, you will leave this room in a body bag," Ventress snarled. Before Dr Tellick could even respond, Ventress plunged the short blade of the pocketknife into his back just below his left shoulder blade. Dr Tellick yelped in pain.

"Okay, okay, okay! It was Moetsky! He told me in confidence over a couple of drinks a while back. He threatened to make me sick like he did to Dr Spazzi if I told anyone!" Dr Tellick was a blubbering mess and tendrils of pain radiated outwards from the blade, shooting across his entire back.

Dr Moetsky specialized in radiation therapy and he was a part of the rotational team of doctors assigned to Outpost Zulu. He primarily worked on developing medicine to reverse the effects of radiation exposure and he was the head of pharmacology at PAR. Some had speculated that the untimely death of his predecessor, Dr Spazzi, the former head of PAR pharmacology, was linked to foul play. Dr Moetsky was a real no-nonsense kind of guy; he always kept his head down and worked hard. He did not strike Ventress as someone who would suddenly develop a pesky moral compass and he was the last doctor that she would have suspected. Still, she believed Dr Tellick nonetheless—he was a spineless worm and a terrible liar. She believed that his words were truthful, even if it had taken some coercion to get to the bottom of things.

"There. That wasn't so hard, was it?" Ventress asked softly as she got off Dr Tellick, leaving the pocketknife embedded in his back. Dr Tellick slowly brought himself to his feet; his left arm hung limply at his side.

"Guards!" Commander Ventress shouted with authority.

Wolf and Ghost promptly entered the room with their weapons at the ready.

"Take the good doctor downstairs. He will be coming back with us tomorrow, but for now lock him up in one of the old holding cells," Ventress commanded.

"Yes, Ma'am," Wolf replied promptly.

"Wait, Ventress, wait! I told you everything I know!" Dr Tellick pleaded as the PAR operatives pushed him towards the doors.

"Thank you for your honesty and your attempt on my life, doctor. You will be rewarded accordingly," Ventress said dismissively as the guards ushered Dr Tellick out of the room.

Ventress looked down at the bloodstained carpet and scowled. The carpet had been a beautiful mixture of light blues, greens, and reds. Naturally, Dr Tellick's blood had stained some of the patches of blue and green, missing the red accents entirely. Dr Moetsky had done fantastic work for PAR. In fact, he was the reason that Ventress was able to stay so healthy and fit, along with the other high-ranking members. She rubbed the back of her neck as she contemplated what Dr Moetsky had to gain from his betrayal. Morality seemed to be too flimsy of an excuse; at least that's what Ventress thought. She would deal with his treachery when she returned from Outpost Zulu; for now, she had a speech to prepare. She walked back over to her desk and refilled her small teacup from a kettle that was resting on a portable gas camping stove behind her desk. She then retrieved a pad of paper and a blue pen from one of the desk drawers and began to write.

***

Joseph was shuffling across the road towards the Courtview Hotel when a loud voice amplified by a megaphone rang out through the streets.

"A MANDATORY MEETING WILL TAKE PLACE TOMORROW AT NOON IN FRONT OF THE COURTHOUSE! ALL RESIDENTS MUST ATTEND! NO EXCEPTIONS!"

Joseph looked to his left and spotted a tall man with a megaphone accompanied by a small group of PAR guards. He repeated his message again and continued strutting down the main street towards Joseph. Joseph's head hurt and the obnoxiously loud man armed with a megaphone wasn't helping. He pushed open the heavy oak doors and entered the lobby; the doors closed behind him and muffled the irksome voice that was booming out of the megaphone. The lobby was dim; it was still too early for the candles to be lit, but the natural light from outside was beginning to fade quickly. It had been a particularly gloomy day to begin with and Joseph was actually surprised that it hadn't rained.

He began his slow ascent up the stairwell to the third floor and then down the hallway to room 314. After missing the key slot several times, Joseph finally managed to get his door unlocked. He clumsily kicked off his battered boots and collapsed onto his mattress. He lay there for a while, looking up at the ceiling and watching the room spin as if he had just gotten off an unusually fast carousel. He began to think about Tom and how Big Mike had confirmed that there was indeed a man named Tom who had vanished without a trace. Well, not really without a trace, not with those photos stashed across the hall. Joseph wanted to know what Aaron was planning to do next, and Big Mike certainly had done nothing to alleviate his curiosity.

The photos and Big Mike's affirmation of facts kept leading Joseph's thoughts down a dark path. He wanted desperately to refute Aaron's claims and to forget about the pictures. He liked it here; so did Greg and Hillary. If PAR really was responsible for the photographs and the disappearances, was there anything they could even do about it? It was a cruel world that Joseph lived in now and the rules had been rewritten. Still, Joseph was adamant on talking to Aaron tonight. He had always believed that knowledge was power, but right now sleep would give him all the power that he could possibly want. Joseph closed his eyes and spiralled into unconsciousness.

***

Reaper left the bar not long after Joseph. He had just finished off his second glass of bourbon when a rowdy group of guards came barging into the bar demanding shots of tequila. Much to Reaper's displeasure, the group seemed to have already been drinking while at their posts. Their undeniable lack of discipline disgusted Reaper. To him, self-control was the highest form of power. A man who could control his needs and desires in order to accomplish a seemingly impossible task was a man not to be trifled with. These guards were a disgrace, unable to even stay sober for their watch duties. Reaper was aware of the irony as he sat there two bourbons deep while technically on duty. He was undercover though; it was different. He began heading towards the doors as the three drunken guards were hooting and hollering. One of the oblivious guards took a careless step backwards and collided with Reaper.

"Hey, watch it, bozo!" the guard shouted. The guard was a young man who did not yet have a need to shave. His companions, one female and one male, looked to be around the same age. Young punks.

"You bumped into me, kid," Reaper snarled as he continued on his way out.

"Who you calling 'kid'?" the young man said, placing a hand on Reaper's shoulder and turning him around.

Reaper didn't think—he just reacted, winding back and punching the guard in the mouth. It sent him stumbling into his companions, who in turn drew their holstered pistols. Several patrons sitting at various booths and tables rose to their feet; two of them also drew pistols out from their waistbands.

"Hey, hey, hey!" Big Mike boomed as he came around the bar. "Take it outside!"

"Those damn guards are always looking for trouble! They think they're untouchable!" one of the patrons with a pistol shouted.

"Shut up, scum! You're not supposed to have a gun!" the female guard shouted back as she aimed at the armed man.

"Oh boo hoo! And you're not supposed to drink on duty, coward!" the man rebutted.

Reaper stood in the middle of the verbal crossfire, dumbfounded at what was transpiring.

"Yeah, you guys are a joke! Acting like guardians of the peace with your matching little uniforms. We know what you're really up to!" another patron shouted, this one also on his feet but without a weapon.

"Oh yeah? What's that?" the guard that Reaper had punched asked, while wiping blood away from the corner of his mouth.

"I said, that's enough!" Big Mike boomed. "You three are cut off!"

"What? You can't do that! We'll have you arrested!" the second male guard shouted at Big Mike.

"Oh yeah, tough guy? I'd like to see you try," Big Mike snarled as he towered over the guard, a full foot taller and at least a hundred pounds heavier. There were murmurs of agreement backing Big Mike up. The three guards, who were rapidly sobering up now, decided to cut their losses and leave without further confrontation. Reaper locked eyes with the young man that he had struck in the face as the man walked past him and out the door.

"Free drinks on the house!" Big Mike shouted and the bar erupted in applause.

"Sorry about those guys," Big Mike apologized as he turned to face Reaper. "Always looking to cause trouble. Thanks for what you did—it's about time we started standing up to them."

"Don't mention it. The kid needed a lesson in manners," Reaper said as he watched the group of guards from the window slink down the street like a bunch of dogs with their tails tucked. He turned for the door once more to leave, a task now proving to be remarkably difficult.

"Hey wait, I haven't seen you around here before. You new?" Mike asked.

"Yeah, just passing through," Reaper replied.

"Care for that free drink, stranger?" Mike offered.

"Maybe next time—I'm real tired. Thanks though." Reaper pushed open the heavy iron door and was free from the clutches of BAR at last.

Reaper followed the same path that Joseph had taken: across the street, through the dimly lit lobby, and up the noisy metal staircase to the third floor. Reaper entered his own respective room: 312. The heavy hotel door slammed shut behind him, as most hotel doors tend to do. He stood in the doorframe and observed the out-of-place scene taking place in front of him. Klein was propped up in his bed with the hood of his sweater up, eating beef jerky while watching something on a laptop that had been hooked up to a mobile charger courtesy of PAR. Klein disturbingly reminded Reaper of a teenage girl watching Netflix and snacking away after a messy high-school break-up.

"Working hard or hardly working?" Reaper scoffed as he entered the room.

"Says the man who got to hang out at a bar all day," Klein replied without looking up from his screen.

"Yeah, it was great," Reaper said without any enthusiasm.

Reaper came over to the side of Klein's bed to see what he was watching. There were four separate screens on Klein's laptop, three for each hotel floor and one for the lobby. Klein was watching a security feed.

"Is this live?" Reaper asked.

"Yes. While you were out drinking, I set up a handful of wireless security cameras that remotely connect to this laptop. Now I can see the comings and goings of everyone here," Klein informed him as he continued to study the screen carefully as if he were hunting for ghosts.

"Has anyone ever told you how creepy you are?" Reaper jeered.

"Did you achieve anything today?" Klein asked, ignoring Reaper's rhetorical question.

"Yeah, and your cameras will be a big help," Reaper said as he rummaged through a duffel bag and pulled out a full bottle of unopened water. He took a few deep gulps before continuing. "I overheard a conversation with Big Mike."

"Surprise, surprise," Klein replied sarcastically.

"Yeah. Well anyway, I couldn't quite make out the entire conversation—that bar is a hub of locals—but I heard enough. Pictures, PAR, and experiments—ring a bell? The best part is that the guy that I was listening to came here after his drinks. You should have him on your feed," Reaper said, as he continued to enthusiastically drink from his bottle of water.

"How long ago did he leave the bar?" Klein asked.

"Ten minutes or so before I did," Reaper replied with a shrug.

Klein began a series of rapid clicks as he rewound the camera feeds.

"It's a little blurry, but is this your guy?" Klein asked, turning his laptop around for Reaper, who was now standing at the foot of his bed. Reaper moved in for a better look and squinted at the screen. He couldn't quite make out the face, but the weather-beaten leather jacket was a match.

"Yeah, that's him," Reaper said with a nod.

Klein studied the camera feed carefully. After a few minutes he finally said, "Room 314—he's our neighbour. Let's go."

Klein closed the lid of his laptop and put it on the nightstand to his right.

"Whoa, whoa, whoa, easy there, cowboy," Reaper said with a laugh. "We're looking for the pictures, remember? If we chase after every looky-loo who might have seen them it'll get us nowhere."

"It's the only lead that we've got," Klein stated matter-of-factly.

"No. He had mentioned something about meeting up with someone again tonight. I don't think our buddy next door has the photos, but I have a feeling that he just might lead us to whoever does. We should watch his room with your cameras and see where he goes later," Reaper informed his partner as he finished off his water and tossed the bottle into the corner of the room.

Klein mulled it over and rubbed his smooth bald head beneath his hood as he thought. Reaper was right, but he didn't want to admit it. After a few more moments he finally agreed and opened his laptop back up. He put the camera feed back on live and watched room 314 with great interest.

Reaper lay back on his bed with his hands behind his head. It had felt good punching that kid in the face; he was a real arrogant piece of work. For a moment Reaper had forgotten all about the mission at hand and PAR. He just saw a young punk that needed to be set straight. Reaper smiled as he replayed the punch over and over again inside his head. It reminded him of a much simpler time, a time when the world wasn't a charred pile of rubble, death, and decay. A time when he had truly known what he had wanted in life and who he was meant to be.

***

Joseph had no idea how long he had been asleep for, but his room was now almost completely dark. He was parched, but all the supplies were in Greg's room, safely tucked away in that little black backpack. He slowly sat up and rubbed his eyes as he adjusted to the lack of light. He then shambled over to his window that had a perfect view of the courthouse at the end of the main street to his right. The lights were on and he could make out a handful of figures on the front steps, presumably guards. He looked immediately downwards and could see that the bar across the street was just as lively as ever. It wasn't totally dark yet, but it would be soon. Joseph moved away from the window and stuffed his feet into his unforgiving boots. The arch support was non-existent now and any remnants of padding had been worn away. If he could see the insides of his boots, Joseph would be able to observe the plethora of bloodstains from countless blisters that severely discolored the interior fabric. Fortunately, his battered boots did not yet have any holes, which was nothing short of a miracle.

Joseph left his room and locked the door behind him, despite not having a single possession that needed to be kept safe. He wondered what time it was as he made his way down the hall to Greg's room. It was impossible to tell these days; his watch battery had kicked the bucket months ago. He had never been able to tell time by the location of the sun, but even if he could it would have been all for nought, as the sun was constantly hidden behind the gloomy cloud coverage that never ceased. Joseph gently knocked on Greg's door and waited for a few seconds. No answer. He knocked again, this time with a bit more force. Still no answer. He knocked a third time, this time pounding on the door.

"Coming!" a startled voice shouted from within the room, and a few short moments later a groggy-eyed Greg answered the door.

"Did I wake you?" Joseph asked with a sincere chuckle.

"Yeah...what's up?" Greg asked as he wearily rubbed his eyes.

"I need some water," Joseph said.

"Oh, right." Greg motioned for Joseph to come in and yawned.

Joseph helped himself to Greg's backpack and rummaged through their supplies until he found what he was looking for. He took three generous sips before putting the bottle of water back. They were going to need more water soon; he could tell that Greg and Hillary had already enjoyed some of the refreshing liquid, as the bottle was now only a quarter of the way full.

"How'd the sightseeing go?" Joseph asked as he zipped up the bag, which had been carelessly tossed onto the floor.

"It was actually pretty cool! I've never seen an aircraft quite like it, not even before the war. It was kind of hard to see it out back, but we still managed to get a good look," Greg replied as he sat down on the edge of his bed.

"You know what kind it was?" Joseph asked as he peered out of Greg's window, which had a similar view to his.

"I used to fix trucks, Joseph, not airplanes," Greg said with a characteristic grunt.

"Oh, right. Anyways, I talked to Mike after you two left," Joseph said while watching a man and a woman walk into Big Mike's bar holding hands. "About the pictures. He seemed to know what I was talking about and he strongly implied that I should follow up with Aaron tonight."

"Ah geez," Greg sighed as he rubbed his prickly bald head.

Joseph turned around with his hands deep in his pockets. "Don't you think it's a little strange?"

"What is? Your mysterious neighbour across the hall? Yeah, that's strange alright," Greg sarcastically replied.

"No, the fact that Mike knew what I was talking about. And there's something else. Aaron told me about a guy that he knew, a drunkard named Tom. He said that he was the person in two of the pictures that I saw. Guess what? Big Mike also knew this Tom," Joseph told Greg as he attempted to make eye contact with him in the rapidly receding daylight.

"Why do you care so much?" Greg asked with a sigh. "I mean, it's not our problem. I don't want to sound cold or anything, but why get involved? We've got a good thing going here, Joseph."

It was true—they did have a good thing going, and Joseph wanted nothing more than to forget about his encounter with Aaron last night. But he couldn't. Those pictures had genuinely disturbed him and they were permanently imprinted into his brain. Not only that, but Joseph hated the whole 'ignorance is bliss' attitude. It was in his nature to know both sides of a story; that's what had made him such a damn good lawyer. Even as a kid debating politics or religion at an uncomfortable family gathering, Joseph had made sure that he did his homework. He would study up on what he knew his opponent's viewpoint would be, or in that case, what his arrogant aunt's opinion would likely be. Nothing drove Joseph more crazy than being kept in the dark and not knowing the full story. His hunger for knowledge was insatiable. Besides, if Outpost Zulu really was covering up a dark secret, then it would be in his best interest to know what he was truly up against here.

"Listen, I'm not asking you to come with me. I'm literally taking a few steps across the hall so that I can finish hearing him out. You're more than welcome to go back to sleep if you're not interested," Joseph assured his sceptical companion.

"No, no, I'm going with you. Just in case, y'know? You're not a big guy or anything." Greg spoke as if he were a parent about to chaperone a child.

"Thanks, Greg, I appreciate it," Joseph said with a smile that was impossible to see in the dark.

There was a quick little knock on the door that interrupted their conversation. Joseph and Greg exchanged worried glances before they heard Hillary's voice from the other side.

"Guys, it's me!" she shouted.

Joseph went and opened the door, letting Hillary inside.

"Surprised you're not asleep," Greg said with a chuckle.

"I might have been if I wasn't so thirsty!" Hillary exclaimed as she unzipped the backpack in search of hydration.

"Joseph and I are going to talk to that guy he met last night," Greg informed her.

Hillary finished off the last of the water bottle before replying. Now there was only one full bottle left.

"Seriously? Again?" she asked in a tone that indicated she was less enthused than Greg.

"Yeah, seriously," Greg replied, matching her apathetic tone.

"Okay, well, count me in. Can't let you two have all the fun without me," Hillary said, eager not to be left behind. "When are we going?"

"I figured that we should wait at least until nightfall, which won't be long. Seems appropriate," Joseph said as he returned to the window. He was relieved that his friends were coming with him. He wasn't afraid of Aaron—Big Mike had vouched for him after all—but it never hurt to have someone watching his back. An unknown soul had lit the lanterns on the main street below and Joseph enjoyed watching their comforting orange glow illuminate the sidewalk.

Joseph, Greg, and Hillary conversed for the next 30 minutes or so. There wasn't anything else to do to kill time, and the trio enjoyed each other's company anyway. Unbeknownst to the group of talkative friends, their room was being watched by two highly skilled killing machines who were preparing to strike.

Chapter 11

A Storm Is Brewing

Reaper and Klein had observed their neighbour from room 314 enter room 308, joined shortly afterwards by a girl from 306. They had been moments away from mobilizing when they saw a group of five hooded figures move quickly down the hallway and enter room 315. A perplexing development in the situation to say the least. Reaper and Klein unanimously decided that the best course of action would be inaction, at least for the time being. And so, the two seemingly incompatible partners shared half a bag of beef jerky and continued to closely monitor Klein's laptop as they waited for their perfect opportunity to pounce.

***

Joseph, Greg, and Hillary heard a cluster of footsteps and hushed voices move past Greg's room, followed by the unmistakable slam of a door at the end of the hall.

"That sounded like it came from Aaron's room," Joseph remarked, rising to his feet.

"Are you sure you want to do this?" Greg asked as he hesitantly got off the edge of his bed.

"Yeah, I'm sure. I've got this anyways," Joseph said as he opened his tattered leather jacket to reveal the pistol that was tucked into his waistband.

"Alright, let's get this party started then," Hillary said with a hint of excitement in her voice.

The trio made their way out of Greg's room and down the hall. To Joseph's surprise, the communal lantern had been lit once more and the hallway was now basked in a warm orange glow. He wondered who was responsible for the good Samaritan act, but his thoughts were short-lived as he was suddenly standing in front of room 315. Joseph took a deep breath and knocked. The door opened just a crack and Aaron peeked out into the hall.

"Oh good, you came! And you brought friends. Come in, come in," Aaron said quickly.

Aaron held the door wide open and the trio entered the candle-lit room. There were four people standing in the middle of the room wearing oversized green raincoats with their hoods up. Surrounded by candles, the hooded figures resembled members of some kind of cult, and they were soaking wet. If it was raining it would be imperative that Joseph and his friends collect rainwater after this meeting; their water supply was running dangerously low. Aaron rejoined the congregation, also sporting a dark-green raincoat, and clutched his envelope of horrors just as he had done when Joseph first met him. Joseph grimaced at the thought of what was inside that stained yellow envelope.

"Okay, that's everyone for tonight," Aaron declared. "Joseph, have you filled your friends in?"

"As much as I could," Joseph replied.

"Good. Here, these are the pictures," Aaron said, handing Greg the envelope. "Take a look for yourself."

Greg resisted an eye-roll and removed the pictures from the envelope. His eyes couldn't roll now even if he wanted them to; in fact they widened in horror as he took it all in. The limbless man lying on a blood-soaked hospital bed in apparent agony, the second photo of the same man now with mechanical arms, and the third photograph of a row of tortured patients equipped with a variety of artificial appendages and circuitry lying next to the woman who had retained her biological limbs but had her skull filled with wires, her face canvassed with a lifeless expression. He numbly passed the photos over to Hillary who audibly gasped in shock. She held a hand over her mouth as she studied each photo carefully. Hillary quickly handed the pictures back to Greg, who in turn stuffed them back into the envelope and returned them to Aaron.

"Are these…" Greg cleared his throat before continuing. "Are these real?"

"They came directly from an esteemed member of PAR. Also everyone here, with the exception of you three, knew the man in the first two pictures. His name was Tom," Aaron answered sombrely as the four other people wearing dark-green raincoats nodded in unison. The room fell quiet and Joseph could hear rain pattering against the window; his mouth felt dry now.

"Our plans are being accelerated," Aaron said, finally breaking the silence.

"What exactly are your plans?" Joseph asked.

"We're taking over the outpost. No more will we be PAR's guinea pigs! If we can secure the outpost for ourselves, we will also secure our safety." Aaron spoke with supreme confidence and candlelight reflected off his dark-brown eyes.

"What about supplies? We get most of that from PAR," a woman in a raincoat quietly asked.

"We can find our own supplies! We've got more than enough to go around for months to come and we can send out scavenger parties. Scavenger parties that don't disappear because of PAR. Other less-equipped settlements do it—why not us?" Aaron said decidedly.

"One of the guards told me that the speech tomorrow would be given by Commander Ventress herself," a short and stocky man in a raincoat with a lisp declared.

"If we take her out, PAR will no longer be controlled by a sadistic dictator," Aaron chimed back in. "According to our PAR informant, the one who leaked the photos, most of the Commander's subordinates are appalled by her experiments but they're too afraid to stand up to her. With Ventress out of the picture, PAR will be forced to find a new leader and they will likely revert back to their roots: helping survivors rebuild civilization, not terrorizing them for twisted militaristic gains."

Joseph and Greg looked at each other with a mutual feeling of disbelief at what they were hearing.

"We've got most of the outpost on our side and ready to fight. A good handful of the guards are ready to turn too," Aaron continued. "Once we take her out, we can secure the outpost and we will finally be safe."

"This is crazy!" Greg exclaimed.

"Yeah, I don't want to rain on your parade but how do you expect to defend against a counter-attack? Surely they will strike back," Joseph asked sceptically.

"Without Commander Ventress at the helm, I sincerely doubt that PAR will retaliate. Regardless, we've been smuggling weapons in through a hole in the eastern wall for weeks. A couple of survivors stumbled upon an abandoned military camp in the forest north of the city and it had a stockpile of weapons. If they do strike back, we'll be ready," Aaron explained.

Joseph had no idea that he was walking into an insurgency meeting tonight. He wasn't a killer and he certainly didn't like the idea of having to take turns defending this outpost from Orvilles, bandits, and PAR. The whole situation seemed like a disaster. He had hoped Aaron would have had a more diplomatic solution, but the young Hispanic man clearly had a much more radical mind than Joseph.

"My friends and I have been taking weapons to as many sympathizers as possible. The more armed we are, the better," Aaron said.

"So that's the plan? Shoot the Commander mid-speech like the President Roosevelt assassination attempt and take over the outpost?" Joseph asked doubtfully.

"Essentially, yes. Listen, you three don't have to take part but we can use all the help that we can get. This is about protecting people who cannot protect themselves, people like

Tom. Do you want to see the pictures again? Would you like to see why we're doing this again?" Aaron asked as he angrily extended the envelope towards Joseph.

"No, I'm good," Joseph said quietly.

Aaron turned to the short man in the raincoat with the lisp. "Richard, we're going to go speak with Big Mike. Stay here and protect these with your life."

Aaron handed the cursed envelope to Richard, who proceeded to put it in the nightstand drawer and took a seat on the edge of the bed beside it.

"Help yourself to weapons and ammo before you go. Even if you're not looking for a fight, it's better to be prepared for one just in case," Aaron said as he pointed at the green duffel bag in the corner of the room.

"Thanks," Greg replied absentmindedly.

"C'mon, you three. Let's go," Aaron ordered the three people in dark-green raincoats. The weather-protected trio followed Aaron out the door, leaving Joseph, Greg, Hillary, and Richard alone in the hotel room.

"One pistol each and one clip of ammo each," Richard instructed with his prominent lisp. A sawn-off double-barrel shotgun had magically appeared on his lap. Joseph deduced that the oversized raincoat had more than one purpose, protection from the elements being the less important one.

The trio of companions shuffled over to the duffel bag and Hillary grabbed a snub-nosed revolver along with a handful of bullets. Greg selected a Glock 17, a popular weapon for pre-war police officers. Joseph, already armed with his Colt 1911, helped himself to a second clip of ammunition for his pistol. Richard slowly nodded at the group, indicating that it was time for them to leave. The trio was anything but heartbroken that it was time to go and they scurried out of the room, quickly entering Joseph's room, which was directly across the hall.

"What the hell did you drag us into?" Greg asked as soon as the door slammed shut behind them, his voice full of exasperation.

"Well, I certainly wasn't expecting that!" Joseph replied as he ran a hand through his unkempt hair.

"Those poor people! Someone has to help them!" Hillary exclaimed as she nervously bit her fingernails.

Joseph slumped onto the corner of his bed and held his head in between his hands. The entire outpost was about to be turned upside down just when they thought they had finally found someplace safe to stay. Greg plopped himself down onto a desk chair on wheels, the chair sliding a foot back from the force of his dramatic flop. Hillary was much too antsy to sit, pacing back and forth along the length of the window, which was now streaked with droplets of rain.

"Maybe we should help them," she said, more to herself than to her two companions sitting in the almost pitch-black room.

"No way, this isn't our problem. We should just lay low and stay out of it," Greg said as he leaned back in the black leather chair and it creaked beneath his weight.

Joseph wasn't sure what to do. Hillary was right—someone did have to help those people, or at the very least make sure no one else was victimized. Did it really have to be their responsibility though? How much help would a lawyer, a mechanic, and a high-school girl really be? One thing was for certain: a storm was brewing in Outpost Zulu.

"Do you think they'll actually do it? Assassinate the Commander?" Greg asked, his question directed at Joseph.

"Yeah. Aaron strikes me as a man of his word. He's invested in his cause." Joseph paused for a second. "With that said, I don't think Aaron and his sympathizers have thought this whole thing out very well."

"Exactly! This place needs PAR; they'll never be able to provide enough resources and security without them. We all know how long most settlements last these days," Greg said, reflecting on his previous travels.

The life expectancy for any settlement was short. Very short. Without proper protection, mutants and raiders would drive settlers out in a matter of days, weeks at best. At least Outpost Zulu had a wall; Joseph had never seen such a wall in the last couple of years. But even so, it would likely only be a matter of time before the outpost became overrun just like countless ones before it. There was really no surefire solution. Remove the PAR presence and protect residents from potentially being abducted, but expose them to everything that lurked beyond the wall and force them to fend for themselves. Let PAR continue to operate, and risk becoming a living part of those godless photographs. Joseph supposed that it would be possible to defend the outpost without PAR, assuming that they had enough weapons to go around. However, he was still concerned about what kind of retaliation PAR might take if their leader was assassinated. If Joseph had learned anything from world history, it was that forcibly removing a dictator from power often only paved the way for an even more tyrannical leader to emerge from the shadows.

"Well, you heard them! They've been smuggling guns through the wall! I'd rather take our chances with protecting the outpost ourselves than have one of you two"—Hillary choked up as she spoke—"go missing."

A single tear ran down Hillary's cheek and glimmered for a brief moment as it caught the faint light coming through the window from a lantern outside. Joseph went over and embraced her, and that's when she really let the tears flow.

"Hey, hey, we're alright..." Joseph reassured her as he looked over to Greg so that he'd offer some consolation, unsure of what to say himself.

"Yeah, we're okay! As long as we stick together, we'll all be fine," Greg said, coming over to rest a reassuring hand on her shoulder.

The trio stood like that for a while. It was easy to forget just how young Hillary was in comparison to Joseph and Greg. The young girl had been through so much over the last couple of years; they all had. What mattered most to Joseph was sticking together. He became aware of the fact that the rain had stopped and that the trio had missed their opportunity to replenish their fluids. It would be okay, Joseph thought. It always was in the end.

Hillary pulled away, sniffling and rubbing her eyes.

"Sorry...I don't know where that came from."

"Don't be sorry—you've been through a lot. We all have," Joseph said sympathetically.

"Yeah, and tonight didn't help," Greg added.

"We could all probably use a good sleep; we can figure things out in the morning," Joseph said, his eyes beginning to feel heavy.

"You going to be alright?" Greg asked Hillary.

She nodded and forced a smile. Greg and Hillary said goodnight to Joseph and returned to their rooms, leaving Joseph alone in the darkness.

Joseph just stood in the dark for a while, contemplating what tomorrow would bring. He was rudely interrupted when a brilliantly bright bolt of lightning lit up his room. Joseph jumped, startled by the unexpected illumination. A bellow of thunder echoed through the air and gave Joseph a faint vibration in his chest. He had always enjoyed a good thunderstorm, growing up, and right now he absolutely loved it.

Joseph fumbled clumsily in the dark, his hands exploring the dresser. He remembered seeing a bright-blue coffee mug earlier in the day and wondering how many of the people who drank out of that very mug were no longer in the land of the living. Joseph clumsily knocked the mug off of the dresser, but the soft oriental-themed carpet provided enough cushion to prevent it from breaking. He picked the mug up and raced over to his window, turning the hand crank to open it. The window only opened a couple of inches, but it was enough for Joseph to slide the mug halfway out onto the thin windowsill. The mug caught one raindrop, then another, and another. He smiled triumphantly and made his way to bed.

Joseph kept his jacket on, as a cool breeze from the brewing storm wafted through the open window. He didn't mind; in fact he welcomed it. The smell of rain on concrete soothed his very soul. Another flash of lightning lit up his room, followed by the angry roar of thunder. Joseph lay on his right side so that he could face the window, his head resting on his right bicep as he curled into a tight ball. He used to be a pretty muscular guy, but not so much any more, and his bicep wasn't as comfortable to lie on as it once was. Still, he was relatively cosy and perfectly content watching the storm that was raging outside his small window. He closed his eyes and listened to the rain pounding against the glass. It took him back to being a kid.

He remembered being out at camp with his mother. It was a family camp, meaning that the entire extended family had access to it. The building itself was quite small and painted a light shade of baby blue to match a similarly coloured deck. All of the paint had begun to peel away and expose the rotting wood beneath, but the quaint little camp still held an intrinsic rustic charm. The camp consisted of a small kitchen that was attached to the living room. There was a saggy rust-coloured couch in the living room that had been a bed for countless family members when the actual beds had been full. The little box television that was situated at the end of the heavily used couch was rarely turned on. There were two bedrooms, one with a bunkbed and one with a more traditional twin-sized bed. Only the bravest or the most ignorant family members used the shower. Those who showered were never truly alone, accompanied by spiders, earwigs, and perhaps even a bit of mould. Joseph always opted to bathe in the large lake in front of the camp. He would take a bottle of soap and shampoo into the lake, letting them float beside him as the cool water refreshed his spirit.

There had been a particularly stormy evening when only Joseph and his mother were at the camp, which was rare considering the fact that the camp was usually bustling with relatives. Joseph was 5 years old at the time and they had just returned from a small local shop just ten minutes down the highway. Joseph had a fixation with moose, despite never seeing one in person. So naturally, his mom had bought him a stuffed moose and a picture book all about moose. They were sitting in the camp on the rust-coloured couch reading the book when a violent storm blew in off the lake. Brilliant purple lightning zig-zagged across the sky while the sun began to set, the water reflecting a mixture of fiery oranges from the sunset and vibrant purples from the lightning. Joseph and his mom had stopped reading in order to watch the storm churn the lake and light up the sky. That's when they spotted a little tin motorboat in the middle of the lake.

The boat was dwarfed in comparison with the gargantuan waves and looked to be in great danger of capsizing, but capsizing was the least of the captain's concerns. The dazzling purple strikes of lightning had locked in on the lone boat, firing bolts from the heavens at the defiant little vessel. Joseph and his mother had watched that motorboat fly across the water towards shore, crashing through the white-capping waves, all while that furious purple lightning continued to chase the tin coffin. The boat did eventually make it to shore, despite numerous lightning strikes that barely missed it—by what appeared to be only a few feet.

This is the childhood memory that Joseph thought about as he lay alone in his dark and desolate hotel room. It was a comforting thought, and the storm outside made him feel as if he was reliving that sacred childhood experience. A tear escaped the corner of his eye, yet he couldn't help but smile. Joseph drifted off into a deep sleep while he continued to replay that fantastical memory and think about his mother who had always been there to comfort him in his times of need.

***

Reaper and Klein had been studying the security feed on Klein's laptop closely as they waited for their perfect opportunity to strike. Discretion was fundamental to their mission, so both men had been waiting for the crowd to thin out before engaging. According to Klein there was only one person remaining in room 315, the room in which eight unidentified individuals had congregated, including their neighbour from the bar who had returned to his own room a few minutes ago with two of his companions. Reaper and Klein were just about to mobilize when their neighbour's two companions, a large man and a small girl, emerged from room 314 and returned to what appeared to be their own respective rooms nearby. Everyone from the party that had taken place in room 315 was now split up; it was time to strike.

"Quick and quiet. No witnesses," Klein said, still monitoring the laptop.

Reaper knew what 'no witnesses' meant: any soul unfortunate enough to catch the two operatives in the act needed to be eliminated—no loose ends. Reaper had never given much thought to pulling the trigger; he had a job and he executed. This mission, however, felt a little different. There was something not quite right about it, something inherently vile. Still, Reaper was a soldier and he had his orders. Good soldiers follow orders and Reaper was a damn good soldier.

"Alright, let's do this," Klein said decisively as he closed the lid to his laptop.

The storm outside had become deafening. An angry torrent of rain battered the windows and created a constant hum of white noise as it berated the roof. Frequent blasts of thunder reverberated throughout the building. The storm would work to their advantage, masking the noise that they were inevitably going to create. Both operatives were armed with silenced Walther-PPK pistols and large hunting knives, two silent yet effective instruments of death. In and out, quick and clean, and most importantly: no witnesses.

The duo stepped out into the hall, Reaper coming out behind Klein and ensuring that their door did not slam shut behind them. The two quickly and quietly worked their way down the hallway, the communal lantern flickering wildly as they passed by. Within a matter of seconds, they were standing in front of the room where so many people had previously congregated. Reaper removed a lockpicking kit from his jeans pocket and quietly went to work while Klein kept watch. Reaper was an expert with a lockpick; he had spent many long nights practising on various padlocks for fun. It was like an innocent puzzle for him, a way to pass the time instead of drink. Now it was proving to be a vital skill instead of just a hobby.

Reaper worked at the final locking pin, applying slight pressure until it finally gave way and the door unlocked with a faint click. Reaper quickly shoved the lockpicking kit back into his pocket, disregarding the proper placement for the tools. He abruptly threw the door open and drew his gun in one fluid motion, Klein entering behind him with his gun at the ready. This time, the door did slam shut. A pudgy little man in a raincoat who had been watching the storm outside his window quickly spun around. A sawn-off double-barrel shotgun was resting on the edge of the bed just a few feet away from him.

"Don't even think about it," Reaper said as he slowly made his way over to the bed so that he could secure the weapon.

The little man raised his hands and asked, "Who are you? What do you want?"

"The pictures. Where are they?" Klein asked, keeping his gun trained on the man as Reaper grabbed the shotgun off the bed.

The little man's eyes widened as he realized the severity of the situation. "You're PAR!" he shouted. "Help! Somebod—"

Klein squeezed the trigger, the military-grade silencer effectively muffling the gunshot as a single bullet sailed directly into Richard's forehead, terminating the petrified man's plea for help. The bullet exited through the back of Richard's skull and pierced the window behind him, becoming lost in the stormy night sky as the window cracked violently around the small hole in a web-like pattern. The shot was so precise that there was very little blood at first. A small red dot where the bullet had entered gave way to a slow trickle of blood that began running down the bridge of Richard's nose. Richard blinked twice before his legs buckled and he crumpled to the floor. Reaper grimaced.

"So much for discretion. What do we do with the body?" Reaper asked as he began to search for the pictures.

Klein holstered his pistol and walked over to the still-warm corpse. He effortlessly picked the limp body up by the jacket with two hands. Klein made it look as if he were picking up an oversized doll instead of a full-grown man. He just stood there for a while, holding the lifeless corpse as a now steady stream of blood leaked from both the entry wound and exit wound.

"What the hell are you doing?" Reaper asked with a look of disgust on his face.

"Quiet now," Klein replied eerily.

There was a flash of lightning that dwarfed the light provided by the candles scattered throughout the room. In perfect synchronization with a rolling boom of thunder, Klein tossed Richard's body through the cracked window with tremendous force, sending the corpse plummeting down to a dark side street below. The only organic part of Richard that remained in the room was a small blackish stain of blood that had soaked into the tasteless brown hotel carpet. The dark stain on the equally dark carpet would prove difficult to spot with the limited lighting in the room.

"There, he killed himself. Commander Ventress can dispatch Captain Andor to take care of the body after we find the pictures," Klein said with no sign of remorse as he retrieved the casing from the bullet that had fallen to the floor and was now glimmering in the candlelight.

Reaper gave his head a quick shake and focused on finding the photographs, which didn't take long. He opened the nightstand drawer and to his surprise found the envelope. What a terrible hiding place, he thought. He moved over to a candle before examining the contents.

"Did you find them?" Klein asked, curiously observing Reaper from across the room where he had been searching for the pictures in a spacious closet.

"I think so…" Reaper said as he began to open the envelope.

"Don't. Just give me the envelope," Klein demanded.

"No. I deserve to know," Reaper growled as he removed the pictures.

Klein continued to watch Reaper closely but made no move to stop him. Reaper's left eye involuntarily twitched as he examined the first photo of the limbless man crying out in pain on the bloodied hospital bed. The surgeon that was watching in the background with a face lacking any resemblance to empathy was the same doctor that had patched Reaper up after he caught a couple of bullets in a skirmish a few months back during one of his 'waste management' missions. Reaper flipped to the next picture.

"Just like you…" Reaper murmured as he examined the same man from the first photo who was now wielding cybernetic arms that resembled what Klein had shown him beneath his own skin.

Reaper examined the final photo, the one with a row of mutilated patients affixed with a variety of artificial limbs and circuitry lying next to the woman who had a blank expression on her face as wires snaked throughout her skull. Reaper rubbed his left eye, which refused to stop twitching, before putting the pictures back into the envelope.

"Now you know." Klein's voice snapped Reaper back to the present.

"Now I know," he repeated in a monotone voice.

"Let's go. Quickly. Before someone returns," Klein said, turning for the door.

Reaper reached for his gun, and Klein paused at the door without turning around as if he could read Reaper's thoughts. Reaper's right hand rested on the hilt of his holstered pistol for a moment. His usually sharp mind was scattered. Neither man moved for what felt like an eternity, frozen in time. Finally, Reaper let his hand fall to his side. Klein opened the door and Reaper followed him into the hall. The flame within the communal lantern had almost fizzled out, making the hallway darker than usual. Reaper followed Klein down the hall and back into their room. Once they were inside, Klein made a beeline for the radio that sat on the dresser beside his laptop. Reaper remained in the unilluminated doorframe and carefully observed Klein's every move.

"Commander Ventress, come in. Do you copy?" Klein spoke with clarity into the mouthpiece. He waited several moments before trying a second time: "Commander Ventress, it's Klein. Do you copy?"

There was another long delay. Klein was about to try a third time when finally, there was a reply from the other end.

"This is Commander Ventress. Go ahead." She did her best to speak with her usual bravado, but it was abundantly clear that she had been in a deep slumber just moments prior.

Klein delivered his message quickly and concisely.

"Our mission is complete. We have the package. We need clean-up on the east side of the hotel. How copy?"

"Good copy, excellent work. Check out of your room and bring the package to me immediately. I'll dispatch Captain Andor to deal with the mess. Out," Ventress replied as she clicked off the radio.

'Check out of your room' was code for returning it to its original state for future operations. Captain Andor was responsible for restocking the room with supplies provided by PAR, but it was common military practice to maintain order and tidiness. It was also just common courtesy. Klein immediately returned his weapons to the large duffel bag underneath the window and gently slid the laptop back under the bed along with the mobile charger. He figured that it would likely be advantageous to leave the cameras up permanently and he was confident that they would not be discovered, especially not in such a dimly lit hotel. Reaper finally emerged from the shadow of the doorframe, returning his weapons and the lockpicking set. There wasn't much to organize and the room was back to its original tidy state in less than ten minutes. The two contrasting PAR operatives did not utter a single word to each other in that timeframe.

The duo left the hotel room together, the heavy door slamming shut behind them one last time. They moved quickly; it was only a matter of time before someone returned to room 315 and they were so close to being in the clear. Reaper and Klein briskly jogged down the metal staircase, their heavy combat boots clanging against the stairs. Klein was leading the away and he briefly paused at the door leading to the well-lit lobby as he checked to make sure that no one was there. They were in luck for the time being. They entered the lobby, and the handful of scented candles made the room quite welcoming.

Reaper briskly made his way over to the safe that was concealed by the painting so that he could return the room key.

He carefully removed the painting of the lighthouse from the wall and set it down on a maroon-coloured lobby chair nearby. Klein kept watch, his head on a swivel. Reaper turned the dial on the safe, but the tiny metal door remained locked. He took a deep breath and tried once more but still to no avail.

"Four, twenty-two, four," Klein irritably whispered.

Reaper focused all of his will on that dial and spun it to the correct numbers: FOUR, TWENTY-TWO, FOUR. Click. The safe door gently sprung open, allowing Reaper to safely stash the key away for the next PAR operator who might need it down the road. He closed the safe once more and picked up the painting that he had set down on the nearby lobby chair. Reaper stood there for a moment, studying the painting closely once more. Something seemed off about it now, but he couldn't quite figure out what it was. Perhaps it was the current lighting in the room, or the lack of lighting for that matter, but the beacon from the lighthouse no longer appeared to be shining. How could that be possible, Reaper thought. What would that unpainted ship that surely existed just beyond the shroud of the storm follow now?

"Hurry up," Klein hissed as he peered out of the lobby window, "someone's coming!"

Reaper quickly hung the painting back up over the safe. It was a little crooked, but it would have to do. The lobby doors swung open, allowing a torrent of rain to find its way inside, soaking into the red and gold carpet that led up to the front desk. Two men in dark-green raincoats entered the lobby. Both Reaper and Klein recognized them from the security feed. The four men all awkwardly nodded at one another before the duo from the security feed made their way into the stairwell.

"Our time is up, let's go," Klein said as he pulled the door back open and allowed another burst of rain to enter the lobby.

Reaper followed Klein out onto the main street. It was remarkably dark; all the lanterns that had been lit never stood a chance against the vengeful storm. The only remaining lights came from Big Mike's bar and the unnaturally bright courthouse at the end of the main street. Reaper had the envelope of jeopardizing photographs tucked into his waistband, concealed by his bulky 'A C' hoodie. He was sceptical that it would protect the photos from the onslaught of water, but quite frankly he didn't really care right now. The two promptly made their way down the sidewalk towards the blindingly bright courthouse, which lured them in like moths to a dazzling beacon shining in the night.

The unforgiving wind was blowing from Reaper's left, battering one side of his face with relentless freezing-cold raindrops that felt like miniature needles. His bushy black beard provided some reprieve from the frigid autumn rain, but those pesky little drops still seemed to find their way through his coarse hair. Nobody else was brave enough, or stupid enough, to be on the street right now. Those who were not drinking their sorrows away with Big Mike, or cosying up in the Courtview Hotel, had been shacked up in the rundown buildings that lined the dark side-streets. PAR had initially intended to refurbish the entire outpost, but progress had halted after the main strip had been completed and Commander Ventress took over.

Reaper and Klein were approaching the bottom of the cobblestone steps that led up to the front doors of the old courthouse now. Two heavily armoured guards equipped with M4A1 assault rifles stood on the bottom of the steps, defying Mother Nature herself.

"Halt!" one of them shouted, his command barely audible over the storm.

Reaper couldn't see the soldier's face on account of his ballistic helmet and dark-green fabric face covering that looked uncomfortably soggy, but he recognized the voice.

"Rex," Reaper shouted back. "It's me, Reaper!"

Rex squinted as the unforgiving rain homed in on his eyes.

"Good to see ya, Sir!"

"Oi! Reaper, welcome back!" the second identically equipped guard said. Reaper now recognized him as Beetle. His oversized prescription glasses were completely fogged up, concealing his eyes entirely.

"Good to see you boys," Reaper said as he gave them both a quick fist bump. "The witch herself is expecting us."

Klein scowled, but no one seemed to notice or care.

"Careful what ya say, Sir. She locked up the outpost doctor in the old cell downstairs! Guess he knew who took those pics," Rex said with a laugh.

"Speaking of, did you find 'em?" Beetle asked.

"Yeah, and there won't be anything left of them if I stay out here much longer," Reaper said as he began to ascend the slick cobblestone steps.

Reaper and Klein reached the top of the gradually ascending stairs and stood under the white concrete awning for a moment. The storm was showing no signs of letting up and spurts of sideways rain periodically found their way under the protective awning.

"Reaper," Klein said, stopping him from opening one of the cumbersome courthouse doors.

Reaper turned to face Klein.

"What is it?"

"You did well. Just make sure that you don't bite the hand that feeds you," Klein warned.

Klein opened the large courthouse door and held it open for Reaper. Reaper stepped inside and was swallowed up by the bright artificial light that permeated from within the former building of justice.

Chapter 12

For the Greater Good

Reaper and Klein had been ordered to wait in the hallway outside Ventress's chambers until they had thoroughly dried off like a pair of wet dogs. Wolf and Ghost, the two Alpha Squad members responsible for guarding Ventress's room, had been dismissed for the night. Reaper had caught up with them at the end of the hall while waiting to dry off. There wasn't much to catch up on other than the whole debacle with Dr Tellick. Reaper had only met him once or twice around headquarters; he mainly spent his time at the R&D facility or here at the outpost. Reaper always thought of him as a real squirrelly fellow, always rushing around and speaking too fast. It had been apparent that Wolf and Ghost were extremely fatigued, so Reaper wrapped up their conversation fairly quickly. It hadn't taken him long to sufficiently dry off anyway, as the trio had been standing around a wonderfully warm electric space heater. The plethora of generators that the old courthouse had been hooked up to was enough to keep the lights on, but just barely—the lights would periodically flicker as the courthouse's impromptu life-support system strained to sustain power. Space heaters required substantially less power than running the heating unit and as a result only small sections of the courthouse were adequately heated.

After his two battle-buddies had departed to their quarters for the night, Reaper rejoined Klein, who was loitering by another space heater at the opposite end of the hall. There were a few minutes of awkward silence; then they walked back down the hall to Ventress's chambers together. Klein knocked purposefully on the door and the two operatives waited for a response.

"You can come in now," Ventress declared from the other side of the door.

Reaper and Klein entered what used to be the judge's chambers. It was quite spacious and tastefully decorated. A black leather couch sat off to the right on top of a classy rug filled with brilliant blues, greens, and reds. Reaper couldn't help but notice the blackish stain that had formed near the bottom corner of the rug. Blood: a colour that he knew all too well. Behind the couch was a massive dark-oak bookshelf lined with leather-bound books, where a space had been cleared for the radio that Ventress had been using. In front of the couch, on the colourful yet stained rug, was a glass coffee table followed by two leather chairs that matched the three-cushioned couch. The left side of the room had various portraits of former judges on the wall and featured two elegantly tall lamps that looked straight out of the Victorian era.

Commander Ventress sat directly in front of Reaper behind an oversized mahogany desk with the seal of justice imprinted on the front. The top of the desk possessed only Ventress's custom nameplate and one short green lamp that appeared to no longer have a lightbulb. Ventress had her hands interlocked on top of her desk, and the torrential downpour rattled the large window behind her that took up the entirety of the back wall, overlooking what used to be a field of wildflowers but now was home to the sizable CS50 aircraft.

"I believe you have something for me?" Ventress asked as the two field agents approached her desk.

Reaper reached under his hoodie and retrieved the soggy envelope, tossing it onto her desk with a wet plop. Ventress clenched her jaw before opening the abused envelope with a visible look of disgust on her face. She very briefly flipped through the photographs that were inside. The water had stained most of the photos, but they were still identifiable. She tucked them back into the mushy envelope and wiped her hands dry on the sides of her black leather trench coat before interlocking her fingers on top of her desk once more.

"Very good. Klein, you are dismissed. Take a seat, Reaper," Ventress ordered.

Klein nodded and promptly left the room. Reaper sat down on one of the low-set black plastic chairs in front of the Commander's massive desk, his knees audibly popping as he did. The two locked eyes for several moments, neither speaking nor moving. Ventress moved first, opening the bottom drawer from the other side of her desk. She placed two crystal glasses on her relatively empty desk and pulled out a half-empty bottle of Irish whiskey. She stood up to pour the drinks, filling both of their glasses halfway before returning what was left of the golden liquid to her desk drawer and sitting back down. Reaper made no move for the glass at first. Ventress, however, picked up her glass and took a generous gulp. She closed her eyes for a brief moment and relished the calming beverage, tilting her head back slightly.

"Drink," she said sharply as she placed her glass back down on the desk in front of her.

Reaper reached for his glass; a lifetime of obeying his superiors had attuned him to carry forth almost any command without question. Almost. Reaper took a sip, a less generous one than Ventress, and savoured the flavour. He hadn't had whiskey in a very long time. He rarely had access to drinks any more and he preferred to operate with a sharp mind. Reaper took another sip, a bigger one, and then placed his glass back onto the desk.

"So, you've seen the pictures," Ventress stated as she swirled the whiskey in her glass for no apparent reason.

"Yeah," Reaper replied as he felt his pulse quicken. He briskly took another drink before adding, "And I know what you did to Klein."

"What I did? Oh no, that was entirely his choice," Ventress said casually.

"And those people in the pictures," Reaper said, nodding at the envelope that sat in a small puddle of water on the desk, "was it their choice too? Where did they come from?"

"They came from here," Ventress answered truthfully. "Their lives were repurposed to serve a great cause."

"A great cause," Reaper scoffed. "And what great cause would that be?"

Ventress picked her beverage back up and took another sip, the alcohol giving her body a soothing warm tingle.

"Andrew"—Ventress used Reaper's first name, catching him off guard—"don't be naive. You know probably better than anyone else what this world has become. What people have become." She said 'people' like it was a vile word.

"I do what I do…" Ventress paused before rephrasing her explanation. "We do what we do, to preserve what's left of humanity. These…procedures pave the way for groundbreaking medical technology and military advancement. Aid and security that is necessary to govern a peaceful post-war society."

"And how's that working out for you so far? I almost witnessed a lynch mob in the bar looking to go after a couple of lousy guards. I thought they just didn't like those young punks for their arrogance, but now I understand where their hate actually came from," Reaper remarked as he glared into Ventress's emerald-green eyes.

"I take no pleasure in what I've done," Ventress replied while returning Reaper's glare, "but I'm doing what no one else is strong enough to do. I'm securing the future of humanity."

"You're terrorizing innocent lives," Reaper growled. "The time for war is over—it's time to rebuild. What are you going to do if your little speech doesn't woo the masses tomorrow?"

Ventress was growing impatient.

"Don't worry about Outpost Zulu. If the locals don't stand alongside me, I will crush them like the cockroaches that they are." Ventress took a moment to compose herself before continuing. "I have had plans to create a new outpost for quite some time now. A bigger one, a more secure one, an outpost that is genuinely safe for the residents and well-fortified. If the infected continue to converge around the outpost it will only be a matter of time before this place is overrun. One cybernetically enhanced soldier that I can create, like Klein, holds more value than any of the guards here combined. Ideally I can expand on Outpost Zulu and turn it into something that will be prosperous, but if the belligerent locals here cannot be quelled then I will do what I must. I will exterminate the infestation of ingrates and start from scratch."

"So what's the point?" Reaper raised his voice. "Why even bother with this speech? This whole damn operation? If everyone here is so insignificant to you and your plans, why waste your time?"

"People talk," Ventress replied simply, taking another drink as she approached the end of her glass. "Even in this desolate wasteland rumours spread fast. The success of PAR lies in part with our credibility. If I can't win over the masses here, there will always be a risk of civil war when we become more established. So either the people are to support us or..."

"Or you eliminate them." Reaper finished Ventress's sentence.

"Precisely," she said with a charming smile.

"You're tyrannical," Reaper scorned.

"You're no saint yourself," Ventress snarled.

"Thanks for the drink," Reaper growled, picking up his glass and heading for the door.

"Andrew," Ventress said sharply. Reaper stopped, one hand resting on the gold doorknob. "I'll want that glass back in the morning."

Reaper opened the door without saying a word and slammed it shut behind him as he left. Ventress could hear the distinct sound of glass shattering and knew that she would not be getting her crystal glass back. She irritably tapped her fingers against the mahogany desk and finished off her whiskey.

Ventress sat there for a while, continuing to tap her fingers against the smooth wood and listening to the rain pattering against the window. It would be a shame to lose Reaper, as losing Reaper would likely mean losing Alpha Squad as well. But at the end of the day, Reaper and his squad could be replaced just like everyone else. Except for Ventress of course; she was irreplaceable.

Ventress reached for the weather-beaten envelope and grabbed a small purple lighter from her upper desk drawer. She was seconds away from setting the envelope on fire when she paused. Ventress set the lighter down on her desk and removed the photos from the envelope. She spread the three large pictures out on her desk, studying them one more time. Dr Moetsky had done a nice job of capturing the terror painted onto the faces of the patients. Their eyes wide and mouths ajar, their suffering immortalized within these three photographs. Ventress believed every word that she had said to Reaper. She knew that what she was doing was ethically wrong, but she also believed that military supremacy was the only logical route to take in order to secure the future of the human race. If she was in absolute control and no one could oppose her, she could ensure that humanity thrived once more. But there was more to it than that. The truth was that Ventress liked what she did; it gave her ecstasy. It made her feel like a god. Her marvellous green eyes gobbled up the pictures one last time, ignoring the various water stains. Commander Ventress smiled from ear to ear.

***

A magnificent reverberation of thunder had drowned out the pounding on Joseph's door. Joseph was in a deep sleep and the persistent knocking had gone unheard for several minutes. Finally, during a break in the thunder and downpour of rain, Joseph jerked awake at the sound of the perpetual rapping at his door. He sat up quickly, rubbing his eyes and squinting around the room. It was still dark and he had no idea how long he had been asleep for. He knew that it hadn't been long enough though, as his eyelids were desperately trying to close again. The knocking continued. Joseph forced himself out of bed and made his way over to the door. He hesitated to open the barrier that separated him from the anonymous knocker.

"Who is it?" Joseph called through the door.

"Open up!" a panicked voice demanded, a voice that Joseph recognized.

Joseph obliged, opening the door. He was met by a disgruntled-looking Aaron, who shoved a pistol into his face, pushing Joseph backwards. There was a second man who entered with Aaron and proceeded to shine an invasively bright flashlight around the room. Joseph backpedalled; his pistol currently sat across the room on his nightstand.

"Whoa, whoa, whoa! Take it easy, pal!" Joseph said quickly as he raised his hands.

"Where are they?" Aaron shouted, cocking his gun to prove that he wasn't messing around.

"Where are what?" Joseph shouted back, his eyes darting to the man with the flashlight who had begun tearing his room apart in search of something lost.

"Don't play dumb! The pictures! What did you do with them?" Aaron demanded to know, his voice filled with rage.

"What? You left them with that guy when you left—Richard," Joseph replied as he tried to lower his voice in order to keep Aaron calm.

"Yeah, and now he's dead! You and your friends were the last ones in the room with him. You killed him and stole the pictures! You're with PAR!" Aaron's eyes were wide and wet, although it was impossible for Joseph to know whether the moisture came from tears or the violent storm raging outside.

"Hey, hey, hey, listen! I had nothing to do with any of that. After you left we got our guns and returned to our rooms. I swear," Joseph said as he slowly lowered his hands, speaking quickly but clearly.

"I don't believe you," Aaron claimed, but there was hesitation in his voice.

"If what you're saying is true, and I murdered your friend and stole the pictures, do you really think that I would go to bed directly across the hall when you know my room number? Why would I hang around and wait for you to come knocking? Think about it...it just doesn't make any sense," Joseph explained.

"There's nothing here, Aaron," the man with the flashlight said as he accidentally shined the handheld beam of light into the corner of Aaron's right eye.

Aaron's hand trembled and the pistol wobbled uncontrollably. Joseph was worried that the unstable man might accidentally pull the trigger, and he slowly put a hand on the pistol, guiding the muzzle down to the floor. Aaron ran an equally shaky hand through his dark curly hair.

"You're right, you're right. I just don't understand how this happened," Aaron muttered as he took a seat at the end of Joseph's bed, hanging his head in both shame and grief. The second man clicked his flashlight off and stood awkwardly in the back corner of the room.

"Tell me what happened," Joseph said to Aaron with sympathy in his voice.

"I don't know," Aaron replied, his pistol hanging loosely in his right hand with his head still hung low. "Me and Al came back to the room. The window was shattered and I could see Richard's body on the ground below in a pool of blood surrounded by guards. The pictures are gone too."

"Do you think he jumped?" Joseph asked, trying to rule out all possibilities.

Aaron gave his head a sombre shake. "Richard wasn't that kind of guy. I knew him well. Even if he did want to kill himself, why wouldn't he use a gun? It would be much more effective than taking a chance on a three-storey fall. That still wouldn't explain the missing pictures anyways. Why would he take them with him to his grave? He was my best friend and a strong supporter of my cause."

In Aaron and Al's haste, they had failed to notice the small black bloodstain on the dark-brown rug near the window that indicated that Richard had indeed suffered a gunshot wound, although this wound was not self-inflicted. Joseph thought that something certainly did seem off about the whole situation, like there was foul play afoot. Those hotel windows were thick, really thick, and Joseph would be surprised to see anyone jump through one, especially that short little man Richard. Committing suicide with a gun surely would have been easier and less of a hassle than throwing oneself through a hotel window. Regardless of the means that led to Richard's end, the missing photos were a reason to be sceptical of suicide. Joseph wondered what difference it would make whether or not PAR actually had a hand in what happened. Aaron was already hell-bent on leading some kind of asinine revolution and this would only further incentivize him. Richard was now a martyr.

"I'm sorry that you lost your friend," Joseph finally said lamely. "What will you do now that the pictures are gone?"

"Most of the people around here saw the photos already and will stand by me. They know the truth. Richard's death will not be in vain." There was conviction in Aaron's voice and Joseph knew that the young Hispanic man would do exactly what he said he would do: assassinate Commander Ventress.

"Aaron..." Joseph began, before changing his mind. He desperately wanted to persuade Aaron to take a more peaceful route. Perhaps if all the locals came together and stood up for one another then some kind of agreement could be made.

"Yeah?" Aaron replied as he slowly rose to his feet.

"Be careful tomorrow," Joseph said, stifling what he really wanted to say.

"You too, my friend. Sorry about all...this." Aaron motioned to Joseph's ransacked room.

"Yeah, don't worry about it. I doubt housekeeping will mind." Joseph cracked a smile and so did Aaron.

The two disruptive men left the room, leaving Joseph alone in the dark once more. He stood there for a while, contemplating the potential murder that had just occurred across the hall from him while he slept peacefully on his mattress that was stained with an array of bodily fluids. He wondered if he would have been able to intervene if he had been awake. Regardless, Joseph wasn't particularly sad; death was a common occurrence in this new and merciless world. He didn't even know the man who had killed himself or had been killed across the hall. Joseph was, however, slightly disturbed that something so severe had occurred without his knowledge less than 20 feet away from where he stood now. Joseph wasn't entirely convinced that PAR was responsible for Richard's death, but it certainly seemed to be a strong possibility. If PAR was involved, those deeply disturbing pictures would be validated. Not only that, but the untimely disappearance of the photos made the whole situation at Outpost Zulu even more suspicious.

Joseph's thoughts shifted to what would transpire tomorrow during the Commander's speech. There would surely be bloodshed, but Joseph wasn't sure which side would come out on top. History had proven time and time again that you can't end a violent regime with more violence. Putting down one tyrannical dictator by force would only open the doors to further chaos and violence. Just look at what happened in Iraq after Saddam Hussein was taken out. The country was plunged into a state of perpetual civil war, which is how the country remained right up until nuclear warfare—spearheaded by the United States and Russia—decimated the entire planet. The harsh truth was that sometimes an oppressive dictator was a better option than the runner-up or creating conditions conducive to a state of total anarchy.

Joseph yawned and licked his dry lips; it took a lot to faze him these days. He hurried over to the window and retrieved his mug, now full of rainwater, being careful not to spill even a drop. He gulped the cool water down in a matter of seconds, the liquid temporarily quenching his seemingly eternal thirst and leaving a residual metallic taste in his mouth. The rainwater that fell from the radiated clouds above couldn't be good for his health, but his longevity was the least of his concerns these days. He placed the mug back down on the ledge, the rain showing no signs of letting up any time soon. Joseph contemplated what the best course of action would be tomorrow. Avoiding the speech entirely would likely be the safest of options, but a painfully curious part of him wanted to see how things would transpire. He felt like he was in some kind of surreal movie where a ragtag band of rebels were about to take on an evil empire.

A flash of lightning temporarily blinded Joseph. He gave his eyes a thorough rub before casting a wayward glance over to the brightly lit courthouse. He continued to watch the storm for a while as his bright-blue mug steadily collected more contaminated rain. Joseph took another drink of the tangy water before returning the mug to its perch once again and heading back to bed. He lay there staring up at the ceiling for a while, seemingly unable to switch off his brain. He eventually forced his eyes shut and focused on the soothing sound of the autumn storm outside. The rain continued to noisily strike Joseph's window, but he enjoyed the white noise. In Joseph's pre-war life he had always kept a fan on when he was trying to fall asleep as a mental distraction. Now there were no such luxuries. The rhythmic sound of the rain would have to do, and it did just fine as it gently lulled Joseph back to sleep.

***

There was no irksome knocking to disturb Joseph's sleep this time, allowing his fatigued body to determine when it was time to wake up naturally. Joseph slowly opened his eyes, which still somehow felt as if they hadn't had a rest in days. He lazily looked around the room until his bloodshot eyes settled upon the unspectacular blue mug that was still perched on his windowsill. It had finally stopped raining, but the dark cloud coverage continued to loom ominously in the sky and looked as if it were ready to expel another torrent of rain at any second. Joseph forced himself out of bed, a routine struggle, and shuffled over to his mug of rainwater. He took a sip, the water carrying the same distinct tang as it had last night, the tang that was similar to the taste of iron or blood. Joseph didn't mind; every sip of water was precious regardless of the aftertaste.

Joseph watched several droplets of rain slide down his window, occasionally conjoining with other raindrops that were also descending towards the windowsill, indicating that it had only recently stopped raining. He couldn't even fathom a guess as to what time it was, as the sun was completely concealed behind the seemingly impenetrable coverage of clouds.

Joseph peered out of his water-streaked window towards the old courthouse. He had a great view, only having to turn his head slightly to the right. Joseph thought about the events that were likely to transpire today. Part of him wished desperately to forget about the photos, about PAR. To turn a blind eye and continue to enjoy the luxuries that Outpost Zulu had to offer. Deep down, however, Joseph knew that he couldn't turn a blind eye. He had defended murderers, thieves, and liars in his previous life. He felt as though he had been on the wrong side of justice one too many times. Maybe today he could put a stop to his pattern of defending the supposed 'bad guys' because it was easier or more lucrative to do so. He had made a living off deceit and manipulation, and now he had absolutely nothing to show for it, only the persistent guilt that he carried within himself. Today he could join Aaron's revolution and finally be a part of something bigger than himself, for the greater good. Joseph could be a hero.

Joseph took another sip of water, savouring the liquid, and gave his head a shake. Delusions of grandeur would get him nowhere. Survival was a gift granted to those who thought logically and selfishly. Sticking your neck out for others was a good way to get your head chopped off. Still, Joseph couldn't help but admire Aaron. A man doing what he thought was right in a world completely void of morals. Risking all the comforts that he had been provided with, and potentially even his own life, to take a stand against forces that he saw as truly evil. The photos that Aaron had shown Joseph were irrefutable proof that there was an inherent darkness surrounding PAR. The untimely death of Richard and the disappearance of those photos gave Aaron's cause for action more credibility and indicated that PAR did in fact have something to hide. As much as it pained Joseph to do so, he had to admit that PAR could not be trusted.

Joseph threw his head back and gulped down the remainder of his water. He decided to leave the mug on the windowsill, just in case it happened to rain again. Joseph turned to head for the door when he caught something out of the corner of his eye and froze. Right where his head had been, just moments prior, was a small pile of hair. His hair. He rubbed the back of his head and looked at his hand—now full of hair. This hadn't happened before; Joseph always had thick luscious hair that all the barbers used to compliment him on. He frowned, looking at the fistful of hair in his hand. His days were numbered and he knew it. He couldn't even imagine how much radiation he had been exposed to over the last two years. Ironically enough, he felt pretty good today. He was hungry, but that distinct pang of hunger was just a part of Joseph's daily existence and for once it was not accompanied by nausea.

Joseph left the room, trying to ignore his uncharacteristic hair loss. He locked the door behind him and paused in the hallway across from room 315. Poor Aaron. Joseph doubted that he had slept at all last night and he wondered what the guards had done with Richard's body. He took a deep breath and walked over to Greg's room. Greg answered the door almost immediately after Joseph knocked, as if he were expecting him.

"Morning, Greg," Joseph said as cheerfully as he could.

"Hey Joseph," he replied, somewhat groggily.

"I've come for the tuna," Joseph said as his stomach noisily growled on cue.

"We also have a can of baked beans which might be more suitable for breakfast," Greg said with a yawn.

"Yeah, that works. I'll go see if Hillary is hungry too," Joseph said.

Joseph knocked on the next door to the left. Hillary was much slower to answer, and when she did, her blond hair seemed to defy the laws of gravity, sticking up in every possible direction. She lazily rubbed the sleep out of her dark-brown eyes.

"Want some breakfast?" Joseph asked, his stomach rumbling once more.

"Do you even have to ask?" Hillary replied as she pushed past Joseph and headed towards Greg's room.

The two entered Greg's room together and watched Greg struggle to open the can of baked beans with a knife. It was a crude technique, but Greg was eventually able to expose the savoury beans. Nobody had bowls or utensils, so the group sat cross-legged on the floor surrounding the can of beans like a group of campers surrounding a warm fire on a cold winter night. They wiped their hands as best as they could on their grimy clothes and ate directly from the can by hand. It was messy, and quite frankly gross, but it was also delicious. The trio polished off the can in a few minutes like a small pack of feral dogs. Joseph wiped his now sticky fingers on the very bottom of his filthy jeans. He was surprised that he didn't get sick more often, with the lack of sanitation and all. He had chalked up his relatively good health to the absence of germ-spreading people. Although right now, he'd rather have a stuffy nose than lose his beautiful hair.

"Quite the storm last night," Greg remarked.

"Yeah, that was crazy!" Hillary exclaimed, her eyes full of wonder.

"Yeah," Joseph said before changing the topic to something much more serious. "Guys, something happened last night. You remember that little short guy named Richard who was overseeing us when we picked out our guns?"

"Don't...don't say 'overseeing'. It reminds me of that guy," Hillary said with a shudder.

"Sorry," Joseph apologized with a cringe, also not enjoying that word any more. "But you remember who I'm talking about?"

Both Hillary and Greg nodded.

"Okay...well, he was killed last night. It's possible that he killed himself, but I highly doubt it. All of the evidence seems to suggest that there was foul play involved, that it was a murder of sorts. Not just that, but the pictures have gone missing too," Joseph informed them.

"What? How?" a cross-legged Greg asked.

"I don't know. Aaron barged into my room last night. He thought I did it at first," Joseph replied.

"You would never!" Hillary said with confidence.

"I know, and he knows that now too. Apparently he came back to his room shortly after we left and found his window smashed, with Richard's body lying in the street below, surrounded by guards," Joseph informed his friends. The trio was still sitting on the floor surrounding the now empty can of baked beans.

"Do you think he jumped?" Greg questioned, the same thought that Joseph initially had.

"I thought so at first too, but Aaron was adamant that Richard wasn't that kind of guy. Plus, why wouldn't he just use a gun? It would have been much easier and probably a lot less painful. Even then, that still wouldn't explain why the photos went missing. Aaron claims that they were best friends and that Richard supported him fully." Joseph leaned back on his hands, his legs also still crossed.

"It's PAR! It's got to be!" Hillary shouted abruptly.

"Well, we don't know that for certain…" Greg began but was cut off by Joseph.

"No, I think she's right. I've been thinking about it a lot and it's becoming harder to deny that PAR can't be the good guys."

"So what? Are you going to join Aaron's crusade now?" Greg spoke with sarcasm, a tone that Joseph wasn't fond of.

"I'm at least going to see what happens today. I want to hear what the Commander has to say and I'm also curious to see if Aaron will follow through with his plans," Joseph answered.

He had no doubt that Aaron would at least attempt to follow through. The truth was that he was also genuinely interested to see how PAR could possibly attempt to justify the kidnappings and inhumane experiments to an outpost filled with residents ready to grab their pitchforks and torches. It reminded him of when he had to try to defend one of his clearly guilty clients against a bloodthirsty jury in search of sadistic forms of justice.

"I'm going to the meeting, or speech, or whatever it is too," Hillary declared.

"You two are just asking for trouble," Greg muttered.

"Greg, relax, it'll be fine. We'll just hang out near the back and if things get violent we'll slip back to the hotel," Joseph said reassuringly.

"Alright, alright, fine. But how about we visit the bar again for a little pre-game drink?" Greg suggested.

The trio unanimously decided that a little pick-me-up was in order and headed out. Joseph, Greg, and Hillary were going to need every drop of liquid courage they could get their hands on.

Chapter 13

Setting the Stage

Commander Ventress tightened the Velcro straps on the sides of her black bulletproof vest. The vest was heavy, but she had grown accustomed to the weight. The weight of the cumbersome vest was a comforting reminder that she was protected, similar to the sense of security that a child suffering from anxiety would receive under the familiar heaviness of a weighted blanket. She then slipped into her black leather trench coat. The coat was not weathered, as Ventress ironically wore it inside the majority of the time. Today, however, it looked as though more rain would be in the forecast and that her jacket would become more than just a fashion statement. The heavy black clouds appeared to bulge with precipitation, building up to a satisfying release of frigid autumn rain that was sure to come.

Ventress began to do up the large black buttons; the coat had been designed as a piece of luxury apparel rather than a practical jacket. As a result, the top button resided just below Ventress's chest. But instead of a provocative sight, the top of the thick bulletproof vest that protected her internal organs stole the spotlight. Over the top of her heart on the jacket was a single letter, the letter 'V' stitched in gold that she had sewn on herself. She also wore a pair of nicely fitted cargo pants, although the lengthy trench coat extended down to her knees, effectively covering most of her lower half. She had recently polished her black combat boots, the toes reflecting any glimmer of light that shone down upon them.

She ran a brush through her long black hair, ensuring that there wasn't a single knot or tangle to be found. As a kid, other children had often made fun of her dark hair and fair complexion. They had said that she looked like a crazy old witch. As Ventress got older she grew into her looks, as people often do. She also grew into somewhat of a sadistic monster. As soon as she turned 18 Ventress had joined the military, a typically honourable and courageous profession. However, unlike most of her comrades, Ventress did not join to protect the free world and fight for democracy. She couldn't care less about those things. Ventress joined because she was filled with an unquenchable lust for blood that had tormented her from a very young age.

She had chosen the infantry division and saw heavy combat before she was 20. She loved every second of the battlefield. The thrill of knowing that her life could end at any moment was exhilarating, and the power that she felt when she took a life was intoxicating. Her prowess on the battlefield was chalked up to be the utmost form of valour, swiftly propelling her through the ranks. As she continued to climb the hierarchical military ladder, she saw less combat and more bureaucratic work. It had bored her half to death, but the pay was good. It was through the military that she had been able to connect with Alexander Reznoff, an ex-Soviet general who had fled to Canada. The Post-Apocalyptic Republic was Reznoff's brainchild. One lonely Friday night, Ventress had charmed Reznoff over a handful of 'work-related drinks'. One thing led to another and before she knew it Reznoff was practically begging her to lead the military department of PAR.

Ventress had been reluctant to leave the Armed Forces at first, but PAR was generously funded through private investors and was much more lucrative, so she agreed in the end. She agreed just in time too, as nuclear tensions between the US and Russia were escalating exponentially. Reznoff gave Ventress full control over the military, including recruitment. Ventress initially focused on recruiting soldiers who had prolific track records in combat, such as Reaper, but she quickly had to become more lenient as to who she recruited as nuclear Armageddon began to appear imminent. When the nukes finally started to fly, PAR wasn't even close to being ready. Half of the members were still scattered across the country and never made it to the bunker. Once it was time to transition from the planning phase to the action phase, it became clear that Alexander Reznoff was unfit to lead. At least it was clear to Ventress.

Reznoff had been holed up in his quarters for weeks, suffering from a complete mental breakdown and leaving PAR without a competent leader. Ventress had seduced Reznoff to finally open his thick steel door and to let her in with the rather provocative promise that she could help take his mind off things. Once they were alone inside the vault-like room, Ventress alleviated Reznoff's worrisome thoughts by blowing his brains out with her golden .50 handgun. She had set the crime scene up to appear as a suicide, even leaving a sappy suicide note on his desk. A handful of Reznoff's loyalists had suspected that Ventress was behind his death, but they were a small minority. With Reznoff out of the way, Ventress had been able to assign emergency military power to herself and promptly deal with Reznoff's remaining loyalists, silencing their loose tongues once and for all. This emergency power was only supposed to be temporary, but days turned into weeks, and weeks into months. So now here she was, the leader of a Post-Apocalyptic Republic that she could run however she wanted. Ventress had seen first-hand what humankind was capable of and she recognized that people needed to be told what to do. Free will is what ended the free world. So, through superior military technology and pure force of will, Ventress would tell the new world how to act and they would listen to her like a bunch of domesticated dogs.

Ventress put the little brown hairbrush back into her upper desk drawer, beside her stash of whiskey and her now partnerless crystal glass. Maybe if she told the people the truth then they would understand that what she was doing was in their best interest, that she could protect them from external threats and create a sustainable long-term outpost, one that resembled a pre-war life. Her work was almost complete and soon she wouldn't need any more involuntary volunteers for her experiments. She would be able to create a singular enhanced warrior worth more than an entire section of highly trained soldiers. She was so close to perfection, and Klein was living proof of that. No, she thought, stick to the script. Their feeble minds could never understand the bigger picture. If humans were wired for bigger-picture thinking, elected leaders wouldn't have destroyed the planet.

Ventress shuffled through a few cue-cards that she had kept in her outer trench coat pocket. She genuinely hoped that the locals would believe her, or at the very least be wilfully blind to what had occurred at the outpost. She wanted these people to understand that sometimes sacrifice is necessary in order to achieve greatness. Ventress took a deep breath and glanced out the window; a light drizzle had begun to descend from the sky. She would smooth things over—the people of Outpost Zulu would believe her propagandist speech. If they didn't, Ventress would cleanse the outpost and create a new one filled with occupants who would appreciate what PAR stood for and, by extension, appreciate what Ventress stood for.

***

Klein's personal quarters in the courthouse were situated in a repurposed public attorney's office. It was much less spacious than Ventress's chambers, but it suited Klein just fine. A foldable green military cot had been placed to the left of a lopsided maple-wood desk and was equipped with a dark-green waterproof sleeping bag. The crude sleeping arrangement had served its purpose well and had blessed Klein with a good night's slumber. He was currently focused on what had been laid out on the desk for him by his commander. He had been too tired the previous night to fully investigate the gift within his room, but now he was recharged and felt like a little kid on Christmas morning. Klein stepped over to the desk and picked up a piece of white paper that held a short message written in beautiful cursive:

Klein,

It's time that you wore this in the field. I suspect that you might need it.
—Co. Ventress

Klein began to undress immediately and donned the custom-made combat suit that he had been generously gifted. The base of the suit was a tight black Kevlar-infused fabric that covered his entire body from his neck to his wrists and ankles. The fabric would prevent most small-calibre bullets from penetrating his flesh, but would offer very little cushion to soften the blunt impact a bullet would have as its trajectory came to an abrupt halt against Klein's sculpted body. In other words, a bullet might not cause life-threatening damage to Klein, but it would certainly still hurt like hell. Fortunately for Klein, the tight black Kevlar-infused fabric was only the base layer. The exterior of the suit was covered in titanium alloy plates connected by a second and much thicker layer of Kevlar, completely concealing the skin-tight base. These plates were painted a matte black with the single acronym 'PAR' painted in dark red over his left pectoral plate.

The suit also came with matching specialized boots and gloves. The top of the combat boots, also black and lined with Kevlar, joined seamlessly with the bottom of the titanium alloy plates that covered Klein's shins. The dark Kevlar-lined gloves with reinforced knuckles were similarly flush with Klein's titanium wrist gauntlets. This state-of-the-art armour would have been far too heavy for an ordinary man to wear. Even Klein, a physical specimen, would have succumbed to the cumbersome armour's weight if it weren't for his cybernetic enhancements. His artificial appendages allowed him to carry the weight with relative ease, but he could still feel the heavy armour pressing down against his muscular torso. Klein reached his armoured arms for the crown jewel of the combat suit: the helmet.

The helmet had also been painted matte black and was lined with layers of Kevlar and Twaron. There was a large, angled, rectangular visor constructed out of ballistic glass that had been tinted a dark and reflective shade of crimson red. The visor's overall appearance resembled the expression of a scowling machine. The helmet itself encompassed the entirety of Klein's head and was a technological masterpiece. On the interior of the helmet Klein would be gifted with a plethora of military gadgetry displayed on an inner visor that was made out of advanced smart-glass technology, protected by the exterior layer of ballistic glass. Night vision, infrared, target identification system, short-range radar, adaptive brightness, and a built-in air filtration system were all included. These tactical enhancements were controlled through a combination of intuitive design and basic voice commands that had been programmed to only obey Klein's distinctive voice. The wondrous combat helmet also had an exceptional battery life and was able to last nearly seven days without needing to be recharged. Klein had tested the suit out several times at the R&D facility, but he had never had the opportunity to wear it in the field. The helmet was also remarkably intuitive and could indicate escape routes, possible threats, as well as where to aim when in a firefight in order to compensate for user error. This, paired with Klein's already lethal accuracy and cybernetically enhanced limbs, made Klein the most dangerous man in the world.

Klein stood there in the middle of the old public attorney's office, feeling out the combat suit. It felt good and Klein felt powerful. He caught a glimpse of himself in the reflection in the window. He looked more like a machine than a man. He supposed that's what he was on track to becoming with his cybernetic limbs. The suit and the limbs were only just the beginning; Commander Ventress had plans to replace more and more of Klein with militarized technology, transforming him into a literal killing machine. Klein looked around the room, his reflective crimson-red visor adjusting to the various sources of generator-powered light. Klein struggled to pick up his M4A1 assault rifle that was lying on the floor beside the foldable cot. The trade-off for becoming a nearly unstoppable juggernaut was a sacrifice in mobility, a flaw that still had no workaround. Klein practised aiming at various objects around the room as he began to familiarize himself with the feel of the hefty suit once more.

Right now, standing in a cramped repurposed office, Klein was the apex predator. Not *an* apex predator, but *the* apex predator. Klein looked at his reflection in the window again. Head to toe he was dressed entirely in black, minus the splash of red on his chest and visor. The large titanium alloy plates broadened his already immensely thick frame. His technologically advanced visor made a slight adjustment and sliced through his reflection so that he could no longer see himself; he could now see only the slight drizzle of rain that had begun pattering on his window. Klein didn't need to see himself anyway. He knew what he was and what he was capable of. Klein began to inspect his weapons and ammo, humming a pre-war tune that escaped his helmet as an unintelligible mechanical rasp.

***

Alpha Squad's barracks resided within the former courtroom itself. It was abundantly spacious for the four operators and their fearless leader dubbed 'Reaper'; a codename which

Andrew Rodriguez was increasingly becoming detached from. A small handful of Captain Andor's guards were protecting the courthouse, which allowed Alpha Squad to catch some sleep and gear up together as a complete unit. Their military apparel was much less imposing than what Klein was wearing upstairs and a tad more conventional. Sticking to the theme of black, Alpha Squad was dressed in combat gear similar to that of your traditional infantry soldier. Kevlar vests, combat boots, ballistic helmets, and a plethora of pockets. Each soldier had a black balaclava that they could optionally wear underneath their helmet, but the face covering was only mandatory for Andrew. If he were to be identified by someone in the crowd, Commander Ventress would have even more questions to answer, like why PAR had an undercover agent sneaking around the outpost. Rex, Beetle, Wolf, and Ghost were loading their weapon clips and bantering. Andrew was unusually quiet, slowly loading each bullet with tactful care.

"What's up, Reaper? We usually can't get you to stop running your mouth," Wolf probed in good humour.

Andrew snapped out of his trance and asked, "Why'd you join PAR?"

Andrew's question was directed at Wolf, but the remaining three soldiers ceased their chatter.

"I got recruited like the rest of us," Wolf answered with an uncomfortable laugh. Despite all the time that the squad had spent together, they rarely deviated from mission-related topics or banter. It was easier that way; all five men had suffered enough personal loss to last at least three lifetimes.

"Yeah, no kidding. But why'd you take the contract? You could've kept fighting overseas, working your way up the ranks. Why leave all that behind?" Andrew continued to ask.

"Money," Wolf said gruffly.

"Yeah, and how's that working out for you?" Ghost remarked with a snarky tone.

"I joined because I thought I could be a part of something bigger than myself. To maybe help those in need if the world went down the drain. Kind of the same reason why I joined the army." It was Rex who spoke as he continued to load his magazines without looking up.

"Of course it's the medic with some sad sap story." Beetle laughed, prompting everyone except for Rex and Andrew to laugh too.

"No, he's right," Andrew said sharply. "Yeah, the money was good, but I joined because I could see that nuclear warfare was inevitable. We all could. I wanted to be a part of building humanity back up, protecting the weak."

"What's your point, Reaper?" It was Wolf who asked, clearly not sharing the same values as Andrew or Rex.

"My point is that most of us, deep down, signed up so that we could do some good. Maybe to make up for the bad shit that we did prior to the bombs dropping, or maybe 'cause we're damn good people." Andrew could feel his pulse thumping in the side of his neck as he spoke.

"Why're you bringing this up right now?" Beetle asked as he pushed his glasses further up the bridge of his nose.

"Boys, I saw the pictures. I spoke with Ventress. PAR has been abducting people from this very outpost and using them for these sick medical experiments. Hacking off their limbs and shoving mechanical appendages into their torsos so that Ventress can make human-machine hybrids. We ain't the good guys we thought we were." Andrew's guard was completely down now, letting everything come out.

"That's a bunch of garbage," Ghost said, waving a dismissive hand in the air.

"Why would I lie? I know what I saw in those photos. And you know that stick-in-the-mud, Klein? He's living proof. His arms and legs are cybernetics. He's a freak," Andrew scoffed.

"So what?" Wolf asked, but in a way that made it sound more like a statement.

It was a good question. So what? What was to be done? It was a dog-eat-dog world now, more so than ever before. Either you hung with the big dogs or you got turned into dog chow, or in this case an ungodly scientific experiment. But was PAR really the big dog? They weren't as well equipped as the locals might think. Sure, they had a handful of aircrafts, but did any of the five birds have guns? No. The military that Ventress was so proud of consisted of fewer than 100 troops as a result of an accelerated nuclear Armageddon. Maybe PAR was just a rabid dog that needed to be put down so that a new alpha could lead the pack. It occurred to Andrew that PAR wasn't even really the problem; it was Ventress. Ever since she took command, the trajectory of PAR had done a complete one-eighty. It went from an organization designed to unite survivors under one peaceful banner to a militaristic empire hell-bent on expansion and oppression.

"I just thought you boys should know who we're protecting today. What she stands for and what we stand for by extension," Andrew replied as he went back to inspecting his weaponry. The former courtroom fell silent, and the only noise coming from within the room was the rhythmic sound of bullet cartridges being loaded into M4A1 magazines.

***

There was a small shack that had been constructed out of various sheets of rusted tin and wooden planks of all lengths. This shack was situated to the right of the entrance to Outpost Zulu on the interior of the wall and acted as a makeshift guardhouse for the PAR security force. Guards could store their equipment here in between watches and take refuge when the weather was particularly unpleasant. The shack could comfortably hold about five men plus their kit. There were presently ten guards crammed into the lopsided shack, one of them being Captain Andor, who was briefing his security force about the day's duties.

"Alright, men, listen up." Andor spoke with authority. "The Commander will be giving her speech in about thirty minutes. We've gotta round up the townsfolk and make sure we get a good turnout."

"Or else what? Is she gonna make us disappear too?" one guard said with an eye-roll, prompting multiple guards to snicker.

"Shut your mouth," Andor barked. "If all this goes smoothly, there's a bunch of promotions on the line."

The snickering stopped on account of the promise of promotions.

"Yeah, that's right. Don't screw this up and we could finally get the hell out of this outpost," Andor said enticingly.

There were murmurs of approval now.

"Still doesn't make her any less of a witch!" a female guard near the door shouted.

"Yeah, surprised she's even giving her speech in the rain—she might melt!" another guard chimed in, followed by a couple of laughs.

"I couldn't care less what any of you think. If it weren't for her, you wouldn't have guns or even a wall to protect you. Do your damn job and you'll be rewarded," Andor declared, shutting down any more snarky remarks.

"You, you, and you," he continued, pointing to the few guards that he actually trusted, "come with me. We're going to clear out the bar. It's going to be busy, so keep your eyes open and stay frosty."

The three selected guards nodded in acknowledgement. Captain Andor then divided up the remaining six guards within the shack into two teams of three. Three to clear out the local shops and three to clear out the hotel the best that they could. Once Captain Andor's two groups of guards had cleared out the shops as well as the hotel, they were to link up and assist a separate group of three troops who were already hard at work clearing out the treacherous side streets. Captain Andor had placed only two guards at the front gate, figuring that his resources would be better utilized operating as crowd control. Six other guards were currently protecting the courthouse, accounting for a total of 20 security guards within the outpost under Captain Andor's command. Twenty had always been a good number for Outpost Zulu. It allowed for large rotations of ten or smaller rotations of five, the latter being more common. Today, everyone was on duty and would have to be on their best behaviour. Unfortunately, Captain Andor truly trusted less than half of the men under his command. He was well aware of their disdain for PAR, especially for Ventress. Hopefully the false promise of getting promoted out of outpost patrol would incentivize the guards to perform their duties diligently.

In truth, Andor had no idea when his security force would finally get out of Outpost Zulu, or when he would get out himself. He had been stationed at Outpost Zulu for just over a year. The guards under his command had been here anywhere from two weeks to several months. Some guards got promoted out of the outpost under Andor's recommendation and others died in the line of duty defending the outpost from raiders. The mutants typically avoided attacks on the outpost, sticking to easy prey travelling through the city. Captain Andor had not been informed yet of the fact that the infected had been converging around the outpost for months now. The guards had nicknamed the downtown strip 'The Gauntlet', as travellers who made it to that godforsaken strip had to combat both bandits and mutants alike in order to reach the outpost. There had been rumours that somewhere along The Gauntlet there was a cannibalistic cult who would cut a pinky finger off the people that they indoctrinated. Andor didn't believe such horror stories, but the city beyond Outpost Zulu's walls was certainly treacherous.

Captain Andor took his three selected guards, the three who he had been working with the longest, and departed from the dilapidated shack. It had begun to rain again, although this time it was much less intense than the torrential downpour that had come down with fury the previous night and filled the streets with large puddles. It was more of a light drizzle than a true rain, but the autumn sprinkle was bone-chilling nonetheless. The abundance of puddles were like miniature lakes in comparison to the tiny raindrops that fell into them and left little ripples in their wake. Andor and his men tried to avoid as many small lakes as they could, but eventually they had no choice but to get their feet wet.

Chapter 14

Hold Your Applause

Joseph, Greg, and Hillary strolled out of the Courtview Hotel shortly after 11:30. The miniature droplets of rain tickled Joseph's weather-beaten face as he took a deep breath of the cool, damp air. He could smell the distinct aroma of water on asphalt, a smell that he could not quite explain but a smell that brought him back to the rainy summer nights that had filled his childhood. With Joseph's head in the clouds, he was unaware of the impending puddle that he proceeded to plant his right foot squarely in the middle of. The water surged past his ankle and over the edge of his boot, chilling his entire foot before he awkwardly hopped back onto a dry patch of road. Greg and Hillary were in front of him, paying no attention to his soaking fiasco.

When the seemingly inseparable trio entered BAR, Joseph was shocked to see how busy it was yet how paradoxically quiet it also was. The group headed over to the main bar itself, which was completely empty. All the other patrons were huddled around various tables and speaking in hushed tones; the entire room was filled with a sombre aura. Big Mike glanced over at Joseph, Greg, and Hillary as they approached, but his usual carefree expression had been replaced with one of solemnity.

"Hey Mike," Greg said chipperly as he began to unsling his backpack so that he could retrieve something worthy of trading, "we're thinking three pints today."

"It's on the house," Mike said quietly as he poured two cans of warm beer into each pint glass and proceeded to slide the glasses over to the unsuspecting group.

"What's up, Mike? Why's everyone so blue?" Joseph asked as he took a sip of the warm yet strangely refreshing beverage.

"Didn't you hear what happened? With Richard?" Big Mike answered Joseph's question with a question.

"Yeah, I heard," Joseph replied sombrely.

"Well, Aaron has completely lost it—he's hell-bent on taking over the outpost. Today, like right now," Big Mike informed the trio, who already knew all about Aaron's plans.

"At the speech, right?" Hillary blurted.

Big Mike gave an approving nod as he replied. "Yeah, that's right. I love the guy and I support him—I just wasn't expecting things to kick off so suddenly, y'know? I kind of like this gig. Don't get me wrong, we've got to put a stop to this madness, but I was hoping to enjoy the perks of being in PAR's good graces for a little while longer. Does that make me a terrible person since I know what they've been up to?"

"No, Mike, that makes you a survivor. This entire thing is brainless," Greg remarked.

"Let me be clear," Mike continued as he subconsciously began to dry a nearby glass that showed no signs of dampness, "I hate PAR. They deserve to be run out of town for what they've been doing to us...for what they did to Tom. I just don't know if this is the right route to take. It's risky."

"But it's the right thing to do," Hillary said with confidence. "PAR has just become another bully! You see it in high school, in the workplace, and you saw it with our world leaders before the war. I'm sick and tired of bullies pushing everyone around."

"The girl's got more moxie than me," Big Mike said with a smirk.

"Damn straight," Hillary declared with a wink as she sipped on her beer.

"Yeah, you're right, Hillary. It's the right thing to do," Joseph agreed as he suppressed a carbonated burp. "It's easy to ignore the bad stuff until that bad stuff happens to you."

Everyone nodded in agreement. There was a whole 'out of sight, out of mind' mentality that people liked to adopt. Take cancer as an example. Nobody thinks it can happen to them until it does. Joseph remembered seeing commercials for Sick Kids and hearing stories about cancer survivors, or cancer victims. It was sad, sure, but it didn't affect Joseph's life. Until one day it did. His best friend was diagnosed with stage four brain cancer in his final year of university. Nobody saw it coming and it escalated quickly. In what felt like a blink of an eye, Joseph's best friend had ceased to exist. Just in time too, Joseph had morbidly thought; at least he didn't have to watch the world burn. Joseph figured that this whole PAR situation was kind of the same thing. Everyone who knew what was going on thought it was horrible, but until someone they personally knew was victimized they could just continue to indulge in the luxuries that PAR provided and turn a blind eye.

"This thing might get rough," Big Mike said, interrupting Joseph's line of thought. "Maybe you three ought to lay low until this blows over."

"My thoughts exactly, thank you!" Greg exclaimed.

Joseph was beginning to realize the severity of the situation and was starting to second-guess his idea of attending the speech. The entire outpost was like a metaphorical nuke prepared to blow at any second. Joseph was listening in on the conversations behind him, hearing whispers of 'a new era' and 'payback'. The outpost had reached its boiling point, and Joseph and his companions were about to get splashed by the scalding waters. Before any further conversation could be had, the doors to the bar barged open with a tremendous crash. A lanky man dressed in a black hoodie and cargo pants was accompanied by three PAR guards; all four men were toting M16 assault rifles.

"Alright, time to clear out! Make your way to the courthouse — let's go!" the tall man barked. His three companions were wild-eyed and twitchy as if they were expecting a fight.

"Or else what? You gonna shoot us?" an intoxicated woman shouted.

"Don't be stupid, lady! It's a quick little speech—it won't kill you. Now let's go!" Captain Andor shouted, his voice booming despite being such a slender man.

"Let's go, ladies and gents!" It was Big Mike's turn to deliver a command with booming authority. "I won't tolerate any fighting in my bar!"

The crowd, respecting Big Mike's authority more than Captain Andor's authority, began to shuffle out of the bar, collectively grumbling as they did so. Two of the guards went onto the street to make sure that everyone was shuffling over to the courthouse and not whatever crevices they had emerged from. Eventually the bar was cleared out except for Joseph, Greg, Hillary, Big Mike, Captain Andor, and one additional guard.

"You four, let's go!" Andor ordered.

"Listen, I think we're going to sit this one out, big guy. We want to finish our drinks," Greg said as he locked eyes with Andor. Even Hillary had gotten cold feet about attending the speech, and a sick feeling in her stomach was now present.

"Listen to the Captain! We have our orders!" a stocky guard with an M16 shouted, definitely a PAR loyalist. He raised his gun, flicking the safety off.

"Whoa, whoa, whoa! Easy there, tough guy!" Big Mike boomed as he raised his hands and turned to face the nervous trio seated at his bar. "It's probably best we all get going without a fuss. Just stick close to me."

The group slowly got up off their tattered bar stools, but not before the three friends gulped down a bit more liquid courage first. Big Mike led them out of the bar, while Captain Andor and the other guard followed behind, making sure that the group did not deviate from their designated course. As Joseph and company were marched down the street by Captain Andor and his goon, Joseph focused on not plunging his feet into another puddle. As he walked with his head hung low, he could begin to hear an unintelligible hum of voices, the kind of steady buzz that you would hear in a food court in the centre of a busy shopping mall. Joseph looked up to see a large crowd of people gathering just below the courthouse steps. He hadn't seen this many people in one place since prior to the nuclear war and he couldn't help but wonder where they had all been hiding for the last couple of days.

Joseph, Greg, Hillary, and Big Mike kept marching onwards until they merged with the mass of people, becoming one single living organism. Captain Andor and three of his guards began to spread out behind the crowd, keeping an eye on things. Joseph surveyed the large gathering, his small stature doing him no favours, and searched for Aaron. He couldn't pick him out anywhere, and Joseph guessed that there had to have been close to a hundred people packed into the crowd.

"Jeez, Mike, where were all these people hiding?" Joseph asked with a bewildered expression.

"In my bar!" Big Mike answered with an out-of-place thunderous laugh. "In all seriousness, a lot of the long-term locals shack up in the abandoned buildings off of the side streets. Out of sight, out of mind."

Out of sight, out of mind, Joseph repeated in his head. He continued to survey the crowd, becoming aware of the fact that they were completely boxed in by local security guards on each side of the large gathering, and he wondered how many guards were actually still watching the front gate. There were five soldiers dressed entirely in black about halfway up the white cobblestone steps, separating the front of the crowd from the entrance. They looked significantly better equipped than the local security guards and carried an air of professionalism.

"Hey, aren't those the guys from the farm?" Hillary asked excitedly.

"You're right! It definitely is!" Greg exclaimed.

Hillary and Greg were acting as if they had just spotted a group of long-lost friends instead of a squad of hired mercenaries working for an inherently vile organization. Joseph recalled how relieved he had felt after they had come to the rescue like real-life superheroes. Now he wasn't sure what he felt. Fear? Anger? Excitement? The precipitation falling from the sky began to pick up, the gentle drizzle turning into an irksome light rain. A large group of stragglers that had been collected from the nearby side streets were escorted to the back of the crowd, putting a couple rows of people between Joseph and Captain Andor's guards. The constant hum of the crowd came to an abrupt halt. Joseph peered over the mass of heads in front of him, having to rise up onto his toes to get a clear view, and watched as the courthouse doors swung open.

***

Commander Ventress anxiously paced back and forth across the length of her chambers with her hands clasped firmly behind her back. She was well prepared to deliver her speech, and her contingency plan was set if things went south. Despite what her subordinates might think about her, Ventress knew that violence couldn't solve every problem that she encountered. She did believe, however, that violence was a viable solution for most situations. The less-than-stellar relationship between PAR and the residents of Outpost Zulu was one of those rare situations that Ventress would prefer to resolve peacefully rather than resorting to acts of hostility. She was determined to avoid any unnecessary bloodshed at all costs. Ventress was ready to do whatever needed to be done in order to fix negative relations between PAR and Outpost Zulu, but if push came to shove she was also willing to make the entire problem disappear. She sincerely hoped that the locals would be receptive to her message; it would be in their best interest.

There was a firm knock on her door, followed by a deep, raspy voice.

"Ma'am, it's time."

And so it was. Ventress walked purposefully towards her door and opened it to reveal the towering mechanical menace that was Klein. His broad frame was exaggerated by the combat suit and he took up the entire doorframe. Klein towered above Ventress as the light from her office glimmered off his dark, crimson-red visor.

"I see you found my gift," Ventress remarked as she looked Klein up and down, quite impressed with the imposing figure standing before her.

"Yes," Klein said, his voice barely recognizable. "Thank you."

"Remember your job, Klein. You are to protect me at all costs. Trust no one...not even our own." Ventress looked confidently up into Klein's visor, attempting to make eye contact.

"Yes, Ma'am, I will assume anyone and everyone to be a threat. I will not let you down," Klein replied with authority.

"I know you won't. That's why you have this," she said, gesturing to his grandiose armour.

The determined duo made their way down the courthouse hall and towards the grand spiral staircase that would lead them down to the main floor. The walls were lined with pictures of former judges and attorneys, their smiles bright yet artificial. The floor was covered with a dark burgundy carpet, the kind that would get lighter or darker depending on which direction a misplaced footstep happened to scuff it from. The height difference between Commander Ventress and Klein was nearly a full foot; Klein was a formidable 6 foot 4, but the combat suit generously inflated that number to about 6 foot 7. The lopsided pair made their way down the spiral staircase, Ventress's left hand running gently along the elegant granite handrail. They made it to the bottom of the stairs and paused at the front door for a moment.

The stage had been set and everyone was in position. Alpha Squad would be Ventress's frontline of defence, keeping their eyes on the crowd. Captain Andor's security force had the crowd boxed in from every angle; if anyone tried anything uncalled for, they had permission to open fire. Klein would be Ventress's shadow and keep an eye on everyone, including Andor's shaky security force. Ventress had her two pilots standing by at the CS50 aircraft in case she had to make a hasty departure. All she had to do now was manipulate a collection of belligerent locals and smile. How hard could it be? Commander Ventress took a deep breath and opened the heavy courthouse doors, strutting out with confidence and determination.

***

Andrew was scanning the crowd and looking for possible threats. The irony was that the entire crowd looked like a possible threat. Virtually everyone appeared hostile as they wore a combination of misery and anger on their gaunt faces. Andrew wondered how many of these people knew someone that Ventress's goon squad had abducted for ungodly experiments. His rifle's safety was switched off, but his index finger was placed tactfully away from the trigger. Rex had approached Andrew privately after they had finished gearing up in the old courtroom. He had told him that at the end of the day he took orders from Reaper and that he'd stick by his side, regardless of what happened. Andrew 'Reaper' Rodriguez wasn't so sure about the remaining three members of Alpha Squad. The group had bonded extensively over the last few months, but these were difficult times where doing the right thing was often just a luxury of the past.

Andrew noted that Captain Andor's guards looked shifty and nervous. They weren't well trained and their loyalties were up in the air right now. Ventress's speech would not just need to woo the general crowd; it would also need to have a substantial impact on the local guards, who had spent as much time in this outpost as any citizen in the crowd had. Alpha Squad had been given a very simple mission brief: 'Neutralize any hostile threat. Lethal force is allowed.' It didn't matter whether or not that threat was one man with a knife, or several men with guns. Neutralize any potential threat and keep the Commander safe at all costs. The Commander who was responsible for what the former world would consider to be crimes against humanity. Reaper had his orders and good soldiers followed orders, but Andrew Rodriguez was not just a good soldier. He was a good man.

***

A striking woman dressed entirely in black emerged from within the old courthouse, her long black hair and lengthy, black leather jacket flowing gracefully behind her in the cool autumn breeze. She walked with confidence to where a battery-powered microphone had been set up at the top of the stairs, protected from the light rain by a large cobblestone awning that was previously a beaming shade of white but was now more of a dreary grey eyesore. Joseph's eyes widened in awe at the towering mechanical menace that followed closely behind her. The lethal-looking man-machine hybrid was a stark contrast to the exquisite lady who was currently adjusting the microphone to better match her height.

"What *is* that thing?" Joseph whispered to Big Mike.

"I'm not entirely sure," Big Mike replied, while not taking his eyes off the large enforcer.

The woman in black finished adjusting the microphone, observed the crowd, and then finally spoke.

"Residents of Outpost Zulu, I am Commander Ventress, leader of the Post-Apocalyptic Republic. I stand here before you today seeking to repair damaged relations through transparency and candor."

There were a few murmurs among the crowd. Ventress spoke clearly and with an inherent authority that made Joseph feel as though he were a kid again listening to a lecture by the school principal.

"I have been informed that a terrible rumour has been spread about PAR by radical anarchists who seek to destroy all the positive progress that we have worked tirelessly to achieve," Ventress continued. "It deeply saddens me to know that there are people out there who would rather keep civilization in tatters than see a new and safe republic be built."

"Liar!" an anonymous voice from within the crowd shouted.

Ventress clenched her jaw tightly before continuing.

"I want to assure everyone here, guards and residents alike, that PAR has been created to benefit and serve the people. We seek to rebuild a safe and civil society; we are friends of the common folk and mean no harm to any of you. Whatever defamation you may have heard about us, I assure you it is not true. Yes, we conduct experiments in the field of medicine, but no differently than previous medical professionals did before the bombs dropped.

"We have been working tirelessly to create treatments for radiation sickness, treatments that can help prevent people from falling ill and perhaps even reverse the damage done to the truly deranged sick that live just beyond these walls. We have worked on perfecting medical procedures designed for treating people with grievous injuries. This very outpost has gotten a taste of these medical advancements; our doctors have provided excellent healthcare to all of you."

"Where are the doctors now? Where's Doctor Tellick? Have you made him disappear too?" another unidentifiable voice called out.

"Doctor Tellick has been sent back to headquarters to continue his research; his rotation here is over. I assure you I will have another doctor take his place when his scheduled rotation comes back around," Ventress replied, while maintaining her intrinsic charm.

In reality, Dr Tellick was clinging to life in a mouldy jail cell 15 feet beneath the old courthouse and precisely underneath Commander Ventress's gleaming combat boots. She had deliberately left her knife in his back, both as a reminder of his betrayal and to limit his blood loss before he could be taken back to the R&D facility where he would be disposed of properly. Blood still managed to ooze out from the wound around the blade of the knife, and his body was dangerously close to entering shock. Dr Tellick knew better than anyone else that his chances of survival continued to plummet with each passing hour.

"As a token of goodwill, I will personally ensure that this outpost receives a large shipment of anti-radiation medication that has just passed all of its trials, and we intend to supply the outpost with goods for free, moving forwards. That means you will no longer have to trade for essential services such as food, water, and medical aid," Ventress declared with a seductive smile.

There were hushed whispers of excitement and Ventress surveyed the crowd triumphantly; everything was proceeding according to plan.

"What about the pictures?" a woman cried out.

"I have heard about these supposed pictures and I assure you that they are not from us. I have yet to see any compromising pictures, but if they are real, I assure you that they have been falsified by radicals," Ventress replied with a calm and collected demeanour.

"Bullshit!" A man's voice rang out near the front of the crowd, a voice Joseph recognized as Aaron's. "We got the pictures from one of your doctors! Doctor Moetsky!"

Ventress took a moment to collect her thoughts before giving her rebuttal.

"Doctor Moetsky is an anarchist; he has been plotting the downfall of the Post-Apocalyptic Republic from the very start. He is a brilliant young scientist and a master of deception. He was recently removed from our affiliation after we discovered that he had poisoned one of his superiors in order to attain a higher position of power. Moetsky always despised what PAR stood for and I would not put it past him to spread lies, or falsified photos for that matter, so that he could drag our reputation through the mud. He is the kind of man who is perfectly content to watch the world burn and hoard our supplies for himself. He believes that PAR should be completely self-sufficient and separate from the outside world. That is why he wanted to turn folks against PAR. Moetsky wanted to forcibly drive a divisive barrier between PAR and the rest of the remaining population, making positive mutual relations impossible and forcing PAR to operate purely internally with no contact with survivors who are not members of our organization. I will not let that happen, I promise you. PAR is here to help everyone."

Ventress lied effortlessly and there were approving whispers throughout the crowd. Aaron could tell that he was starting to lose supporters. It was becoming easier and easier to dismiss tangible evidence and believe false promises. Ignorance is bliss.

"Then how do you explain Tom? A lot of us knew him, and he was in the photos, the photos that you had stolen from my room last night when you had my friend Richard killed!" Aaron roared.

There were more whispers, these ones filled with anger and hatred. Whispers that escaped the lips of those loyal to Aaron and those who knew Tom or Richard.

"I assure you that any likeness to someone you may know is purely coincidental. The photos are not real and I certainly did not have anyone killed, or even harmed for that matter. PAR exists to serve you, the people," Ventress declared as she gestured to the crowd.

"You're full of lies!" Aaron screamed.

"Tom was real and so were those photos!" another man shouted.

"You had Richard murdered!" an unidentified woman yelled.

"I saw your guards take my little brother away!" a belligerent voice cried out.

The volatile crowd was shifting like a pendulum, buying into Ventress's speech for one moment and then wanting revenge the next. Right now, the pendulum was all the way back on the revenge side, and Aaron was about to take full advantage of the hostility that was brewing once more. Aaron reached into his waistband and drew out a snub-nosed revolver. He got two shots off before a single bullet, courtesy of Klein, popped his skull open in a burst of red mist. Aaron fell back at the exact same moment that Ventress collapsed behind the microphone, clutching at her chest. Various screams rang out among the crowd, but everyone stood frozen in place, anxious to see what would happen next.

Klein crouched down beside Ventress, who was gasping for air. Her bulletproof vest that had been concealed beneath her fashionable trench coat had done its job well, catching the two bullets that should have ended her life. The shots had been fired from such a short range that the impact of the bullets colliding with the Kevlar had cracked three of Ventress's ribs, but she was otherwise okay. Klein offered her a hand, which she swatted away as she forced herself to her feet on her own accord. Alpha

Squad was scanning the crowd with their guns raised, but the mass of bodies made it exceptionally difficult to identify potential shooters. Another bullet flew from the crowd, this one glancing off Wolf's ballistic helmet.

"Second shooter!" Wolf shouted, but the squad couldn't locate the source of the shot.

Another bullet whizzed by Ventress, smashing into the cobblestone pillar inches to her left. Klein stepped in front of her, his visor locating the shooter within seconds and allowing him to take an effective shot. Multiple members of the crowd looked to flee the scene, but found themselves staring down the muzzles of the M16 assault rifles being held by Captain Andor's guards. Ventress pushed Klein out of the way and grabbed the microphone once more.

"I came to you today offering peace and prosperity!" Ventress wheezed as she clutched at her broken ribs. "We are not your enemy! The radicals among this crowd who seek to undermine everythi—"

Yet another bullet was shot from somewhere within the crowd, and this one found its home in Ventress's left shoulder. Without hesitation Ventress ripped her golden .50 Desert Eagle handgun from its holster, which was located on her left side beneath her jacket, and fired several rounds in the direction of the gunshot, striking numerous unarmed bystanders in the process.

"Open fire!" she barked, the microphone picking up her voice that was now filled with blinding rage.

"We don't have a clear shot!" Andrew shouted.

Ventress shoved her pistol back into the holster and ripped the M4A1 from Andrew's hands despite her recently acquired injuries, emptying the clip into the mass of bodies in front of her and setting off a vicious chain reaction of events. Captain Andor and a handful of his guards began firing wildly into the crowd from all angles. Numerous locals who were caught in the crossfire drew their own weapons, weapons that they had acquired either through the hole in the eastern wall or by smuggling them past intoxicated guards, and returned fire. Some of the guards began to turn on one another and it became impossible to tell which ones were fighting for or against PAR. Wolf, Ghost, and Beetle started taking aimed shots at the armed citizens in front of them.

Andrew and Rex took cover behind one of the thick cobblestone pillars near the top of the stairs, Andrew now only armed with his sidearm. Klein shielded Ventress with his nearly indestructible body and started escorting her back up to the courthouse. The crowd surged forwards and up the steps, forcing Wolf, Ghost, and Beetle to open fire on full auto at the moving mass of bodies. A slew of bullets sent from the furious crowd struck the trio of Alpha Squad soldiers from almost every direction and sent them tumbling down the hard cobblestone steps. Their bodies were trampled as the enraged gunmen and gunwomen began running up the courthouse stairs. Andrew and Rex fell back into the courthouse after Ventress and Klein, locking the heavy doors of justice behind them.

Chapter 15

Curtain Fall

Everything had happened so fast. When Aaron shot Commander Ventress and subsequently was killed himself, all Joseph could do was blink in disbelief. Aaron had been so adamant on assassinating the Commander and Joseph had believed him, yet this moment had come as an absolute shock. When Aaron was shot down, Big Mike shouted out in rage and began pushing himself closer to the front of the crowd, his intentions unknown to Joseph, Greg, or Hillary, but his apparent fury was well known. Two more shots were fired from the crowd in rapid succession, and the mechanical menace quickly incapacitated whoever the second shooter was in a similar fashion to how the machine-like man killed Aaron—with lethal precision. The Commander was back on her feet and reaching for the microphone once more.

"Time to go," Joseph said to his companions, and neither of them had any objections.

It seemed like numerous onlookers had the same idea in mind as a large portion of the crowd turned to flee down the main street. Captain Andor and his guards foiled their plan quickly as they cocked their M16 rifles, commanding the crowd to stay put. It was now that Joseph began to realize that his demise might be on the very near horizon.

"Come on!" he shouted to his friends. "Let's get closer to the middle, away from the guns!"

The trio pushed through the crowd, putting more and more human shields between themselves and Captain Andor's firing squad. They were only a handful of rows deep when Commander Ventress was shot a third time in the middle of her sentence about "...offering peace and prosperity". The infuriated Commander returned fire into the crowd in the blink of an eye and Joseph instinctively ducked even though the bullets were far in front of him and off to his right.

"Open fire!" the Commander's enraged voice rang out, amplified by the nearby microphone.

Joseph looked up just in time to see a wild-eyed Commander Ventress beginning to fire a machine gun from her hip into the crowd. People started to scream and seemingly every second person was reaching for a concealed weapon of some kind. The PAR guards were now firing blindly into the crowd—bodies were dropping left and right. Three people immediately behind Joseph collapsed from bullet wounds of varying degrees of severity; none of them were dead yet, but they were all closer to death than life.

"Get down, get down!" Joseph shouted as he grabbed Hillary by the back of the neck and rather forcefully shoved her onto the growing pile of writhing bodies behind them.

Greg took the hint and dove down as well, covering Hillary with his large body. Joseph hit the asphalt hard and his shoulder found yet another puddle, only this puddle wasn't the same blackish-grey colour as the previous puddle he had stepped in. No, this puddle was an opaque brownish red, almost like an oil spill. Only it wasn't oil; it was blood that had leaked into the irradiated waters from the surrounding dead bodies that continued to rapidly grow in numbers. Joseph lay there with half of his face stained red with the blood of strangers, bullets whizzing over the top of him and plunging into nearby survivors. Joseph could see two guards wrestling over a rifle near the back of the crowd, only 20 or so feet away. The bigger of the two wrenched the rifle free and shot the smaller guard point blank in the face, his head exploding like a watermelon that had been dropped from a great height. The victorious guard then turned the muzzle on another PAR guard, only to catch a bullet to the back from Captain Andor, who then proceeded to fire into the crowd a little too calmly as if he had done this before.

A bullet sent from one of the Outpost Zulu locals struck Captain Andor just above his left kneecap, sending him down to one knee. Captain Andor was not done fighting and he continued to fire, even taking a moment to reload so that he could continue sending small projectiles of death into the crowd. Joseph slid his hand into his jacket, feeling the eroded hilt of his Colt 1911. He focused on Captain Andor as he began to slowly draw his pistol, while remaining relatively hidden from behind the corpse that he was lying beside. Joseph pulled his pistol up and awkwardly aimed, while still lying on his right side. He took a deep breath and slowly squeezed the trigger. Captain Andor raised a hand to his chest and looked around for the shooter. Joseph shot again, his bullet this time making it through Andor's neck. Andor dropped his rifle, now on both knees, and clutched his throat so tightly that it looked as if he were trying to choke himself. Blood spewed between his dark fingers, dripping into the nearby pools of water. Andor finally located the shooter, locking eyes with Joseph for what felt like an eternity.

Joseph watched Captain Andor fall over onto his side, neither man breaking eye contact for even a second. That's how Captain Andor died, locking eyes with a stranger in the crowd until his soul finally left his body. Andor was too surprised to be afraid; everything seemed surreal. He stared into the bright-blue eyes of the man who had shot him for a few more moments, while lying on his side, and then he released his final earthly breath. Joseph began to shake uncontrollably, still clutching his pistol. The shooting was dying down and people were beginning to flee in every direction. Joseph felt as if his brain had detached itself from his body and was floating up into the sky; his vision began to narrow and lock in on Captain Andor's now emotionless face, his chocolate-brown eyes void of all life.

"Joseph! Joseph!" Greg shouted as he shook Joseph by the shoulder. "Joseph, are you okay?"

"Yeah. Yeah, I'm good," Joseph replied numbly as he rapidly blinked his eyes and tried to ground himself back into reality. Hillary had sat up and her huge brown eyes were gobbling up the carnage. She did not cry or speak; she was simply taking it all in.

"I'm hit, Joseph, I'm hit! Those bastards got me," Greg shouted.

"What?" Joseph responded with a dumbfounded look.

"My back, I can't see it. How bad is it?" Greg nervously asked.

Joseph gave his head a shake and forced himself off his side, now crouching in the expanding pool of blood that had soaked his clothes as well as half of his face.

"Turn around," Joseph instructed Greg, who was kneeling next to him.

Greg turned around and allowed Joseph to examine his wound. A large gash travelled the length of his shoulder blade and partially down his back. Whichever bullet Greg had been hit by had fortunately only grazed him. The laceration was deep and narrow. It wasn't life-threatening, but an infection would be easy to come by if the wound was not properly treated.

"You'll be okay, Greg. The bullet just grazed you, buddy," Joseph assured him.

"Just grazed me? You say that like it doesn't hurt like hell," Greg scoffed, but Joseph could hear the relief in his voice.

"We should get something to clean the wound and cover it up. There's a medical tent nearby," Joseph suggested.

Joseph cautiously rose to his feet. Those who had not been shot had now dispersed and the gunfighting had come to an end just as abruptly as it had started, allowing Joseph to embrace the full extent of the carnage that had accumulated around him. Dozens of bodies were scattered throughout the street, some squirming in pain and others not moving a muscle. A small group of PAR guards were attempting to tend to the wounded, including the guards who had defied their orders and turned on their former brothers-in-arms. The street was literally running red with blood as the dark-crimson substance that leaked from bodies had mixed with the flowing trickle of rainwater. Joseph watched a group of a dozen or so men and women pound on the courthouse doors. A couple of innovators were attempting to climb the tall iron-rod fence off to the side that protected the back of the courthouse, but they had no success; the skinny iron poles were impossibly slick from the persistent rain. They kind of reminded Joseph of the Orvilles, desperately trying to catch their prey in a blind frenzy of bloodlust. Joseph could see the dark-green tent down the road and off to the left of the courthouse with the universal medical aid symbol: a red cross with a white background.

Greg offered his hand to Hillary, who took it without saying a word as he helped her to her feet. She looks shell-shocked, Joseph thought, and quite frankly she probably was. A handful of people were weeping, crouched next to their fallen friends and family. One of the PAR guards tried desperately to stop the bleeding coming from the stomach of an elderly lady, only to realize that she had succumbed to her injuries long ago.

"Don't look down, sweetheart. Keep your eyes on the tent," Greg said in a fatherly voice to a traumatized Hillary.

Hillary tried to obey the simple instruction that Greg had given her, but she kept tripping over various human appendages, some of which were attached to corpses and others that were connected to soon-to-be corpses who were crying out for help. Greg couldn't believe how quickly everything had happened. One minute he actually caught himself buying into the Commander's speech, and the next he found himself caught in the middle of a warzone. Ventress had been persuasive. She had an excuse for everything and she was good at making people forget about what had been going on. At least Greg thought so. Now he saw what Commander Ventress was capable of, what her subordinates were capable of. There was no remaining shred of doubt in Greg's mind that PAR was just as much an enemy as mutants, bandits, or cannibalistic psychos. The trio stumbled past a PAR guard who was holding the hand of a young boy as his life essence drained from a hole in his chest. Greg immediately went back on his previous thought. Commander Ventress was the enemy—PAR was just stuck in her stranglehold.

The trio carefully made their way through the minefield of bodies, taking great care to avoid stepping on anyone, either living or dead. The medical tent wasn't far, but progress was slow. Joseph could see the group of vigilantes had resorted to ramming the massive doors to the justice building with their bodies. The failed innovators had given up on climbing the slick iron fence and had joined them. To Joseph's surprise, the doors actually seemed to be giving way. It was truly remarkable what a collective of strong-willed and hate-fuelled individuals could accomplish, such as decimating an entire planet for example. He could hear the engine of the large aircraft parked out back firing up and Joseph assumed that the tyrannous Commander would live to see another day. Her life was of no concern to him now. His priority was reaching the flimsy green medical tent that was flapping fiercely in the wind that had begun to howl with a vengeance as if Mother Nature herself had been enraged by the bloodshed. All Joseph cared about was making sure that his friends were okay; he cared more about their lives than anyone else's, including his own.

***

Andrew and Rex slammed the hefty courthouse doors shut behind them and turned the pair of deadbolts into the locked position. The locked doors would certainly slow the lynch mob down, but it was only a matter of time before they forced their way through. Ventress had dropped the empty assault rifle by the door and was currently struggling to reload her pistol. Her left hand was drenched with her own blood that had trickled down the smooth sleeve of her leather trench coat from the oozing wound in her shoulder. She cursed beneath her breath and winced in pain as the new clip of ammo slipped from her grasp, clattering to the floor. She retrieved another clip of ammo from the interior of her coat, the prospect of bending over with three cracked ribs too daunting, and finally managed to reload her signature golden gun. Klein watched the cumbersome courthouse doors shudder under the impact of the angry crowd who were trying to barge their way through.

"What the hell was that?" Andrew shouted as he stormed furiously over to Ventress. "You got three of my men killed!"

"You can thank those ungrateful animals for that. They're the ones who shot first," Ventress snarled. Andrew and Ventress were nose to nose now.

"Maybe they were right to shoot first, you bitch." Andrew unleashed all of his fury into a single punch that connected squarely with Ventress's petite nose, sending her backpedalling.

Klein raised his M4A1 assault rifle and aimed it at Andrew. Rex aimed his matching rifle at Klein, forcing Klein to deviate his attention from Andrew and aim back at Rex instead. Both of Ventress's nostrils were spewing blood; she wiped her nose with the back of her hand that held her gold pistol, only to slightly interrupt the flow of blood before it continued streaming profusely once again. She could taste that familiar metallic flavour of blood on her lips and smiled, the dark-red liquid staining her typically pearly-white teeth.

"Andrew, Andrew, Andrew. What happened to you? You had so much potential. I could've given you everything you could have ever possibly wanted," Ventress said in a scornful tone, although she sounded much less assertive now as she spoke; her broken ribs and shattered nose gave her voice a sickly congested drawl.

"I'm not going to be a part of your savagery any more, Ventress. You will pay for what you've done," Andrew growled.

"What I've done?" Ventress fell into a bout of maniacal laughter that escalated to the point where even Klein cast her a subtle glance of concern from behind his visor. "Have you forgotten who you are? What you do? You collect souls for a living, Reaper, you always have. You follow orders like a good boy and you've never once hesitated to pull the trigger."

"You're right, Ma'am, pulling the trigger has never been an issue," Andrew said coldly.

In a blur of rapid movement, Andrew fired his pistol wildly from the hip and sent a barrage of bullets towards Ventress. Most of the shots slammed into her bulletproof vest, but one lucky bullet found its way through her trapezius muscle that connected her left shoulder to her neck. Ventress fell to the ground and landed on her back, temporarily stunned by the overwhelming amount of pain that had been suddenly inflicted upon her. Klein turned to shoot Andrew, only to be met with an aggressive burst of gunfire from Rex's assault rifle that struck his right shoulder and the side of his head. None of the bullets penetrated the armour, but it was enough to temporarily stun Klein and crack his ballistic visor. Andrew turned his gun on Klein to finish the job, only to have a bullet whizz cleanly through his right calf muscle—courtesy of the wounded Commander who was currently lying on the floor in a growing pool of blood. Andrew's pistol clattered to the floor as he collapsed, clutching at his lower leg. Klein turned back to Rex, who was now desperately trying to clear an untimely weapon jam. Klein effortlessly swatted the gun out of Rex's hands and delivered a bone-crushing kick to his chest, sending him careening across the slick marble floor and incapacitating him as he whacked his head off the unforgiving tiles.

Andrew, now on all fours, lunged for his pistol. Ventress fired another shot while still lying on her back; this time the bullet sloppily removed four fingers on Andrew's right hand. Andrew howled in agony as Klein kicked the pistol out of reach and quickly moved to assist the grievously injured Commander Ventress. Her left arm was completely immobilized as a result of the shoulder wound, paired with the more recently acquired bullet hole that had completely torn her trapezius muscle apart. Over half of her 24 ribs had been broken and she coughed up a blackish splash of blood, indicating that at least one of her lungs had likely been pierced by her broken ribs. Klein offered his hand to help Ventress to her feet, and this time she took it. She could hardly move and Klein more or less just yanked her to her feet like a ragdoll.

The once seemingly secure doors were rocked as another violent surge of enraged locals smashed against the already battered entrance. The massive courthouse doors bulged inwards, looking ready to burst open at any second. Ventress stood over the top of Andrew and looked down at him in disgust as he looked back up at her with hatred in his eyes. She attempted to belittle him but couldn't manage any words; instead an involuntary gob of blood fell from her mouth and splashed across his face. That would suffice, she thought. The compromised doors that separated Ventress from an angry mob hunting for her head were visibly cracked now and the wood itself was starting to creak. Ventress was consumed by pain and fury as she fired a barrage of bullets at the doors. Multiple shots penetrated the thick wood and struck unsuspecting vigilantes who were on the other side. She then aimed the pistol at Andrew, who was clutching his mutilated right hand while still defiantly looking up at her from his knees. His face was splattered with Ventress's internal blood, his eyes full of resentment, and his demeanour entirely feral.

"Do it, you coward," he hissed.

"My"—Ventress wheezed painfully as she tried to speak—"pleasure."

She squeezed the trigger, but her last shot had already been sent through the courthouse doors just moments prior in her characteristic episode of blind rage.

"Time to go, Ma'am," Klein said as another surge of bodies collided violently with the doors.

Ventress gave Andrew a forceful kick to the face, sending him sprawling backwards and giving him a broken nose that matched her own. She suppressed a yelp of pain as the motion from the kick sent shockwaves of agony throughout her entire torso. She moved as quickly as she could down the long marble hallway towards the back door. Klein kept a hand on her back, gently ushering her to move faster. She heard the doors finally submit to the will of the people with a thunderous bang followed by an outburst of shouting. Ventress began to jog down the hall, her left arm dangling uselessly by her side and her vision beginning to cloud. The back door leading to the once flourishing field of wildflowers that had hosted countless lunch breaks for courthouse staff, and where the CS50 was currently parked, was only a few more feet away. Klein stopped and turned, firing shots at the group of vigilantes who had breached the courthouse and were in pursuit. They returned fire, but their real target, Commander Ventress, was already outside and quickly shambling towards the aircraft. The pilots had pre-emptively begun firing up the engines shortly after hearing the gunfire and had also lowered the ramp.

Ventress collapsed on the cold metal ramp, the gentle incline being too much for her ravaged body to handle. Klein barged through the back door and sprinted over to the aircraft with inhuman speed, his protective armour proudly wielding multiple scuffs from bullets that were unable to penetrate his combat suit. Klein grabbed his commander by the collar of her jacket, dragging her up the ramp and into the large cargo bay. Through the windows that lined the back wall of the courthouse, he could see the gunmen and gunwomen barrelling towards him. He opened fire while on one knee, his body acting as a human shield for the now unconscious Commander Ventress.

"Get us out of here!" Klein roared as he continued to shoot through the glass windows and the livid vigilantes began to return fire once more.

The thrusters of the CS50 engaged and the aircraft slowly began to levitate while the loading ramp started to fold upwards. Just before the ramp could fully protect Klein, a well-placed shot from Big Mike struck his already compromised visor. The visor shattered, destroying both the durable ballistic glass and the fragile smart glass beneath. Jagged shards were sent careening into Klein's face, and his right eye was deeply gouged by a particularly sharp piece of glass. He let out a guttural shout of pain as he fell back and the landing ramp was finally sealed, creating a thick metal barrier separating Klein from any more gunfire. The aircraft continued to ascend for several more moments, before the thrusters fluidly adjusted their trajectory and propelled the aircraft forwards at a tremendous speed, transporting the tattered Commander Ventress and her bloodied enforcer to the unholy R&D facility.

***

Andrew was lying on his back stunned and in a great deal of pain. His eyes were involuntarily watering and he could feel his nostrils forcefully expelling blood, which made him want to sneeze. He forced himself to slowly sit up and watched his assailants make their getaway towards the back door. Ventress was shambling like a bona fide zombie and Andrew doubted that she would survive the flight back. He looked down at his right hand, finally having a chance to thoroughly examine the damage. His thumb was completely unscathed, but all four of his remaining fingers had been sheared off to make one flush line of bloody nubs that were situated just above his knuckles. His mangled fingers, or lack thereof, spewed blood and it felt as if his entire right hand was engulfed in flames. He swore and clutched at his injured fingers, the pressure only making the pain worse. Andrew's wounded calf throbbed and felt unnaturally hot, but the pain was still less than that of his amputated fingers.

A thunderous crash rang out behind Andrew, temporarily distracting him from his physical trauma. He looked over his shoulder, still clutching his right hand, and watched as a surge of a dozen or so firearm-toting vigilantes busted into the lobby of the courthouse. Members of the bloodthirsty group were armed with various pistols, and their heads were on a swivel. It only took them a few seconds to catch sight of the immoral duo rapidly retreating to the back door.

"Over there!" a man almost as large as Klein bellowed.

"Don't let them escape!" a tough-looking woman with a buzz cut and face tattoos shouted.

The crowd flowed past Andrew as if he were just a slightly inconvenient stone that had been placed in the middle of an otherwise obstacle-free stream. Their quarrel was not with Andrew, at least not yet. The angry mob started to charge down the hall, a few of them absorbing bullets from Klein and collapsing mid-stride. The crowd would not be denied and returned fire as they continued their pursuit all the way to the back door, where another firefight broke out.

"Reaper!" a voice yelled from Andrew's left.

Rex was quickly making his way over while rubbing the back of his head and struggling to catch his breath.

"Reaper, you okay, man?" the medic asked instinctively, despite seeing Andrew's agonizing wounds.

"Yeah, never better," Andrew said with a grimace.

Rex knelt down beside Andrew and examined his injuries. Rex was still dazed from smashing his head on the floor, but over a decade of medical experience in the field had made his movements automatic. He reached into one of his various pouches and retrieved a wad of gauze. He grabbed Andrew's mutilated right hand by the wrist and began tightly wrapping his bloodied nubs. Andrew winced, but did not protest. Rex wrapped what was left of his fingers tightly together, the white gauze already starting to turn red.

"Keep your fingers pointed to the sky," Rex instructed Andrew as he moved on to address his injured calf.

"The bullet went clean through your leg—you're lucky," Rex informed Andrew after a brief inspection of the leaking wound.

"Oh yeah, I feel lucky," Andrew replied sarcastically as he watched the gauze that encompassed his entire right hand take on a sickly reddish-brown hue.

Rex began cramming balls of cotton into both the entry and exit wound in order to slow the bleeding.

This time, Andrew did more than just wince. "Shit!" he yelped as he instinctively pulled his leg away, only to be hit with another searing flash of pain emitting from his calf.

"Don't be a baby—come here," Rex said unsympathetically as he gently pulled Andrew's leg back towards him. Rex plugged up both holes and began wrapping the gauze around Andrew's calf. He then removed his helmet and set it on the ground, allowing Andrew to prop up his maimed leg. Andrew's vision had blurred from the intense pain of having cotton balls shoved into his bullet wound and he was struggling to stay conscious.

"Wait here," Rex said as he got to his feet, his hands now covered in Andrew's blood.

"Where are you going? I don't think that mob will be too happy to see me when they return," Andrew said nervously.

"To get a doctor, a real one. Just hang tight—you'll be fine," Rex assured him.

Rex took off in a slow jog down the hallway to the right, leaving Andrew alone by the courthouse entrance. Andrew glanced over at the pool of blood that Ventress had left behind. Even her blood seemed toxic and unnatural as it covered the expensive marble stone. Andrew grimaced; both his hand and calf were simultaneously throbbing uncontrollably. It felt as if he had a second and third heartbeat in his wounds. He was beginning to feel light-headed and nauseous. Andrew focused on taking deep breaths and not slipping into unconsciousness, although he certainly wanted to. He was not in a safe place to rest. Andrew slid his foot off Rex's helmet, which sent a wave of blinding pain shooting up his entire leg. He cursed and began to slowly slide himself across the slick marble floor towards his pistol that Klein had kicked a generous distance away.

Andrew couldn't see the CS50 take flight, but he could hear it. The firefight that had broken out by the back door promptly came to a halt as the powerful thrusters on the aircraft were engaged, allowing Ventress and Klein to escape the clutches of the bloodthirsty mob. Andrew was beside his pistol now, which he retrieved before continuing his painfully slow butt-scooch over to a cream-coloured pillar that had been erected to support the floor above. Andrew used the pillar for exactly what it was intended to be used for: support. He leaned back on the pillar and allowed the sturdy construction to keep him upright, squeezing his eyes shut as the room began to spin. Then he removed his headgear and balaclava—he was finding it suddenly hard to breathe. He could hear the stampede of vigilantes making their way back down the hall towards the main entrance.

"Hey, look over there!" a voice shouted angrily.

"Get him!" another belligerent voice chimed in.

Andrew forced his heavy eyelids open and saw two gunmen running over to unknowingly finish Ventress's dirty work. Andrew was just about to raise his pistol in defence, but his left arm didn't want to cooperate. What's the point, he thought. If he didn't die today, he would surely die in the coming days from infection or blood loss. At least he would die thinking that he took Ventress to the grave with him. One final soul that Reaper had collected. One of the men snatched the pistol from Andrew's limp left hand.

"Any last words, PAR scum?" the man jeered as he aimed Andrew's own pistol at him.

"Wait!" a familiar voice boomed. "Calm down, son."

A massive man shoved the vicious gunman aside and crouched down in front of Andrew, who was struggling to keep his eyes open in order to maintain eye contact. Andrew vaguely recognized the behemoth of a man—it was the bartender who had served him the day prior. Big Mike never forgot a face and he recognized Andrew from the bar too.

"I served you yesterday, at my bar," Big Mike said as he studied Andrew's menacing complexion. Most of Andrew's face was concealed by a bushy jet-black beard, but the limited skin that was showing was painted in blood. He had messy black hair that was just slightly too long for most military standards, but still short enough to squeak by the less stingy regulations that PAR had.

"Bourbon," Andrew muttered.

"Bourbon, that's right. You're pretty banged up. That woman do this to you?" Big Mike asked.

Andrew nodded. "You should've seen what I did to her."

"I saw her do a faceplant about halfway up the ramp to the aircraft," Big Mike remarked with a deep chuckle.

"Music to my ears," Andrew smirked.

"Is it safe to assume you ain't with PAR no more?" Big Mike asked with a mischievous grin.

"Yeah, you could say that," Andrew answered wearily.

"I say we kill him!" the second gunman hissed. "Make him pay for what he's done!"

Big Mike stood to his full height, towering above the thin pair of furious gunmen.

"Why do you think this guy was shot up? It wasn't for protecting that Commander, I'll tell you that. We're going to need all the help that we can get around here now that PAR is gone." Big Mike spoke with commanding authority.

"But he's PAR!" the other angry gunman protested.

"He was and now he's not. Now piss off—go help the wounded. Better yet, go make sure anyone is even still watching the front gate," Big Mike ordered.

"Fine, whatever." The angry man obliged, but not before shooting Andrew a hate-filled glare as he and his partner departed.

Most of the crowd had calmed down now that Ventress was gone and they had no one left to focus their hate on. There were a handful of injured people lying in the hall that led to the back door being comforted by fellow vigilantes. Most of them would die soon; Klein was too efficient to leave survivors.

"Mike, Mike! We're losing him!" someone crouching over a blood-soaked body shouted.

Big Mike lumbered off and left Andrew to suffer alone in silence once more. He tried desperately to keep his fingers 'pointed at the sky' but he could feel his energy quickly slipping away. The gauze that was wrapped around his four amputated fingers was now more black than red. On the bright side, the bandaging surrounding his calf looked to be holding up a bit better.

Andrew wasn't left alone for long as Rex suddenly appeared by his side.

"Come on, buddy, let's get you moving," he said as he threw Andrew's left arm around his shoulders, hoisting him up and allowing him to stand on his good leg. Andrew couldn't bear any weight whatsoever on his right leg, so he leaned heavily on Rex. Once Rex had him facing the entrance, Andrew could see a doctor stumbling over the front doors, now lying on the floor as a result of the rage-fuelled mob. He only caught a glimpse of the doctor for a second, but the long white lab coat was unmistakable. So was the streak of blood stemming from an apparent knife wound at the base of the doctor's left shoulder blade. Rex helped Andrew make his way to the front door as Andrew hopped on his left leg while keeping his right hand close to his chest.

"What happened to him?" Andrew asked with a grunt as he continued to hop along with Rex's support.

"Ventress," Rex scoffed.

"What a bitch," Andrew sneered as the two battle-buddies made their way out of the courthouse and back into the refreshing perpetual autumn rain.

At first the cold droplets of rain stung tremendously as they soaked into Andrew's wounds, but quickly the cool water began to feel somewhat soothing. The wind had picked up significantly and he suspected another November storm was well on its way. Andrew and Rex stood at the top of the cobblestone steps for a while, taking in the carnage that surrounded them. There were bodies all over the street, and the puddles had been tainted with blood. Rain continued to steadily fall from the sky, which partially cleansed the pavement but also mixed bodily fluids with rainwater to create an abundance of vile concoctions. The wounded were being tended to by a variety of locals and a handful of security guards who had turned on their uniformed comrades when Ventress had given the command to gun down the crowd. Andrew could see his three fallen comrades piled in a heap at the bottom of the slick staircase. Rex helped Andrew slowly hobble his way down the precarious stairs until they were standing in front of their deceased brothers.

Andrew removed his arm from around Rex's shoulders and slumped onto his knees. Rex slowly turned the corpses over onto their backs, their lifeless eyes gazing up to the heavens. Wolf, Ghost, and Beetle had succumbed to their various gunshot wounds before they had even made it to the bottom of the stairs. At least that's what Andrew made himself believe; it was a far better death than being trampled or bleeding out slowly on the street in the rain. The bodies were pumped full of holes, holes that no longer released any more red liquid. Their open eyes were macabre and made Andrew nervous; he anticipated that one of his fallen squad mates would crack a smile at any moment and start bantering with him. There would be no more banter — they were never going to experience any kind of emotion again. Andrew began to close their eyes one last time with his good hand.

"Rest easy, brothers," he said as an unfamiliar lump formed in his throat.

"Those bullets weren't meant for them," Rex said as he wiped a tear disguised as a raindrop from his cheek. "They were for Ventress."

"I know, and I hope to God that I killed her," Andrew replied as he forced himself to stand on his good leg, his injuries now seeming insignificant.

"C'mon, let's get you patched up," Rex said as he allowed Andrew to lean on him once more.

The two shaken-up soldiers slowly made their way through the street lined with corpses, grievers, and soon-to-be corpses. Andrew kept his eyes locked on the dark-green medical tent flapping in the wind and recited a silent prayer inside his head.

Chapter 16

Aftermath

Joseph, Greg, and Hillary were almost at the medical tent now. They had heard a series of muffled gunshots coming from within the old courthouse, and Joseph couldn't help but wonder what was going on behind the large wooden doors that had so far held up against the onslaught of bodies trying to force their way inside. The medical tent was within throwing distance when a cluster of bullets ripped through the massive hardwood doors to the courthouse and struck multiple vigilantes. The act of violence only further emboldened the group as they continued to throw themselves against the resilient doors. Finally, after a few more collective body slams, the once protective doors of justice gave way to the furious mob. The trio paused to watch the rush of people surge into the courthouse. The aircraft out back, which Joseph had heard firing up moments prior, had yet to depart; perhaps the vigilantes would administer justice to the notorious Commander after all. Joseph could hear the increasingly familiar sound of gunshots coming from within the courthouse yet again, and he visualized a scenario that could be transpiring where the exquisite Commander went down in one final blaze of glory.

The shooting dragged on for a while and Joseph began to wonder if there had been a hidden unit of PAR operatives lurking within the confines of the courthouse in the event that something like this were to occur. Before he could contemplate any further, the massive CS50 aircraft ascended above the courthouse and hastily departed from Outpost Zulu. The familiar sound of gunshots subsequently came to an end, giving way to cries of loss and pain once more. Joseph preferred the sound of gunshots to the alternative. The group of friends continued on towards the medical tent.

"Do you think they got her?" Greg asked as he helped guide Hillary around a deceased security guard who had soiled himself.

"Hopefully," Joseph replied, although not really caring all that much. What's done was done; nothing could change that now. Joseph was more focused on the future and what it had in store for them.

The group approached the entrance of the medical tent and it was absolute bedlam. There was a gaggle of wide-eyed folks stuffing their pockets with medical supplies, either for themselves or for the wounded that were unable to reach the tent. A teary-eyed woman with curly hair who appeared to be in her late forties, although it was impossible to tell as people aged horribly these days, clutched a bundle of sterilized bandages and a bottle of peroxide. She bumped past Joseph, only to be stopped by a man clutching at his left arm as blood escaped between his fingers.

"You can't take the whole bottle, lady! Give me that!" he said, reaching for the bottle of bacteria-killing liquid with his good arm.

"No! Get away, I need it!" she screamed as she tried to run off.

The man grabbed her wrist, jerking her back and halting her forward momentum. Before he could do anything else, the wild-eyed woman spun around and plunged a hunting knife into his stomach as she clumsily dropped most of her stolen supplies. The man released her and stumbled backwards. As he did so, the knife slid out of his stomach with a sickening squelch. He looked down in horror and dropped to his knees.

The woman's face matched his terrified expression. "My baby, I'm coming!" she cried out as she quickly retrieved the medical supplies that she had dropped and ran off towards the scene of the massacre in front of the courthouse.

Neither Joseph, Greg, nor Hillary said a word or moved to help the dying man. Instead, they stepped over his body and entered the medical tent. Joseph pocketed a roll of gauze and took a couple of disinfectant wipes. The trio huddled together near the far left corner of the tent, trying to avoid the panicked people who were sporadically coming and going. Joseph and Hillary helped Greg remove his tight shirt to reveal the gash that the bullet had left on his back. It wasn't terrible, but it was bad enough that it needed to be looked after, especially if he were to avoid an infection. The bullet had grazed Greg from the top of his right shoulder blade and made its way halfway down his burly back before continuing on its course.

"I can do this part," the once aspiring nurse said.

"Are you sure?" Joseph asked, somewhat relieved since he had no medical experience whatsoever.

Hillary nodded as she took the gauze and disinfectant wipes from Joseph. The excess blood made the wound appear worse than it really was. Hillary wasted no time, quickly wiping down the wound with the alcohol-based wipes. Greg held back a cry of pain, but a faint hissing sound escaped between his clenched teeth. Once Hillary was satisfied with the cleanliness of Greg's laceration, she began to wrap the gauze over his shoulder and around his torso, effectively dressing the wound. She did a good job, a much better job than anything Joseph could have done, and the wrapping actually looked semi-professional.

"We'll want some extra bandages and disinfectants, y'know, for changing the dressings and such," Hillary said, admiring her handiwork.

"Thanks, kid. You would've made a good nurse," Greg remarked as Joseph helped him ease back into his shirt.

"I know," Hillary replied, forcing a smile.

There was a babble of chatter coming from the entrance to the spacious medical tent. Joseph looked over to see an ashen-faced doctor being followed by an entourage of desperate people in need of medical aid. The doctor looked around in horror at his ransacked medical headquarters. He was a nervous man who required order. Everything needed to be in its designated place. If something did not have a designated place, Dr Tellick would ensure a special place would be created in accordance with his pre-established order.

"Everyone, please," the doctor pleaded with exasperation. "I can only help one person at a time! If you are well enough to stand, there are likely others in more dire condition who need my help first."

The entourage of medical aid seekers did not let up; some people were literally tugging on Dr Tellick's lab coat. Dr Tellick stumbled forwards, not looking too great himself. He turned to face the growing crowd filled with terrified faces, revealing his own wound to Joseph and his companions as he did so. "The doc needs a doctor," Joseph remarked.

The crowd began to part like the Red Sea as three armed security guards escorted two PAR operatives dressed entirely in black over to a nearby cot. One of the operatives was badly wounded and leaning on his similarly dressed partner, unable to bear weight on his right leg. The bandages on the injured man's right hand were beginning to come undone and he left a thin trail of blood wherever he walked. The crowd closed back up and continued to pester the wobbly doctor as the former PAR affiliates eased the bloodied man down onto the cot.

"Those are the guys from the farm, the same ones we saw on the courthouse steps," Hillary whispered to her companions.

Once Andrew had been placed on the cot, the three security guards approached the growing crowd surrounding the doctor.

"Back up, back up, everyone! Back up! We need to form a triage!" one of the guards shouted.

"Or else what—you'll shoot us too?" one man shouted.

A few members of the crowd began to draw their weapons. The three guards looked at each other briefly and then tossed their weapons onto the ground, where they were quickly snatched up by the locals.

"We're not with PAR any more and we played no part in what happened out there!" the guard claimed.

"We had to fight our own men to keep as many of you alive as we could!" a second guard added.

"But we still need to maintain a level of order!" the second guard continued. "We only have one doctor and only God knows how many wounded. If you can walk, you need to go help retrieve those who cannot!"

Multiple people began to grumble and lower their weapons, but made no move to leave the doctor alone.

"Please, people, listen to them! I too was an affiliate of PAR," Dr Tellick said, "before I knew what they were up to. We were blinded by lies and secrecy, but I assure you that we want to help! We are on your side."

Perhaps it was Dr Tellick's inherently non-threatening demeanour, or maybe people still respected the authority of a doctor. Whatever the reason, the crowd began to disperse. A handful of injured folks hung out by the entrance, as others rushed to retrieve the more grievously wounded people that lined the blood-filled street.

"You three should help gather up the wounded as well," Dr Tellick said as he turned to the guards. "Might help those uniforms look a little less...evil."

The guards unanimously agreed and were eager to start making things right. They were about to leave when Dr Tellick stopped them.

"And boys, please be smart," he added. "Not to sound callous, but use a bit of discretion. Don't bring me the ones who are knocking on death's door. I'm a doctor, not a priest."

The three guards nodded at the exact same time like a single machine before scurrying off. Dr Tellick turned to face Rex, observing the dark-red cross on his right shoulder.

"Before I can help your friend here, or anyone else for that matter, I'm going to need some help myself," Dr Tellick declared.

"Yeah, Ventress stuck you pretty good," Rex remarked as the doctor lay down on his stomach on the cot next to Andrew. "Can one of you three give me a hand?"

Rex was asking Joseph, Greg, and Hillary. Hillary quickly walked over to the medic before anyone else could respond. With a pair of surgical scissors, Rex widened the hole that had been created in the lab coat by the knife, allowing him and Hillary to slip the coat off the doctor. The doctor's bloodstained undershirt would be much harder to salvage, and Rex carefully cut the shirt off. The wound was slowly expelling both blood and pus; it was not a sight for those with weak stomachs. Joseph and Greg both sheepishly avoided looking directly at the wound. Removing a blade embedded in the human body was tricky business, but fortunately for Dr Tellick the pocketknife that Ventress had stabbed him with had a relatively short blade.

"I don't believe the knife struck the axillary or cephalic vein. Still, the bleeding will increase exponentially once the knife is removed. One of you will need to immediately disinfect the wound. Once that is complete, one person will stitch while the other dabs away any excess blood." Dr Tellick spoke as if he were giving a lecture to a couple of med students. His voice was surprisingly calm given the considerable amount of pain he was about to endure.

"Ready, doc?" Rex asked as he reached for the handle of the knife and Hillary cracked open a bottle of peroxide.

"Let's get this over with," he muttered in response.

Rex quickly removed the short blade, and the wound began to ooze with fresh blood that the blade had been preventing from escaping. Hillary quickly began to rub the blood away with a sterilized wipe and applied small splashes of peroxide to the wound as she did so. She was a bit more thorough cleaning the doctor's wound than she had been with Greg's injury given the fact that Dr Tellick was clearly battling the early stages of infection. The doctor groaned in pain but remained very still.

Once the wound was thoroughly cleansed, Hillary applied firm pressure to the injury while Rex retrieved his suture kit from one of his limitless pockets, a kit specifically designed for closing up lacerations.

"She's a natural," Joseph whispered to Greg.

"She sure is," he agreed.

Joseph and Greg watched in admiration. The small and seemingly vulnerable girl that they had both felt responsible for protecting was putting them both to shame as they continued to squeamishly look away. Rex had begun administering the stitches; Dr Tellick had always believed this to be the most uncomfortable part. The entire process took less than 15 minutes, but it was a rather unpleasant 15 minutes for Dr Tellick. All things must come to an end, including the torturous procedure of having a knife wound cleansed and stitched closed.

"You did great," Rex said to Hillary as the doctor slowly eased back into his lab coat. His lack of undershirt that exposed his thick chest hair gave him the appearance of someone who would give you a two-for-one special on the black market for human kidneys.

"Thanks," she replied shyly.

"We could use all the help that we could get right about now," Dr Tellick said to Hillary as he nodded at the first of many wounded who were being brought into the tent.

"Yeah, okay. I can help," she said instinctively.

"Great! Stick close to me and you can give me a hand," Dr Tellick said before turning to Rex. "If you could deal with some of the lesser injured patients, that'd be fantastic."

"Yeah, no problem. You better patch my guy up real good though, doc," Rex said as he nodded at Andrew, who returned his nod of respect.

"Don't worry, he'll be in good hands. I think that young man over there could use a medic," Dr Tellick prompted as he pointed at a teenage boy who had been unfortunate enough to catch a bullet to his foot. "Stabilize as many as you can. We'll take care of the rest the best that we are able to with what this tent has to offer."

Rex hurried off to assist the young boy as Dr Tellick and Hillary moved over to Andrew. The doctor began to unwrap the soggy bandages that covered Andrew's fingers, or lack thereof.

"If you two don't have anything better to do, I'd suggest you help round up the wounded too," Dr Tellick said without looking up. Joseph and Greg instinctively looked over to Hillary, not wanting to be split up.

"Go," she mouthed without saying anything from behind the doctor, as if she were trying to dismiss a pair of overprotective parents.

Joseph and Greg made eye contact for a moment before swiftly leaving the tent and making their way back to the grotesque horror show that had been put on display in front of the courthouse. The old building looked eerily similar to the courthouse that Joseph had taken his first case in almost five years prior when the world still had laws.

***

It quickly became clear to Joseph that the majority of those who had been shot would likely perish in the coming days. The medical tent had been equipped to deal with relatively minor injuries and illnesses, not a mass casualty event and certainly not surgery, which is unfortunately what most of the victims required. At least half of the crowd, which had consisted of almost a hundred locals, had been graciously gifted with injuries varying in degrees of severity as a result of Commander Ventress's orders and actions. Some of the wounded were more than capable of walking to the first-aid station without assistance, but others were not so lucky.

There was an older gentleman—he reminded Joseph and Greg of William—who had suffered two bullet wounds to his left leg. The lack of stretchers made transporting this individual particularly difficult and at first they had attempted to carry the man by his arms and legs. That idea was quickly scrapped as the pain of having his left leg even touched was excruciating to the elderly man. In the end it turned out that the least painful way to transport him was to simply drag him by his arms. By the time the duo had gotten the man to the medical tent, he had already succumbed to his injuries and his body had to be dragged to a growing pile of corpses situated behind the former building of justice where the PAR aircraft had been parked. This was a common occurrence. Although the doctor had advised against bringing those who were near death to his medical tent, it was difficult to ignore the desperate pleas for help. Joseph and Greg would often attempt to rescue one of the more seriously injured victims only to have them pass away before they could receive any medical care, having to then drag their limp corpses through the courthouse and out back to the growing pile of bodies.

It wasn't all doom and gloom, however. Joseph and Greg were able to successfully transport numerous people to the tent who then received reasonably successful medical attention courtesy of Dr Tellick, Rex, and Hillary. The remaining PAR guards had been hard at work with the same task that Joseph and Greg were partaking in, while some of the locals watched the front gate. The entire outpost pitched in, for the most part, but it had still been a gruelling task. The trio of healthcare providers had it the worst. Hillary was drenched in blood from various strangers; even her long blond hair had been dyed red. She was surprisingly calm despite the grotesque injuries that she was dealing with and the alarming number of deaths that occurred mid-procedure. She felt like she was finally doing something meaningful for the first time since the end of the world had begun. She was proud of herself, and so were Joseph and Greg.

Supplies had run out before everyone could be treated, which is why the triage system had been so imperative. Despite multiple protests from minorly injured individuals, the trio focused on those more seriously wounded yet realistically saveable. It was inevitable that a good chunk of survivors would soon join the corpse pile behind the courthouse in the coming days, but that pile of rotting death would've been substantially larger if it weren't for the medical aid of Dr Tellick, Rex, and Hillary, along with all those who helped out in whatever capacity they could. The final survivor was treated in the morning hours of the next day, almost 24 hours after the bloody ordeal began. It was a man who had severely sprained his ankle; his remedy was to take a couple of aspirin and to keep his leg elevated. The trio of medical workers still had to remain on duty, monitoring the more seriously injured men and women who were clinging to life on the dark-green cots that lined the tent. It had been a sleepless night for the makeshift staff working the medical tent and they were all exhausted.

Around the same time that the man with a sprained ankle was abruptly sent on his way, Joseph, Greg, and a handful of other Outpost Zulu residents began the daunting task of digging a mass grave. The rain had let up early in the night, but the ground was still soft from all the moisture. This made the digging significantly easier than if the soil had been dry, but also substantially messier. Joseph was covered from head to toe in a dreadful mixture of mud and blood, the smell of death invading his nostrils. The pile of bodies was large and would only continue to grow in the coming days, so it was imperative that they dug a generously sized grave. The group of diggers worked as quickly as their fatigued bodies would allow them to, taking brief breaks to have complimentary drinks courtesy of Big Mike. The numbing effects of alcohol made the traumatizing task a little more bearable. It took most of the morning to dig a grave large enough to accommodate the expanding collection of lifeless bodies. Most of the participants, including Joseph, weren't in particularly great shape as a result of years of malnutrition. By the end of it all, everyone was both physically and mentally drained.

Joseph and Greg had just finished tossing the final body into the deep hole to hell when a pair of former PAR security guards graciously gifted the cursed pit with one more sacrifice. The consensus was to keep the grave uncovered for a couple of days. No one said it out loud, but everyone knew that the recently forged pit of death was not yet quite full.

Joseph and Greg made their way back to the medical tent to check in on Hillary. Joseph was appalled by the sight. The interior of the tent was lined with cots occupied by both the wounded and the dead. It was easy to tell which people were dead because they were the only ones not expressing animalistic sounds of distress. The entire floor was one sticky mess of congealed blood. Joseph made eye contact across the tent with Hillary, who was cleaning the wound of a young woman. She had been grazed with a bullet similar to how Greg was shot, but this bullet had cut much deeper and was located on the side of her neck. It was a coin toss whether she was unconscious or deceased, but Joseph doubted that she would wake up either way. At least she looked peaceful, he thought.

It was Dr Tellick who finally persuaded Hillary to take a break, a real break, not pretending to rest on a cot next to a collection of dead or dying men and women of all ages. He assured her that there would still be plenty to do in the coming days and that she would be more valuable to everyone if she recharged her batteries. The filthy trio left the tent together as the sun continued to rise and walked back to the Courtview Hotel. The lack of running water had made cleaning up next to impossible, forcing the shaken-up group to take the blood of the fallen to bed with them. Joseph didn't actually make it into his bed; he collapsed on the floor next to it instead. He was so drained that the floor could have easily been a squishy mattress in a five-star hotel. Joseph desperately wanted a hot shower, a luxury that he had once taken for granted in his previous life. He lay there on the floor, in his filth, and prayed for more rain to come so that he could wash the remains of the dead away from his body.

Chapter 17

New Beginnings

Ventress forced her eyelids open to reveal her dazzling emerald-green eyes that were amplified by the harsh fluorescent lights shining down on her. She squinted slightly on account of the bright lights and lazily looked around the room. She was in the middle of an operating room, lying on a surgical table. The room was silver and sterile; a nearby tray with medical instruments was stationed to her right. She examined the silver metal tray that matched the silver room and saw that the tools were still clean. Her entire body ached tremendously and every breath that she took was achieved with a gruelling struggle. Ventress reached a trembling right hand to her left shoulder and felt gauze that was congealed with blood; her gaping wounds had been packed tightly with the absorbent material. She winced. Even the slightest touch was unbearably painful and a bullet was still deeply embedded in her shoulder. She wondered where everyone was and why she had not yet been properly treated.

Ventress felt as if she had been sedated; the entire room seemed to be spinning, and simply touching her untreated wounds had been a great feat of strength. She tried to speak but her voice was too hoarse. For the first time in her life, Ventress was completely vulnerable. It wasn't a feeling that she enjoyed and a swell of anger mixed with panic rose up from deep inside of her. She tried to call for help, to order someone to come help her, but again nothing escaped her mouth other than an inaudible whisper. She thought about Andrew Rodriguez. The traitor. He was responsible for this mess. Well, partially—the initial shooting had come from some pathetic scoundrel trying to be a hero. Blind ignorant fools, couldn't they see that she was trying to ensure they had a future—that humanity had a future? But Andrew, that was more personal. The betrayal! She should've had Klein dispose of him before they left the courthouse. Everything just happened so fast and she wasn't thinking clearly; the blood loss certainly had not helped with her lack of mental clarity either.

Moetsky. That was the next traitorous name that popped into her mind. The man responsible for this entire fiasco and for compromising Outpost Zulu with his treacherous photos. She'd have his head for this! She had informed Klein of Moetsky's betrayal prior to her speech, and the plan was to discreetly apprehend the doctor upon their arrival at the research facility. Where was Klein? Was he alright? Had he dealt with Dr Moetsky yet? Her eyes suddenly widened in horror. Moetsky! Where was he now? How long had she been unconscious for? As if on cue the door to the operating room slowly opened and a man in blue scrubs with a matching surgical mask entered the room, locking the dead bolt on the steel door behind him.

The man in scrubs made his way over to the metal tray beside Ventress's operating table. He carefully picked up a syringe and filled it with an unknown substance from a vial that he had stored in the outer pocket of his scrubs. He gave the needle a gentle flick to ensure that there were no pesky bubbles hanging around the syringe and lowered his surgical mask.

"Hello, Commander Ventress, I'll be taking care of you today," Dr Moetsky said with a grin.

Ventress managed to scream.

***

Andrew had been recovering at the Courtview Hotel in room 312, the room that no one could ever seem to find a key to. He had decided that some PAR secrets were best kept to himself. He spent most of his time lying on his bed and practising his aim with a Glock 17 by targeting the small silver knobs on the dresser at the foot of his twin-sized mattress. Using his left hand would be an adjustment, but he had plenty of time to practice. His right hand had been professionally sterilized and wrapped by Dr Tellick; his calf too. There was plenty of food, water, and weapons stashed within the room, as well as some basic medical necessities. Andrew was well on his way to a full recovery and was growing a little bit stronger each day. He had spent almost two full weeks holed up in his room without leaving. Rex would pop in occasionally to sleep a few hours here and there, before returning to the medical tent to continue tending to the wounded — a seemingly endless task.

Andrew wasn't entirely sure what his future would have in store for him. For the first time since he was a teenager, he had no master. No one to give him commands, and no orders to carry out. He was a free man. It was both terrifying and exciting. His entire life had been filled with structure. His meals had been planned out, his fitness schedule was impeccable, and his mission objectives were precise. PAR had been a mesmerizing beacon of light that had guided Andrew through a turbulent world scorched by nuclear warfare. He had been blinded by that bright light, unable or unwilling to recognize that he was on a collision course with jagged rocks that would send him plunging into a frothing sea that wanted to consume his very soul. Not any more. Now Andrew would guide his own ship. He was finally in charge of his own destiny.

Andrew was currently balancing on his uninjured left leg by his hotel room window while using the wall as support. He peered out of his window and over to the courthouse. All the bodies had been disposed of and the frigid autumn rains had done a nice job of cleaning up the remaining traces of what had occurred. The carnage that took place two weeks ago was almost non-existent now. The memories, however, were still fresh. They served as a constant reminder of what Andrew had been a part of, what Reaper had been a part of. Andrew raised a can of beer that Rex had picked up for him from the bar and said, "To new beginnings," before taking a sip.

It was a few seconds after that wonderfully warm sip of beer that his door opened.

"Hey Rex," he said, without turning around.

"Hey bud, look at you up and about!" Rex replied as he came over and crashed onto the bed, his blond hair flopping onto the pillow like a halo.

Andrew turned to face Rex, taking another sip of his beverage. "Thanks for this," he said.

"Don't mention it," Rex replied, his eyes already closed.

It was quiet for a while and Andrew went back to looking out the window. In a way he felt like a dog, constantly staring out of that window. He supposed a disturbed recluse would have been a more accurate comparison, but he preferred comparing himself to a dog. A vicious yet noble German Shepherd perhaps. There wasn't much else to do other than people-watch and reflect on his life while he waited for his leg to heal. The window served as his television for now, and the drunkards stumbling in and out of BAR were his nightly sitcom characters.

"Do you think she's still out there?" Rex asked without opening his eyes.

"I don't know. I like to think that I killed her," Andrew replied, knowing that the 'she' Rex was referring to was Ventress.

"She'll come back if she's still alive, y'know. She'll bring her entire military arsenal too," Rex continued.

"If she's still alive, and if she returns, we'll be ready. We'll protect these people. Fight for these people. It's what good men would do," Andrew said before taking another drink.

Rex seemed satisfied with Andrew's answer and refrained from any further chatter, falling asleep within minutes. Andrew continued to gaze out the window as night began to fall. He could see a man in a dark-green raincoat swiftly lighting the lanterns that lined the main street with an already lit candlestick. Darkness was falling, but light would inevitably rise to meet the dark in the morning. Andrew remained propped in front of the window deep into the night, long after his can of beer had run dry. He watched the outpost vigilantly, his outpost. He had never seen such a bunch of resilient folks. The way that the community banded together to help the injured and bury the dead was breathtakingly beautiful. Not to mention their quick acceptance of former members of PAR despite their affiliation with monstrous atrocities. It suddenly became abundantly clear to Andrew what he would do next, what his next mission would be. He was to remain here and protect these people from whatever threats might arise. Andrew would be their protector. He would be their watchdog.

***

It was a particularly cold night and winter was in the air. The first snowfall had come as large fluffy snowflakes slowly descended from the chilly night sky and stuck to the ground for brief moments of glory before dissolving into wet stains. Joseph, Greg, and Hillary were huddled around a barrel fire that had been lit just outside the main gate of Outpost Zulu. They were on watch duty tonight, along with a handful of other locals. It was hard for Joseph to believe that the courthouse massacre occurred over two weeks ago; the entire ordeal still felt as if it had happened yesterday. Despite what he had been through, his spirits were high. After the mass grave was filled in about a week ago, things started to return to relative normality around the outpost with the exception of a few changes.

Without the presence of PAR, locals were now responsible for guarding the gate. Weapons were not an issue on account of the leftover guns from the outpost security detail and the contraband pistols that the late Aaron's rebellious group of vigilantes had smuggled in through the eastern wall. Small teams of scavengers would now take turns venturing into the city for various forms of loot, teams that didn't mysteriously go missing, and the trade system was modified to be much more accommodating. Those who had nothing to trade could volunteer for extra shifts manning the gate or partake in extra scavenger runs. Now that the population had been forcibly reduced by Ventress and her loyalists, the abundance of goods left behind by PAR in the various shops would keep the outpost going for at least a few months. The winter months would be particularly tough, but Joseph was used to having to be tough by now. They all were.

Joseph now saw his travelling companions as a family rather than a group of friends. Hillary spent most of her days working at the medical tent with Dr Tellick and Rex as they continued to treat the wounded. Meanwhile, Joseph and Greg enjoyed manning the gate on account of the free booze provided by Big Mike. For now, things were good. Very good. The three post-apocalyptic family members were currently taking turns sipping from an empty can of baked beans that had been repurposed into a cup; the liquid of the night was hot boiled water. It warmed their bellies and made the chilly winter air feel somewhat cosy. The trio was perfectly content with their current situation and no one had plans to leave Outpost Zulu any time soon. The journey to reach the outpost had been perilous and the first few days at the outpost even more so. Finally, Joseph felt like he could let his guard down. He had a home, a family, and a sense of purpose.

Joseph took a generous sip of the hot water before passing the can to Greg, the soothing liquid travelling down his chest and filling his stomach like a warm hug. He watched the flames dance within the rusty tin barrel and listened to the crackle of the wood burning. Joseph's warm breath mixed with the cold air and visibly mingled with the smoke from the fire in an entrancing dance of carbon dioxide. He smiled as he remembered the countless nights that he had spent around a bonfire with his family out at the camp. Tonight was no different. Greg took a drink from the can before passing it over to Hillary, who finished it off. The family of three conversed around the fire, sharing stories, thoughts, and aspirations. No one knew what the future had in store, but as long as they had each other, Joseph knew everything would work out in the end. For the first time in a very long time, Joseph wasn't merely surviving. He was living.

COSMIC EGG
BOOKS

FANTASY, SCI-FI, HORROR & PARANORMAL

If you prefer to spend your nights with Vampires and Werewolves rather than the mundane then we publish the books for you. If your preference is for Dragons and Faeries or Angels and Demons – we should be your first stop. Perhaps your perfect partner has artificial skin or comes from another planet – step right this way. If your passion is Fantasy (including magical realism and spiritual fantasy), Metaphysical Cosmology, Horror or Science Fiction (including Steampunk), Cosmic Egg books will feed your hunger. Our curiosity shop contains treasures you will enjoy unearthing. If you have enjoyed this book, why not tell other readers by posting a review on your preferred book site.

Recent bestsellers from Cosmic Egg Books are:

The Zombie Rule Book
A Zombie Apocalypse Survival Guide
Tony Newton
The book the living-dead don't want you to have!
Paperback: 978-1-78279-334-2 ebook: 978-1-78279-333-5

Cryptogram
Because the Past is Never Past
Michael Tobert
Welcome to the dystopian world of 2050, where three lovers are
haunted by echoes from eight-hundred years ago.
Paperback: 978-1-78279-681-7 ebook: 978-1-78279-680-0

Purefinder
Ben Gwalchmai
London, 1858. A child is dead; a man is blamed and dragged
through hell in this Dantean tale of loss, mystery and fraternity.
Paperback: 978-1-78279-098-3 ebook: 978-1-78279-097-6

600ppm
A Novel of Climate Change
Clarke W. Owens
Nature is collapsing. The government doesn't want you to know
why. Welcome to 2051 and 600ppm.
Paperback: 978-1-78279-992-4 ebook: 978-1-78279-993-1

Creations
William Mitchell
Earth 2040 is on the brink of disaster. Can Max Lowrie stop the
self-replicating machines before it's too late?
Paperback: 978-1-78279-186-7 ebook: 978-1-78279-161-4

The Gawain Legacy
Jon Mackley
If you try to control every secret, secrets may end up controlling
you.
Paperback: 978-1-78279-485-1 ebook: 978-1-78279-484-4